Notebook Mysteries

Notebook Mysteries

KIMBERLY MULLINS

NOTEBOOK MYSTERIES ~ Unexpected Outcomes

Notebook Mysteries Series

Copyright © JKJ books, LLC 2022

First edition: August 2022

Mailing address for JKJ books, LLC; 17350 State Highway 249, STE 220 #3515 Houston, Texas 77064

Library of Congress Control Number: 2022905659

ISBN 979-8-9859930-0-4 (paperback)

ISBN 979-8-9859930-1-1 (hardback)

ISBN 978-1-7360104-9-5 (ebook)

This is a work of fiction. It is based on historical events within Chicago during the time period of the 1880s.

Edited by Kaitlyn Johnson, Strictly Textual

Cover Art by Miblart

*For Claudia who is dealing with her own unexpected outcomes.
For Joshua-my fellow writer and Jonathan who is the most patient
reader I could hope for.*

CHAPTER 1

1887 AT THE BOSTONIAN BRIDGE

*E*mma woke suddenly, feeling like she was falling. She reached out for Jeremy, and then everything went black.

What's on me? she thought shifting her legs, trying to shift the weight off of her. She forced an eye open. *Where am I? Train! Jeremy!* Panicking, she sat up quickly and immediately regretted that decision. Boom! Boom! sounded within her head. She put her hands up to brace it and waited for the nausea to pass. When the pain finally subsided, she realized her hands were wet. Slowly she brought them down and held them in front of her. *Blood?* Her mind couldn't process what she was seeing and her gaze swept the area around them. The car wasn't just in disarray it was upside down!

The floor seemed very close to her head; she reached up and touched it. There was some room to move but the height of the car had been decreased by at least half and most of the room seemed on top of her. "Jeremy," she said loudly, "where are you?" Continuing to stay still she was unsure how stable their situation was; she remembered falling but nothing after that.

Jeremy, where was he? The weight she felt was their luggage, it had been dislodged when they turned over. She moved slowly, sitting up higher to see if it was safe to move about. Through the broken windows, she could see the rail cars scattered down the hill by the bridge. The sun was high in the east; they must have been knocked out for hours. It had been early morning and still dark when they crashed.

The car stayed still as she tentatively moved. They appeared to be stable, but she would have to get more data before confirming that fact. She moved the debris off her body to determine if she was okay. *I am good*, she thought moving her arms and legs. *Except for the eye and head.*

She started to remove the rest of the luggage and found Jeremy. "Dear-one, wake up," she said as she stroked his face. He stirred and slowly opened one eye; the other one was black.

"Emma," he said slowly, trying to orientate himself.

"Jeremy, are you okay?"

He moved his right arm and grimaced. "Ouch, I don't know. I think it's strained."

"Are you sure it isn't broken?" she asked.

He twisted it slowly and flexed his fingers. "Definitely not broken, probably just deep bruises and strain."

"You'll still need to see a doctor. What about your legs, can you move them?" she asked, concerned about further damage.

He helped Emma move the debris off of his legs, both visibly relieved as he stretched them. There seemed to be no visible damage. "What happened?" he asked, still a bit hazy from the pain in his arm and eye.

"From what I can tell, we were in a train accident," she stated.

"You think so?" he asked wryly, looking around.

She eyed her nightgown. "For now, let me make you a sling. Can you sit up?"

He sat up slowly in the limited space. "We seem to have matching eyes," he said, trying to find humor in the situation.

He noticed her head and said with some panic, "Emma, you're bleeding."

"Oh, still bleeding," she said, reaching up again to touch it. *Enough of that*, she thought. Reaching down she tore two strips off the bottom of her nightgown. She used one to make him a sling and wrapped the other around her head.

"Can you see anything? Are we in any danger in here?" he asked, not able to sit as high as her.

She looked out of the window again and said, "I think we're stable, but I wouldn't move around much until I can climb out and take a look."

"We're somewhat wedged in here," he observed; the wood had splintered inward along with the broken windows.

"Yes, but I think I can get out of that one," she said, pointing to the window next to her; it was compressed but looked big enough for her to exit through.

"Be careful. There's glass everywhere and you're in your nightdress," he cautioned.

She looked down and said, "You know, I just didn't consider that." She saw Jeremy's pants were within reach, grabbed them, and laid on her back to pull them on.

"Hey!" he protested. She was going to leave him without pants.

She paused, gave him a long look, and said, "I need to look around out there and a dress is just not practical. You have your pajama bottoms." She looked around and saw their books strewn about. She grabbed one, using it to knock out the rest of the glass in the small window. It should be just big enough for her to climb out. She located her boots and slipped them on, pulling the laces tight. Turning toward him, she kissed him softly on the lips. "I'll see if I can get some help to get you out."

As she turned to crawl toward the window, he said, "Hey, Emma, I found something." He tossed her hat at her. She grabbed it and found it more than a little crumpled. She pulled out the long knife to check for any damage; when she didn't find any, she slipped it back into its slot.

As she smoothed out the hat, she studied the window and thought, *I can either go face or feet first.* She nodded and said aloud, "Feet."

"Makes sense." He watched as she tossed her hat out the window and edged over to the casing to start through. If not for the wreck, he would have enjoyed the view.

She made her way out slowly, putting her legs through first and felt for ground, easing the rest of her body out, arms last. As she gained purchase, she straightened slowly, her head pounding with the movement. The view made her world tilt; the train was in pieces around her. She stumbled and almost fell before she stabilized herself against the car.

"Are you okay, Emma? Should you sit down?" Jeremy asked, suddenly concerned she may have a more serious injury than they first thought.

"No. I'm okay. I just lost my balance for a moment," she said, taking a deep breath as she took in the massive destruction. She walked further away from the car and looked up toward the bridge. The engine coal cars were upright and still on the rails; other cars were scattered down the incline. The cars made marks on the ground, she followed it and saw one of the sleeper cars appear to have been dragged sideways for about 200 feet and plunged more than 50 feet down a steep embankment before entering the river. Three additional passenger cars were pulled down the precipice by that car, one of those their own.

Emma called an update to Jeremy. "From the placement of the sun, I'd say we were out for a long while."

"Why is that an issue?" he called back.

She walked back to the car, her face strained. "The timing is important because it looks like we went off a bridge. The engine is still on the tracks, and we were pulled by the last cars. That last car has been in the water for a few hours."

"Can you get to them?" asked Jeremy, concerned. He tried to sit up higher.

She shook her head and said regretfully, "I don't think so. The embankment's very steep, and the car fell to its side as it went in. It appears to be fully submerged, and the river looks like it has a strong current. I'm going to look around and see if I can determine anything."

Slowly making her way down she had to be sure that she stayed on even ground. As she got further from her car, she noticed a group of men down by the water. She paused when she realized they were trying to get close enough to see if anyone could be saved. They were lined up, interlocking their arms, forming a human chain. The water proved strong, and she watched them struggling to stay upright. They persevered and reached the submerged car. The first man got to the window; he looked back at the group supporting him and shook his head. She could tell from where she was that the news was bad. *Those poor people,* she thought, wiping her eyes.

She pulled herself together and made her way up the hill to the suspended car. It was better supported than she thought, and. It also appeared to have people in it. Hearing crying, she called to them, "Try not to move! You appear to be safe. I'll go for help."

There's nothing I can do here; we need strong men to help these people from their cars. We also need medical help.

She glanced around and noticed a ragtag bunch of other survivors had made it out. Most wore their nightclothes, three men and two women; they appeared to have cuts and bruises, but no broken bones. They were discussing what to do next when she walked up. Emma listened for a moment before saying, "Hello, I'm glad you're okay."

"You, too," one of the men answered. He nodded to the group around him. "We were talking about how to get people out of the rest of the cars."

A woman in the group spoke up. "We can start by finding out who's mobile and can get out through the windows." Introductions were not necessary.

"As long as it's safe," cautioned Emma. "I told people in that suspended car to stay as still as possible. I wouldn't try to move them until we can get some additional supports to stabilize it."

"I agree. There are other cars we can work on first," the same man answered.

"I think I can go for help. I know the town is about two miles that way," she said, pointing to the east. "We need medical help and equipment to get people out."

They agreed. One of the other men asked, "Do you need someone to go with you?"

"No, I'll make good time on my own."

"Okay, we'll continue to work on getting people out."

She nodded and hurriedly returned to Jeremy's car.

"How is it?" he asked leaning toward her through the window.

"Not great. Jeremy, you mentioned last night that we're about two miles outside of town. I have to go there to get help."

He grimaced when he tried to shrug his shoulders. "I think you're right. Stay with the rails and be careful. Are you dizzy at all?"

She tentatively touched her head as she replied, "I have a headache. but no dizziness."

"Okay, on your way," he said lightly, but concern darkened his eyes.

Throwing him a kiss, she turned to make her way slowly around the wreckage. Several more people had climbed out of the cars and sat looking dazed. She directed them to the group she'd conferred with earlier and told them she was going for help.

Making her way up the hill to where the engine sat, she decided to check on the engineers, hoping they'd survived. With that hope in mind, she grabbed the side rails and pulled herself into the engine room. What she saw caused her to grow dizzy again. Shaking herself out of it, she tried not to let emotion take her over.

The impact had driven both men into the front of the train; neither survived. She shook her head regretfully and turned around to climb back down. Before she started down the rail, toward town, she gave the wreckage one last long look, trying to commit the placement of cars to memory.

She started her walk into town. It would take longer since she was sticking to the raised terrain, it was uneven and her step had to be precise. When she thought she couldn't walk anymore, the town came into view. Her head had started to pound again but she pushed herself forward. Hopefully, they were big enough to have a train stop; some of the smaller towns were just pass-through locations.

The sun was still high, indicating it was still morning and, with luck, someone would be at the station. She headed straight there, thinking, *They should be able to put out a call for help and respond to the wreck.*

She barely noticed the odd looks she received in her night-shirt, pants, and crumpled hat. She trudged those last steps and made her way to the ticket booth, sparing a minute to lay her head down on the counter. The man was turned away from her but startled when he heard, "Sir I've been in a train wreck some two miles from here. Many people have died and others are injured. We need lots of men and tools to get people out."

He jerked himself around. "Oh no," he said hoarsely. He exited the door beside her, where there was a bell and he pulled the rope firmly. They listened to it clang out the notification. When he stopped, he said, "We have this in place in case of emergency." With that, he stood watching and waiting. It took a few minutes before wagons started arriving. The entire town appeared to have shown up to help.

A tall blond man, apparently a leader in the town, jumped down from his wagon and said, "Terrance, what happened?"

"Train wreck," he said, nodding at Emma to give more details.

"We'll need rope to support one car that is still on the embankment. There are additional cars turned upside down or fallen on their sides. We need hatchets and other items to cut into the cars. Some people can't get out of the windows. We need a doctor and the undertaker at the bridge, just two miles from here."

"That's Bostian's bridge; it's located over a creek. Did any cars go into the water?" one of the men in the crowd asked.

"Yes," she said regretfully. "I think one is a loss. We wrecked last night; they've been submerged for hours."

The tall blond man took over directing the group. "You men, go get as much rope as you can find. Harrold, get the store opened. We will need as many hatchets as we can find. Hester, get blankets; bring the doctor and the undertaker."

Terrance said loudly, "We'll also need food and water. I'll get them to open the restaurant to bring baskets to the site."

The tall blond man nodded and, as the group headed out, he said, "Meet back here and bring anyone else you think could help." He turned to Emma and said, "Little lady, I'm Preacher. What's your name? Do we need to get you to the doctor?"

"Emma," she said. "And no, I just want to get back to the site."

"Would you like to ride back with me?" he asked in a kindly manner.

"Yes," she said gratefully. He helped her onto his wagon and waited for everyone to return. The groups made good time, appearing with wagons full of supplies. Word had gotten out and even more people showed up, wanting to help.

They headed to the wreck site; Emma and Preacher arrived first. She climbed down without waiting to be helped and rushed over to the incline. As she hurried down, she could see there were significantly more people standing around than when she had left. She spotted Jeremy and started to run to him. "Jeremy!!" He moved toward her at the same pace. "You're out," she said, relieved.

He bent and kissed her softly. He looked around her and up the hill, saying, "You weren't able to get help?" He was concerned about the people still stuck in the wreckage.

They couldn't see the people she had brought. She looked up the embankment and smiled slightly. "Oh, I brought people." At that moment, men started overflowing the incline, carrying ropes and tools.

Jeremy just watched them descend like a wave. "Wow."

Her eyes shined with tears. "Yes, they came as soon as I asked."

As soon as everyone made it down the hill, Preacher called for the groups to come together. "My name is Preacher, and we'll need to work together to stabilize the one car and get the people off." He looked to the survivors and requested, "If you're able-bodied, please join us." Several of the men left their group to help those in the suspended car.

As they gathered around it, looking a bit lost as to where to start, Jeremy eyed Emma. "You should go help them." He knew she was talented in structural engineering and could assist them in how to respond safely.

"Will you be okay here?" she asked, concerned about leaving him again.

"Yes, go," he said, waving her on.

Emma went to Preacher and said, "I can help with where to place the ropes, to offer stability, while we get the people out." She went on to explain, "I have an engineering background that could be beneficial."

He thought about that and asked, "What do you have in mind?"

"Let me walk around." She noticed the base of the train car

was pushed deep into the ground. She returned the front and called, "Preacher, we could use some rather large logs to help wedge the wheels." He nodded and sent off a group of men to cut down some thick trees.

"What next?" he asked expectantly.

"The rope should anchor from the top." She guided him to the locations where the ropes could be safely anchored. "Wrap them around the heavy structural parts," she directed.

He agreed and waited for the men to bring the logs to the rail car. They had cut wedges into the ends to allow them to be put into the ground and offer some support behind each set of wheels. Next, he took her advice and called out instructions to stabilize the car. The ropes were placed with six men at each anchor point. Once they confirmed they were stable, Preacher and Emma went to the front of the car. "Any more advice?" he asked before they climbed up.

"Yes, have them empty the car, starting with the people in the back first. They need to exit one at a time and slowly."

He nodded, agreeing with the plan.

Once they climbed into the car, Preacher said in a firm, clear voice, "Okay, ladies and gentlemen, we're going to take this slow. We'll start in the back and each person will come up one at a time."

Emma saw people hugging their bags and said clearly, "You'll need to leave your bags in the car. We don't want to do anything that might upset the balance."

"But we need our bags," protested several people.

Emma said, "No, what you need is to get out of here safely. If we can get to the bags later, then we'll get them to you. Please don't jeopardize the people around you for things." That final statement seemed to get through, and bags were put down. They started exiting from the back to the front. The train car groaned but remained steady. There were small children in the car and they were taken out quietly. When the last person had climbed out, Preacher motioned to the men to loosen the ropes. The car started to slip but abruptly stopped a few feet down. The evacuated people screamed in response.

Preacher warned the group, "We don't want anyone near that car at this time. Once we deem it safe, we'll retrieve your belongings and get them to you." He continued, "Those of you who are able, I'll need you to come with us and help with evacuations of the other cars. We need to find other people who are trapped."

With that, they separated, with women and children helping the doctor and the men breaking into groups of five each. Each group was given hatchets and other tools. Working together, they cleared a car at a time, three more in total.

The doctor had set up a triage area on a flat spot near the river. He was setting broken bones and treating other ailments as best he could with the supplies, he had available.

Sometime later, the food arrived. The wives of the men from the town brought enough for everyone. They ate together in silence and rested. After lunch, people who were mobile moved to wagons to be transported to town. The injured followed more slowly, assisted as necessary, or were carried up as needed.

The caretaker had also arrived for the grim task of body recovery. Emma and Jeremy stayed behind, watching the body removal, feeling they should be there. They witnessed the event silently as bodies were lined up on the grass. The number would be higher once the car in the river was retrieved.

Emma and Jeremy approached a tired-looking Preacher, looking at the rows of bodies. "So many deaths," he said, bending his head in prayer. Jeremy and Emma did the same, crossing themselves as they finished.

"We'll need to gather personal belongings and descriptions of each one for identification," stated Jeremy as Preacher finished his prayers.

"Agreed," said Emma. "We also need to look at the rails and see if we can determine why we wrecked."

"Do you both feel well enough to help?" asked Preacher.

Jeremy looked at Emma, who nodded. "I'm good. I'll start with the descriptions. I need…" She looked around.

"Your notebook?" Jeremy teased. "I might have something." He pulled several notebooks and pens out of his pocket. "I found them when I was waiting to be rescued."

She smiled as she took them. "My hero." She moved to the first body. "Let's do this one at a time."

Preacher, Emma, and Jeremy went to each person, with Emma writing descriptions and adding a number to each for identification. Jeremy searched their clothes for something that would help identify them later, and Emma added the items to her description. Preacher went last, praying over each one.

Jeremy looked at the items they were collecting, some were valuable. "We shouldn't leave these with the bodies, they might be taken." He spotted a bag nearby, picked it up, and opened it. It had some clothes but nothing else. "Let's use this." He and Preacher started adding the items to the bag.

The job was arduous but, working together, they completed the survey of the forty people. Preacher took custody of the bag and list. "You should both head to town before it gets too late." They agreed and followed him up the incline. The sun was lower and the day was beginning to turn into evening.

As they reached the rails and looked down at the wreckage, they saw the men had started a fire and set out bedrolls. They looked questioningly at Preacher, and he explained. "We'll stay until the railroad men arrive."

"Good idea. Before we go, I would like to examine the rails where the cars went off," she commented.

One of the men at the fire called to Preacher. "I'll be just a moment," he said and headed down.

Jeremy and Emma continued to walk down the tracks. "How fast do you think the train was moving?" she asked.

"I would expect about twenty to thirty miles an hour," Jeremy said as he walked ahead. He saw something and bent down. "Come here, I think this might be it."

Emma knelt next to him. She reached down and saw that the tie crumbled at their touch. "Rotten ties. The engine was lucky to make it across. It failed on that last car and pulled us down."

Jeremy looked at the late afternoon sky and said, "Emma, we should head into town. We need to send telegrams and let the family know we're okay."

"Yes, you're right," she said, looking around. Preacher had finished his business and was waiting for them. "Though, before we go, I need to talk to Preacher about our case."

Jeremy nodded. "I'll wait here." He was starting to feel his energy wane.

"I'll be right back." She called to Preacher, "Can I get a moment with you before we head to town?"

He waved her over to him. She walked up to him and said in a low voice, "Preacher, we need to make a request. Could you let us know the location of the bags when they are brought to town, prior to their distribution?"

"Can you tell me why?" he asked before answering.

Emma explained in a low voice. He nodded and said, "I'll keep an eye out."

"Ready to go?" called Jeremy from his position further down the tracks.

"Yes," she called back. She looked to Preacher and said, "Thank you for all of your help today."

He nodded and watched her thoughtfully as she walked away with Jeremy. She was unlike anyone he had met before. He shook his head and descended back down the hill to check the luggage.

Emma and Jeremy made their way to town. The walk wasn't

bad but he was still in pain and would need some rest. The best thing she could think of was to head to the rail station for a recommendation on housing.

"Over there," she said, pointing to the rail station building. "The manager was very helpful this morning. Hopefully, he can lead us to some housing."

"Yes," said Jeremy, so tired and in pain, he could only provide short answers.

She looked at him, concerned he needed to get some rest.

They made their way to the office. When the manager saw her, he said with a smile, "So, little girl, you're back?"

Emma asked, "Do you know of a hotel where we could rest?"

He shook his head. "We're full up. Local people have taken in the passengers until we can get another train in here to get them home."

Emma bit her lip, pensive in her worry for Jeremy.

The manager saw her worry and hastened to assure her, "My Martha has prepared a room for you at our house."

Emma let the relief show and said, "Thank you so much for that. I'm Emma and this is Jeremy." She didn't mention their last names, she didn't want to be separated from him at this time.

"It's nice to meet you. I'm Dennis Connor," he said.

"May we go there now?" she asked as she continued to watch Jeremy. He was slumped against the wall, his eyes closed.

"Well, I can't go at this time; I've got to wait for the railroad people. Local stations will be sending men to help clear the tracks and make any necessary repairs."

Emma said, "You might want to mention to them that we think it was rotten ties that led to the derailment."

"I'll do so, thank you. Randy!" he called suddenly.

Feet came running and a boy of about ten said, "Yes, Pa."

"These people..." he started, looking at them.

"Emma and Jeremy," she reminded him.

"Yes," he said with a smile. "Emma and Jeremy need to be

taken to your ma for some rest, food, and from the looks of it, a bath."

She returned the smile gratefully.

Randy said, "We live near here. Are you okay with walking?"

Emma looked at Jeremy and asked, "Can you make it?"

"I can make it," he said confidently, hoping he was right. Emma lifted his unharmed arm and placed it over her shoulder for support. They made their way to a small house colorfully painted in yellow and white, with a well-tended yard and a white picket fence. The front door opened before they could reach it. A pretty woman in her late thirties stood in the doorway.

She said, "Come in, we've been expecting you. I'm Martha. Now, don't say anything, we're going to get you to your room. Randy, bring that water from the kitchen. We have a wash basin you two can use."

Emma guided Jeremy into the room Martha had indicated. She eased him on the bed, careful not to jostle his arm. He was asleep before he hit the pillow. She pulled a cover over him, sat down next to him, and brushed the hair off of his face.

She heard something behind her and turned around as Martha entered with the water pitcher. "For you," she said in a low voice.

"Thank you," Emma replied quietly.

Martha nodded and set it down on the dresser. "I thought you might want this also." She pulled a hairbrush out of her pocket and reached out to give it to her. Emma looked at the brush questioningly but accepted it. Martha waved her hand at Randy to exit the room. They pulled the door closed behind them.

Emma looked at the brush, shrugged, and laid it down. Turning toward the bed, she happened to glance at the mirror above the dresser and saw her hair. *What a mess.* She laughed, finding the humor in the situation. *It looks like a blonde bird's nest.*

She slowly unwrapped the bandage from around her head; it was still sore but the bleeding seemed to have stopped. Leaning forward, she touched her eye lightly with her fingers. It was still pounding and could use some cool water. She took off her top and started washing. When she finished, she felt immeasurably better. The clothes lay in a dirty heap at her feet. She hated wearing the dirty top again but saw no other way. Slipping it on, she sat on the bed, brushing her knotted hair slowly.

When it was smooth, she reached for a wet cloth and placed it on Jeremy's eye. Moving as little as possible, she climbed into the bed and settled in. She didn't remember her head hitting the pillow, yet she slept heavy and long. When she awoke, the room was dark. She lay there for a moment, trying to remember where they were.

"Are you doing okay?" asked Jeremy.

"Yes," she said. She turned toward him slowly so as not to jostle him too much and asked, "When did you wake up?"

"Not long ago," he admitted.

"How's the arm?" she asked, concerned it may have gotten worse.

"Sore, but sleep helped. You?" he responded.

"Me, too. Though I'm feeling my bruises," she said, stretching her arms over her head.

"Can you see about getting me some water to wash with?" he grimaced when he looked down at himself.

"I'll go check the kitchen," she said and rose to grab the basin and pitcher. As she carried it out, she saw the family in the sitting room. *It must not be as late as I thought.*

Martha noticed her and put down her sewing. "We were hoping you would wake up in time for us to get you something to eat." She noticed the basin and pitcher and said, "Randy, take that for her."

He immediately stood and said, "Sure, Ma." He went over to take the items.

"Could we have some fresh water?" Emma asked tentatively.

Martha smiled at her. "Yes, of course. Randy, go ahead and get that for her. We also have your bags. They said you marked them before you left the site."

"Yes, Jeremy did that when he was waiting to be removed from the car," Emma said. "Where was all of the other luggage taken to?"

Dennis folded his newspaper. "Oh, Preacher is managing that. He has it at the church and will work on distributing them to the people. He said to let you know they're doing it tonight."

Emma nodded. "That sounds like a good plan."

Randy returned with clean water and Martha said, "Please take that to their room." She looked back to Emma and asked, "Would you like something to eat?"

Emma's stomach growled, answering for her. They all laughed and Martha stood. "Are sandwiches all right?"

"That sounds wonderful," she said gratefully.

"Why don't you go to your room? I'll get your food organized and bring it to you," Martha suggested.

Emma passed Randy in the hallway on his way back. She smiled and thanked him.

"Any time," he said, breezing by her.

She went into the room and found Jeremy sitting up. "You should have waited for help," she scolded him.

"Randy helped me sit up and said he would help me to the water closet," he explained.

Randy reappeared behind her and said, "I went to get your bags." He set them down and walked over to the bed. "Ready?"

"Ready," said Jeremy and grimaced as Randy helped him stand. When he was steady on his feet, they made their way down the hall.

Emma watched to make sure they didn't need additional support. When the door to the lavatory closed, she went back into the room. Going to their bags, she opened them and pulled out clean clothes for them to change into. When they came back, Jeremy looked steadier. He said, "Thanks for the help, Randy."

"No problem," Randy said and headed out.

Jeremy sat back on the bed as Emma wetted a cloth to help him clean up. His shirt had been ripped off his arm to allow the doctor to check it. She removed the remnants and saw many bruises. She looked into his eyes, saying, "You're sure nothing else is hurt?"

He moved his unhurt arm and said, "I think I just got stiff when I laid down."

She helped him wash and retrieved a white undershirt and a pair of pants. He was dressed when they heard a knock at the door. Emma answered it and found Martha there with a tray of food.

"Thank you so much," Emma said as she took the tray and moved it to the dresser.

Martha said, "We wanted to let you know that we have a telegraph office in town in case you need to send a message. He's staying open late tonight to get all of the messages out about the train wreck."

Jeremy thanked Martha and looked at Emma. "We do need to send several telegrams."

"Let us know when you're ready to leave and we'll give you directions. It's just up the road."

"We'll be ready soon," said Emma. She thought of something and asked, "Martha, where were the wounded taken?"

"A large number of mostly healthy or mobile people were taken in by families in town and by Preacher at the church. The more severe ones are in the school, with the doctor onsite monitoring them."

She shut the door to give them some privacy to let them finish dressing.

Sitting on the bed, they ate their sandwiches and drank their milk. "This case certainly went off the rails," Jeremy said wryly.

"Yes," she agreed with a laugh. She suddenly grew serious and said, "I'm glad we're both okay."

"Come here," he said. He folded her to him, and she leaned in carefully to avoid his hurt arm.

"We need to get those telegrams out," Emma murmured into his chest.

"Yes," said Jeremy, "it'll be nice to walk a bit." He kissed her on the neck and said, "Let's finish getting dressed so we can leave."

She sat up, removing her nightshirt and Jeremy's pants. "I'll miss the pants."

"I like you better in skirts," he commented as he slipped on his jacket.

She smiled and continued to dress, donning her white blouse and dark skirt and adding her slightly crumpled hat.

"Were you able to find out the location of the bags?" he asked in a low voice.

"Yes," she said in a low voice. "Let's head out and I'll tell you on the way."

They finished getting dressed and took their dinner tray to the kitchen. They made their way back to the living room and got directions from the family to the telegraph office and church.

As they exited the house, Emma said, "Preacher agreed to check the bags before they were distributed."

"If he finds anything?" he asked expectantly.

Emma replied, "Then he'll remove the items and place them in a secure location."

Jeremy was thinking of ways this might be found out and asked, "What about the weight difference?"

"Preacher said he would find a substitute. He said that,

unless the railroad representatives had issues, they were going to distribute the bags tonight."

"Telegraph office first," he said and Emma nodded in agreement. Neither wanted their families to worry.

They approached the well-lit office and saw there was no one waiting. "We must have missed the rush," she said as they entered the building and found the telegraph clerk alone at his desk.

As they walked in, he looked up and asked, "Are you from the train wreck?"

"Yes, we need to send telegraphs to our families," stated Emma.

"Yes, of course," he said and hurriedly walked over to the counter, handing them paper and pencils.

Jeremy took them and handed one to Emma. She started: *Dora, our train crashed early this morning near Statesville. We are fine, just minor injuries. We will be staying here until alternate transportation can be arranged. Love to everyone.*

Jeremy looked over at hers and copied the first few lines: *Pops, our train crashed early this morning near Statesville. We are fine, just minor injuries. We will be staying here until alternate transportation can be arranged. We are retrieving the luggage soon.*

Cole knew the code "luggage" meant they had the silver stolen from the bank and would need him to send agents to pick it up. He took his and Emma's information and handed it to the telegraph operator.

Jeremy started to pull out his wallet to pay, but the telegraph operator stopped him. "The railroad will cover the cost."

Emma and Jeremy were surprised but thanked him. The clerk confirmed they would be sent immediately.

"Can you point us in the direction of the church?" asked Emma.

He walked them to the door, opened it, and pointed straight ahead. "It's hard to miss. It's that large white building."

They thanked him again and headed there. It was a short walk and they reached the wooden stairs leading to the main doors. They opened the doors to the large room, the sanctuary was located at the far end. Numerous people sat on the floor on one side and Preacher stood on the opposite side.

He was working on the bag dispersal plan. When he saw them, he nodded and indicated they could take a seat with the others. He waited until they were settled before he started talking. "Okay, everyone. I'd like to start this meeting with a prayer." Everyone bowed their head. "God, we pray for those who were lost and those who are injured and are thankful for the people who are here with us. Amen."

The group responded with an, "Amen."

He looked to the two men in suits on his left and motioned to them to join him. "Okay, folks. Let's get down to business. This is Joe Locke and Mike Carter with the railroad. They're here to make some announcements about the bag distribution."

One man stepped forward and said, "As Preacher indicated, I'm Joe Locke, the Railroad representative. We have a system that makes sure your bags get to you. I'll call on you to describe the bag, then we'll retrieve it from the other room and bring it to you."

A lady raised her hand and said, "What if two are similar?"

Joe went on to explain, "Then we open the bag and you'll identify what it contains."

As they waited for the bag dispersal to start, Emma sat there thinking about how they had gotten here.

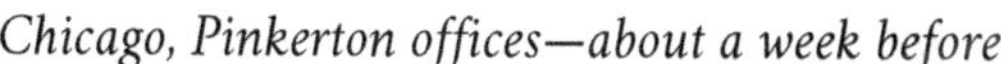

Chicago, Pinkerton offices—about a week before

Emma and Jeremy entered Cole's office. Jeremy asked, "What's up, Pops?"

He looked distracted as he waved them to the seats in front of his desk. "Please, sit. I have a case to review with both of you."

Emma nodded and pulled out her notebook, ready to take down the details as Cole started. "We have information, from a confidential informant, about the two men who robbed the Chambers Bank in Denver, Colorado. They'll be on the train on its way through South Carolina. We know the dates and I would like you and Jeremy on that train."

Jeremy frowned and asked the obvious question. "Why the train, if we know who they are, can't we wait and get them at one of the stops?"

Cole frowned and responded, "Well, we don't actually know who they are. The informant didn't give us that information, just that the two men who robbed the bank will be on the train."

"Who is this informant?" asked Emma.

Cole shook his head. "We do not know that either. A telegraph was delivered from Denver and addressed to this office."

"Can't we find who sent it?" Jeremy asked.

"I notified the telegraph office, but the clerk didn't have a record of the sender."

"What makes you think it's credible?" asked Emma curiously.

"They provided details that were withheld from the public," Cole explained.

"Such as?" inquired Jeremy.

"Such as that it wasn't gold that was taken, but silver," said Cole.

Jeremy asked, "Why take the silver and not the gold? It seems like it would be easier to turn into cash."

"Silver mining's more profitable and popular right now. The Bland-Allison Act, passed in 1878, opened up a new market for silver to be used for minting dollars. I'm sure they assume it will be one big score," replied Cole.

Jeremy saw the glint of mischief in Emma's eyes and asked, "How about a trip, Emma?"

"I would love to," she replied.

Their tickets were secured, and they moved quickly to catch the train leaving that night. They would have to switch trains several times but should be able to make the date mentioned by the informant.

On the first leg of their trip, Emma asked, "What's the plan?"

"We use our observation skills to rule people out," indicated Jeremy.

~

Back to church, after the accident

As the bag dispersal began, Emma and Jeremy watched the process closely. The individuals were called upon to describe their bag; the bag was brought out and confirmed to be the right one. Since they were looking for two men, families were discounted. They had their eye on two passengers who seemed to be together. She had first seen them in the rail car that had to be stabilized. Both were clutching their bags when asked to leave them behind. The first of these two was called up and described his bag as a brown leather carrying case.

Preacher cleared his throat and said, "Of course this way." Emma caught his eye and his slight nod. The man asking for the luggage did not notice the signal. He looked relieved when his bag was brought out. The man carrying the bag commented, "Heavy."

"Just books," he assured him as he took it and went to sit down next to his friend.

The friend was next and went up to describe his bag, similar to the other man's, but it had a black ribbon tied on the handle. It was brought out and the same heavy comment was made. The man explained, "We're booksellers." He moved back to his previous location.

The rest of the bags were dispersed and most of the people opened them to check their belongings. Emma and Jeremy watched the two men, noting they did not open theirs. *That will work in our favor*, Emma thought.

Preacher went to each person, checking on them to see if anything might be needed. When he reached Jeremy and Emma, he ask, "How are you both doing?"

Emma leaned forward and asked in a low voice, "Were you able to remove the item?"

"Yes. I have it put away," he answered in a similar tone. "What happens now?"

"We notified the proper officials and they are on the way to pick them up," Jeremy responded.

A young woman, assisting Preacher, came over to him and said, "We have the water ready."

"Thank you, Eve. I'll let everyone know."

He went to the front of the group and said, "Water is being heated in the bath so you may get washed up; you may go in one at a time. We'll change the water out as each of you finishes, so you can get refreshed."

The people looked relieved and started going in and out of the bathing area. One of their targets took his turn in the bathing chamber. He didn't make a move toward his bag. Instead, he nodded toward his friend and headed in. He returned a little while later, dressed in the same clothes but looking relaxed. His friend left his bag and also returned in the same clothes. It took about two hours for everyone to get cleaned up.

"They aren't opening the bags," Emma murmured to Jeremy.

"Yes," he said in the same low voice. "It gives us more time. We've got the word out and help should be here soon."

Just after everyone finished and was settling down, Mike

Carter came back in and said, "We've gotten word that the repairs will be started tomorrow morning. We hope to have you moving in the next two days."

One of the two men they were watching spoke up, saying, "Is there alternative transportation out of this town? We have to get somewhere." There were a few nods from other people.

Mike answered, keeping his tone polite. "This town is not easily accessible to other towns. I also know the animals that have been used to transport you from the crash site will need rest and feed for at least a day. It's best that you let us do our job and get you on your way."

One of the two men looked like they still might argue, but the other tapped him and shook his head.

Jeremy leaned over and said to Emma, "We should be able to get some Pinkertons here before those repairs are completed."

"So, we wait and hope they don't open the bags?" she inquired.

"We wait," he confirmed.

They settled into their pallets provided by Preacher. He agreed to let them relocate to the church, which allowed a family with a baby to move into their room at the house.

From their pallets, they had a view of the two men. They watched them closely but saw they made no further effort to leave. They seemed content to wait for the railroad to provide transportation.

The two days went by quietly. Jeremy grew nervous that the detectives would not arrive in time to take them into custody. They were hesitant to confront them for fear of hurting the families staying in the church, so they continued to watch and wait.

That third morning, Joe Locke announced to the group, "There's an update for you. The rail has been repaired." A cheer went up. "There is a slight delay because the train is being outfitted to move the injured people who need to lie down and another car for the deceased." Everyone got very quiet at those words. "It will be here in another day." They understood the arrangements and settled in for another day.

Jeremy came to a decision and said close to her ear, "Emma, I'm going to check if there are any telegrams for us."

"I'll stay here and read." She had her book out and covertly watched the whispering men. They looked quite confident in their plans.

Jeremy seemed troubled when he returned. He handed her the telegram and said in a low voice, "They may not make it in time. We'll have to come up with a plan."

Emma mulled that over. "We don't want them to board the train. We will have to stop them ourselves."

"Agreed," murmured Jeremy.

She drummed her fingers on her lips. "It's funny," she said. "I thought we had such luck that they stayed around so we could keep an eye on them. Now, as I see it, they are using the victims as protection."

Jeremy nodded. "We need to find a way to separate them from the group."

As they thought about that, Emma said, "I have a plan. Let's keep it simple." She explained it in detail and Jeremy offered suggestions.

The next day, the newly outfitted train arrived. Everyone lined up to go outside to be transported to the rail station. Emma and Jeremy did not join then and were talking quietly in the corner. Their targets were last in the line. She closed her carpet bag and moved to the first man and asked if she could go ahead of him. He nodded and waved his hand, allowing her in. Jeremy moved to the end of the line behind the second man.

As they started to move, Emma delayed stepping forward and let some distance open up between her and the family in front of her. To further the distance, she dropped her coat and turned to apologize for the delay. She picked it up and then again delayed them by stopping abruptly, causing the men to run into her. These delays caused a significant gap in the line. She continued to walk so slowly that the rest people had exited the room, leaving them behind. The men behind her were starting to grumble about how slow she was but were not yet being pushy.

As they neared the door, it slammed shut. Emma had prearranged that with Preacher and was ready for the move. She turned, her knife pulled and a smile on her face. "Gentlemen, I think we need to talk."

"She's just a girl. You can take her," the second man said with false bravado. They had forgotten Jeremy was behind them. The first man went after her and Jeremy knocked out the second man before he could turn around. He was tying him up while Emma fought the first man.

Emma pointed her knife at him and said, "I think you need to realize you're caught."

He wasn't listening. Instead, he swung his heavy bag to hit her, trying to dislodge the knife. The bag was unwieldy and did nothing other than twirl him around. She jumped back, taunting him. "Ready to give up yet?"

"No!" he tried to hit her again and finally noticed his friend was tied up on the floor. He stopped abruptly and asked, "Zach, are you okay?" He forgot about Emma and bent down to check on his partner. Emma took the moment to jump on his back and push him down to the floor with her knee. Jeremy handed her some rope to secure him.

Jeremy tapped the person he had tied up, saying, "Wake up." He stirred and realized he and his partner were caught.

"You can have it," he said through gritted teeth.

"Have what?" Jeremy asked innocently.

Emma bent over and opened one of their bags. "Look here, Jeremy."

He went over and said with a frown, "All of this for pig iron?"

The two men looked confused.

She opened the other bag and found the same thing.

"Where did it go?" the second man asked.

They heard a knock and saw the knob turn on the door. Preacher stuck his head in and said, "Can I come in now?"

"Yes, Preacher, please join us," indicated Emma.

"I have some company with me." He came in carrying two bags, followed by two men in black suits.

Jeremy raised his eyebrows at the two Pinkerton men. "A bit late, aren't you?"

One of the men looked around the room and took in the two tied up on the floor. "Yeah, but looks like you didn't need much help."

Emma smiled broadly and said, "We had it under control."

"But where's the silver?" one of the men on the floor whined.

"Oh, we have it here," said Preacher as he handed the two bags he was carrying to the Pinkerton men.

"We'll take custody of these two and get the silver back to its owners," one of the Pinkerton men stated.

Jeremy stood and said, "Can I see your credentials?"

"Of course. I'm Edward James and this is Mason Baker. We're from the South Carolina branch of Pinkerton." He pulled out his paperwork and handed it to him.

Jeremy reviewed it thoroughly and handed it back before saying, "This confirms what I was sent from the Pinkerton office in Chicago. Where will you go from here?"

"We'll take them with us and be with you on the train for the next two stops. We'll process them locally and transport the silver back to the bank after their court case," he explained.

Preacher said, "Not to rush you, but they're holding the train for you and they're eager to get going."

The Pinkerton men took custody of the bank robbers and

escorted them out. Emma and Jeremy picked up their bags and followed.

Just before exiting the church, Emma looked over at Preacher and said sincerely, "Thank you so much for everything. We couldn't have done it without you."

"You're very welcome. Please come back and visit us," he said warmly.

"We will," promised Jeremy.

They were finally on the train and sitting with the other passengers in third class. The first and second classes were taken up with the injured or dead. Emma pulled out her and Jeremy's books so they had something to occupy their time during the journey. Jeremy opened his immediately and started to read. Emma found herself distracted by a crying baby. She missed her time with her niece Charlotte. She was a little over a year old now and the night she was born brought a few surprises.

The thunderstorm had been blowing through loudly with lightning strikes booming, but the loudest sound in the house was not the thunder—it was Dora. She was lying in the bed, trying to bring her baby into the world. She'd gone into labor hours earlier; the midwife had been called and the long wait had begun.

The midwife was checking Dora and said, "I think this is it." Tim looked faint but stayed next to her. The midwife gave him more directions. "Get behind her and give her some support." He helped Dora to sit up.

Emma was there, holding Dora's hand, and watched as the baby came into the world. She had never wanted a baby or this experience for herself, but the birth affected her. She felt an immediate love for that red wrinkly mess. The midwife clean her up and gave her to a crying Dora. Tim's face was shining and he didn't seem to be able to stop smiling.

Emma watched the baby with curious eyes. She held out her finger to her, rubbing her little hand. The baby grabbed on and Emma laughed. "She's strong," said Tim, in awe of his new daughter.

"She is," said Dora, touching her face lightly. The baby followed her hand and started rubbing against it.

The midwife had completed cleaning up Dora and covered her back up, saying, "The baby's hungry. You'll need to put her to your breast."

"I'll step out," said Emma, hoping to give them some privacy.

"Thanks, Aunt Emma," said Dora in a soft voice.

Emma smiled and leaned down to kiss her on the cheek. She headed toward the door and turned back. "What's her name?"

Dora looked at Tim and he supplied it. "Charlotte Emma."

Emma's eyes overflowed with tears and she ran over to hug them both. She exited the room to head downstairs to share the news.

Patrick had stayed up to wait for the baby to be born. Dora and Tim had adopted him when his parents were murdered in a child abduction scheme. He danced around the room in the excitement of the impending birth. He spotted Emma and shouted, "Is the baby here?"

Papa put his hands on Patrick's shoulders and said quietly, "Let her tell us."

Patrick was still excited but he waited. Papa prompted, "Emma?"

"A beautiful baby girl," Emma said in a rush.

"Wonderful!" said Papa. "How is Dora?"

"She's also wonderful, tired but wonderful," said Emma with a long sigh.

Jeremy came up behind her, pulling her to him, and said, "You need to rest." He guided her to the settee.

Cole was there as well and Emma sat next to him, saying, "Cole, were you here waiting all night?"

"I was," he murmured. "I couldn't miss out on seeing the newest member of our family."

"Yes, we are family," she said, reaching out to touch his hand.

Tim came downstairs, grinning widely, and inquired, "Would you like to see the baby?"

"I do! I do!" shouted Patrick, running up to him.

Tim swung him up in a big hug and looked around. "Where's Jake?"

Papa said, "Jake said it was time for bed, so we told him we would tell him about the baby in the morning."

Tim frowned but knew Jake had his schedule. He would make sure he felt included in the morning. Lifting Patrick onto his shoulder, he led everyone upstairs to see the baby. He knocked lightly on the door. Inside, Dora sat up, holding a sleeping baby. "Come in," she said to the group, "and meet Charlotte Emma."

Tim took Patrick off his shoulders and walked him to the bed. He had grown quiet as Tim took him closer. "Patrick, this is your new baby sister," he said.

"My sister?" he asked, fascinated.

"Yes, your sister, your family," Dora confirmed.

"Can I touch her?" he asked, looking at the small creature in his mom's arms.

"Lightly," she cautioned.

He put out two fingers and gently touched Charlotte's arm. "She's so soft."

Dora looked up at Tim and said, "He needs to go to bed."

Tim leaned down and kissed her on the forehead. "I'll take him. Bedtime big guy."

Patrick yawned broadly and said, "Okay, night, Charlotte. Night, Mom. I love you,"

"I love you, too, Patrick," she said and wiped her eyes, watching them leave the room.

The rest family moved toward the bed to see the baby.

They received word that the storms had brought more than Charlotte. Claire and Thomas had a surprise that night as well. Their baby Mary Elizabeth had also been born that same night.

Back to the train

Jeremy asked, "Did you want to stop somewhere and rest?"

"No," she said. "I'd like to go home."

"Then, that's where we shall go," he said as he pulled her closer.

It would be more than a week of train travel and communications to get them there. The train finally pulled into the Chicago station in the early morning and they exited to make their way home. Suddenly, their names were being yelled across the platform. "Emma! Jeremy!"

They looked toward the voices and saw their family. *Yes,* she thought, *all of our family is here. Papa, Cole, Dora, Tim.* As they started hugging her, Emma said, "You all came."

"Of course, we did. We're family," said Cole, kissing her on the cheek.

Cole saw Jeremy was in pain and said, "Let's get them to the boarding house so they can eat and rest."

Jeremy nodded, grateful they were there for them.

Dora linked arms with Emma and said, "I'm glad you weren't hurt worse than you were. Though that eye is still looking bad."

She gently probed it and said, "Yes, it's probably colorful. I'm so glad to be home." She changed the subject after they climbed into the waiting carriages. "How is Charlotte?"

"She's sleeping, finally. The colic is better." Charlotte had suffered a bout of colic that kept everyone awake.

"Was Jake able to move back into the boarding house?" Jake had been forced to relocate to Cole and Ellis' house for a while. The crying had upset him and disrupted his schedule.

Dora nodded. "It was better for him to be away while Charlotte was loud, but he is back now. We missed him." She hugged her close and said, "I missed you, too."

"I can't wait to see her," Emma said as she laid her head on Dora's shoulder until they arrived home.

CHAPTER 2

The next morning, Cole sat at his desk, reviewing the information from the silver case. He looked at Emma and Jeremy and said, "Thank you both for coming in to discuss this. I know you are fatigued from your travels."

"No, we don't mind getting out some. We need the exercise," said Jeremy. Emma nodded in agreement.

"Okay, then I will get on with it. Good job getting the silver back and arresting the two people involved. As I understand it, the Pinkertons who arrived in Statesville didn't have to do much."

Jeremy and Emma laughed. "It was an interesting couple of days."

Emma looked at Cole and asked, "Did you find out who gave us the information that led to the arrest?"

"Family," said Cole simply. "We did some checking into the telegraph operator once we had the bank robber's information. One of the robbers was named Michael Cannon. It turns out his sister Martha is married to Jerry Stanton, the clerk who sent the note."

Emma asked unexpectantly, "Cole, where does Martha work?"

"Why do you ask?" Cole asked, curious what she was thinking.

"The bank robbers didn't seem intelligent enough to pull this off on their own," Emma commented.

"That's worth looking into," Cole acknowledged. "I'll have the Colorado office check into it."

A few days later, Cole sent over a note that said, *An accounting of the silver showed it wasn't all recovered. Martha did work at the bank and was involved; she and the husband are missing. They're now persons of interest in the case.*

Emma had answered the door and was walking back into the sitting room while she read the note. She sat next to Jeremy, who noticed it and asked, "Who sent it?"

"Cole," she said, absently handing it to him. As he read it, she said, thinking out loud, "Jeremy, I think there's a chance to catch them. We know they're on their way to Washington D.C. since that's where the buyers are located. I'll bet that train crash also delayed their arrival." Train schedules had to be changed after the wreck.

"There may still be time to intercept them," he said, following her line of thought. "But why turn the brother and friend in?"

"I'm assuming to give them time to escape. We went after Michael and Nick, not knowing the others were part of the plan. They would have made it without being detected."

"Except for the train wreck," he said thoughtfully. They couldn't have known they would have a significant delay in their schedule. "I'll head over to the Pinkerton office now and let Cole know what we're thinking. Do you want to come with me?"

"No," she said. "I have to help with the baking. We have the meeting tonight for the charity."

"Okay." He grabbed his hat and carefully put on his jacket. He walked over and gave her a quick kiss. "See you soon," he promised.

"Count on it. Watch that arm," she reminded him.

"I will."

"Emma," called Dora from the kitchen.

"On my way," she called back. She looked around and saw a flash of pink run behind the chair next to her. She called out teasingly, "Lottie, where are you? We're going to do some baking in the kitchen."

She heard a squeal and one-year-old Lottie wobbled out from behind a chair.

Emma caught her up and tickled her as they moved to the kitchen. As they entered, they saw Dora gathering the ingredients. "What are we making?" asked Emma.

"Chocolate Lebkuchen," said Dora. She looked at Lottie and asked, "And you, little lady, will you be helping today?" Instead of responding, Lottie giggled and buried her head in Emma's shoulder.

CHAPTER 3

They sat around the large table, waiting for the board meeting to begin. They were snacking on the Chocolate Lebkuchen that Emma and Dora had brought. Papa looked at the shape of the pastry and asked Dora, "Are these different types of lebkuchen?"

"No," she said with a laugh. "Emma thought it would be fun to have Lottie help with the shapes."

"Oh," he said with a smile. "It doesn't seem to affect the flavor."

Emma and Jeremy sat near Cole, talking quietly about the bank robbery while they waited for Clair to start the meeting.

"Any word yet on the sister and husband? Have they been seen in D.C.?" asked Jeremy.

Cole answered in a low voice, "Pinkerton has the train station monitored with agents and others are assigned to watch for the black-market contact. They already had an idea of who the contact might be. We should know something in the next few days."

"We can't discount alternative transportation given the disruption in rail," suggested Emma

"Yes, that's why they have agents watching the most likely persons to be involved in the case," indicated Cole.

Clair entered the room with Thomas. They took their seats and the room quieted. "The first order of business," said Clair, "is to settle on a new name for the charity. We have been calling it "the charity" for long enough."

Emma looked at her with interest and asked, "What do you suggest?"

"I was thinking of naming it after our benefactor," Clair said.

"You're right, we should have done this earlier," agreed Emma.

"I'm calling for a vote," stated Clair in a businesslike manner. "Those voting yes," she looked around the table and documented all hands were raised. "The yesses have it. The charity will now be called the Carlyle Foundation. I'll submit the paperwork to our lawyer tomorrow."

Clair read down her list, looked up, and said, "The second item on the agenda. I would like to start organizing a gala to raise money."

"Why?" asked Emma. They had always kept the charity based solely on investments of Mr. Carlyle's money.

Clair laid her list down and said, "I've been discussing this with our lawyer and our accountant." She nodded at Tim and received a nod back. "We need to fundraise to make us more visible. With more money, we could help more people."

Cole asked concern etched on his face, "Are we having money problems? Have we had a business loss?"

"No." She laughed. "Since we got rid of Sam, the accounts have been perfect and they are making money." Sam had been Clair's assistant when the charity first opened. The money disappeared from accounts and he was caught, admitting it had been part of a private vendetta.

"Who would we invite?" asked Emma, unsure how to

proceed. They didn't occupy the same circles as people who could donate large sums of money.

"The elite of society, the people who have money to spend and to donate. I have a list of prospective donors for us to review," said Claire firmly.

"Where did you get the list?" Emma asked curiously. "We don't have a social register in Chicago."

"I made a list similar to that one in New York. I used the paper's society section to build it."

"There's also the University club," stated Cole. "I believe their goals and the Carlyle Foundation's goals match up. Their focus is around the values of a common educational experience."

"We do put a lot of money into education," stated Clair. "Can you inquire if they would be willing to attend?"

"I can. I'm also a member."

"The others on your list, would they come?" inquired Emma.

"I think that, if we list the groups of people we've helped in the past and show the ones we hope to have in the future, then yes," said Clair, positive about her idea. "I planned to put together a package and send it out with the invitations."

Tim looked contemplative and said, "We have several previous clients I believe would attend and encourage friends. I'll get you their names."

"Thanks, Tim. Any other ideas?" asked Clair expectantly.

"My client roster would also be a good start," said Ellis. He rattled off a few well-known names. "Aaron Montgomery—founder of Montgomery Ward; Potted Palmer and Marshal Fields—major department store leaders; George Pullman—Pullman manufacturing, rail cars." He had worked with each to rebuild after the '71 fire.

Clair nodded. "That's an amazing start. Once we approach the first people and get an acceptance, that should open up the door for more donors."

"Clair, have you chosen a venue?" asked Tony, thinking how he could help.

"I've looked around," she admitted. "But I haven't found the right place yet."

Tony said, "The museum would make an excellent location for this event."

Clair looked hopeful and asked, "Do you think Philip would mind?" He was the curator at the local museum and Tony worked as his assistant.

"I'll speak with him. Have you picked some dates?" he asked, knowing Philip wanted to expand the usage of the museum.

Clair pulled out her calendar. "I was thinking of three months from now."

Tony wrote the date down and promised to get back to her.

Dora had been attentive and asked, "What about food?"

"I think we would serve a full dinner," said Clair.

"And desserts," supplied Dora.

"Yes, and desserts." Clair laughed. "We will have tables full of desserts."

"We should cater the dinner and use the bakery to provide the desserts," suggested Dora. "I can also assist in picking them out and setting up the menu." She had some extra time because she had added a cook to their boarding house as her pregnancy progressed, After the baby was born, she kept the new staff on full time. She continued to manage Patrick, the baby, and both boarding houses.

"Are you sure? It'll be a lot of work?" asked Clair.

"I'm sure," confirmed Dora firmly.

"And I'll help her," said Tim, covering her hand with his. She smiled over at him, still so happy he was in her life.

Dora looked over at Jake and said, "Clair, Jake could provide photographs for us also."

Clair said, "That would be excellent. Jake, can you do that for us?"

Dora tapped his book to get his attention. He usually brought one to their meetings. "Can you take pictures at the event?"

"They're not my normal pictures," he stated without answering the question. His pictures were usually murder scenes for the police department. Jake tended to be very literal and sometimes required extra explanation for the easiest things.

Dora explained that it was a part of his role as a board member. Once he understood it was a rule, he agreed.

Clair handed out the assignments:

Tony: to confirm the venue and how many people could be invited.

Emma, Cole, and Tim: to build a guest list.

Dora and Clair: food.

Jake: to take the pictures.

Jeremy and Cole: to review the security setup and provide Pinkerton agents as security guards.

The team worked to organize the event. It was arranged for three months from that day. Philip graciously provided the museum as the venue, and an orchestra was arranged as entertainment. Clair and her assistant secured tables and chairs for the evening, while Claire then met with Philip and Tony to design the setup.

The invitations went out and everything was in place for the big night.

CHAPTER 4

THE NIGHT OF THE GALA

The event came together quickly. Ellis had met with each of his clients and explained what the Carlyle foundation was working on. With that and the information Clair provided, each agreed to be there to support the charity.

Clair was right. Once the news was circulated that Pullman and Fields would be there, they had trouble keeping people out. The list had to be reviewed and trimmed several times. Security at the event would be tight.

The museum was the perfect atmosphere for the occasion. Gas lights offered a glow on the room, the orchestra played throughout the night. The main area floor had been cleared and round tables surrounded the dance floor for people to observe. The dinner had been served with Clair and several guest speakers discussing the projects the foundation was supporting. As that wound down, the dancing had begun.

Ellis and Cole spent much of the evening together. They stood off to the side of the dance floor, watching the dancers twirl by. Ellis listened absently as Cole talked about the follow-up to the silver case. He was saying, "They were able to pick up both the robbers and the buyers."

"That's nice," Ellis said, not hearing him. He noticed Emma and Jeremy dancing. She was lovely in a brilliant red ball gown with black lace trim and Jeremy wore a black tuxedo.

He watched them twirl by, and Emma sent him a small wave. As he waved back, he noticed Tony out of the corner of his eye. He was lounging against the wall, watching Emma and Jeremy dance with a dark expression on his face.

A triangle, he thought. *Emma, Jeremy, and Tony.* He could understand Tony's hurt feelings. That particular triangle reminded him of the past where he and Cole had also pined for one woman. *Funny*, he thought. *I haven't thought about Abbey in years.* Suddenly, the memories flooded his mind, recalling their first meeting.

~

He and Cole were about fifteen at that time and had been living on the streets for a few years. They lived in a structure they had constructed out of wood from various delivery drivers. *Some had been gotten honestly, some weren't*, he thought with a smile. They had been in the shelter that night; the rain pounded down on them as they sat talking. It was at that moment their small door rattled and flew open. At first, they thought it was the wind, but then they saw someone crawling into their space.

"Hey!" Cole said loudly, angry the wind had almost blown out their light. "You weren't invited in here."

The boy closed the door and looked around, saying, "Pretty nice place."

Cole continued to frown. "You're not wanted here."

Ellis saw something Cole didn't and smiled to himself. His thoughts were confirmed when "the boy" whipped off her hat to reveal auburn curls.

Cole finally saw what Ellis saw and said, "Oh!"

"I'm Abbey," she said, introducing herself.

Ellis spoke up and said, "I'm Ellis and this is Cole."

"How did you know we were here?" Cole questioned softly. They were pretty well hidden in the back of the alley.

"I've been following you," she said simply.

"What! Why?" Cole asked, puzzled. What could this girl want?

"You're both pretty good pickpockets," she said. "I was working a few of the same places and watched your technique."

"Yeah, we've been doing it for a while," Ellis answered for them.

"You never thought to move into other things?" she asked innocently.

"What types of things?" asked Ellis cautiously.

"Well, let's just say you could be doing better than this," she said, looking around.

Cole was resolute. "No, we don't want to be involved in something like that. We're getting along fine now."

Ellis had been thinking the same thing; he didn't want to get further into criminal activities.

"Suit yourself," she said and shrugged off the negative reply. "I just thought you might want to make more money."

They sat quietly after that, waiting for the rain to abate. As it let up, she said." I have plans. I'll check back in with you both at a later date."

They nodded and watched her leave. They both knew they had made the right decision.

Over the next few weeks, they were conscious of her being in the neighborhood. She continued to dress as a boy and seemed to know everyone in the area. That day, Ellis was at the fruit stand when Abbey strolled up. She ignored him and started a conversation with the owner of the stand. The owner's back was to Ellis and she kept him talking. *Cover.* he thought and grabbed three apples and put them in his pockets. Starting to move away, he hesitated, wanting to hear what they were talking about.

The vendor asked, "Is your mom getting out soon?"

Getting out, thought Ellis. *Prison?*

Abbey answered in a lighthearted voice, "Sure, Mom will be out at the end of the week."

He realized they were wrapping up, so he strolled in the opposite direction.

Later that night, Ellis mentioned to Cole that Abbey's mom was in prison. "What about her dad?"

"Not sure."

Hmm, thought Cole, *there are layers to this girl.*

They continued to see her throughout the week.

The next Monday, they were in their shelter when once again the door opened and Abbey entered.

"Becoming a habit?" asked Cole wryly.

"Perhaps," she said. "My mom is back and I thought you might like to have a warm place to sleep tonight."

Cole looked at Ellis and he shrugged. "Why not?" They gathered their things, books, and blankets to head out.

Abbey saw what they were carrying and asked, "Books?"

"Yes, we both like to read. We get them from the library," explained Ellis.

She raised an eyebrow at that. "Do you check them out?" She knew they couldn't get a library card without an address.

Cole responded, "We return them when we've finished reading."

They continued to follow her to a small apartment a few blocks away. Abbey opened the door with her key and said, "Mom, I've brought them back with me."

Her mom stepped out. She had similar hair to her daughter, though grayer throughout. She was a striking woman; wiry intelligence shined in her eyes. "Hello, boys," she said. "Tell me your names."

"Cole."

"Ellis."

"Mine is Marjorie. You may call me Miss Marjorie."

"Thank you," both boys answered.

"You can stay with us as long as you want. Though," she said looking around, "it could be better."

"It's fine, Mom." Abbey knew what she was thinking; better meant a job. A job meant a risk of going back to prison and she would like her to stick around longer this time.

Miss Marjorie pretended not to hear her and said, "All right, boys, the evening dinner is a simple event. Cooking's not my forte."

"Anything would be fine," said Ellis, thinking that a warm meal, whatever it was, would be nice. Cole nodded in agreement.

Miss Marjorie wasn't shy about why she went to prison and talked about it at dinner. "I picked the wrong people for that last bank robbery." The boys were fascinated; Abbey appeared to be less so.

Abbey remarked as she finished, "You got careless about the amount of money you were spending, that's why you got picked up."

Miss Marjorie sent her a look and said, "Listen, girl, when I want advice on how to do my job, I'll ask for it."

"I could do better and do it by myself," she muttered.

Miss Marjorie stood and got out the bread. She pulled a knife from seemingly thin air and slammed it into the loaf. "You need to refine your skills more. I need you to be ready to start doing jobs with me."

Abbey said in a low voice, "There's nothing wrong with my skills. I just prefer to work alone."

Miss Marjorie didn't respond to that statement, but she narrowed her eyes as she watched her.

Cole and Ellis sat silently, eating the meal and eyeing them both, not sure what to say.

After a while, a truce seemed to be called and they moved into the small living room.

"You boys can sleep here as long as you want. We have plenty of food and, once I get my next score, we'll move to a bigger place."

"However temporary that will be," Abbey said.

Miss Marjorie glared but chose not to enter into another argument.

The next morning, they woke up and saw that Abbey was already gone. Miss Marjorie was working on lock sets in the small dining room. "Boys," she said. "There's pastry and fruit in the kitchen."

"Thanks," said Cole as he headed that way.

"What's that you're working on?" Ellis asked, interested. He hesitated by the table, watching what she was doing.

Miss Marjorie didn't look up when she said, "Lock sets."

Ellis sat down and continued to watch her.

Miss Marjorie picked one up, handed it to him, and explained, "These are examples of the lock sets used in most homes and businesses at this time. When I plan to enter a building, I like to practice picking ones that are of different ages; they can become trickier to open with time."

He turned it slowly in his hands, examining it, and said, "This slot looks like a flat key."

"Yes, that is the new Yale design," she commented.

"Would a business use only one type of lock?" he asked, thinking of the types of keys used in homes.

"Yes, most have moved to the lock sets that use a pin and tumbler design. Interestingly, the design was an improvement on the simple wooden tumbler lock created by the Egyptians." She looked at him with a gleam in her eye and asked, "Would you like to learn to pick locks?"

Ellis had an interest in how things worked and said, "Yes, please."

They worked together quite happily, taking apart the various locks and putting them back together. Cole called out from the kitchen, "Ellis, you should eat breakfast."

He called absently back, looking at the lock set in his hand intently, "I'll be there in a moment."

Cole knew that tone and said, "I'll bring it to you."

Ellis sat there for the next three days, working diligently on each one. He took them apart to learn how they operated and then worked on the techniques used to pick them. Miss Marjorie stayed with him, working out the details and the questions.

At the end of the week, Miss Marjorie said, "I think you're ready."

"Ready?" he asked absently.

"Yes, ready to help me with the locks on a job I'm planning."

Cole, who was sitting in the room with them, said, "Wow, I don't think he should be doing that." He was always protective of Ellis.

Ellis looked contemplative and said, "I'd like to see if stress in the field affects my performance."

"Seriously, you aren't considering it?" Cole asked, frustrated at this turn of events.

"I am," he said.

"Well, you can't."

"Can't? Cole, you're not my parent," he said simply.

"No, you're right," he conceded. "But we haven't gotten caught yet and doing something like this could get you sent to the workhouse or prison." Cole was always thinking ahead to the possible consequences.

"I know, but I would like to do this."

"I don't support your involvement."

Miss Marjorie looked over at Cole and said in a sarcastic tone, "I don't think you were asked."

Abbey, who was sitting nearby, giggled.

"What are you laughing at?" asked Cole belligerently.

"You. You're a thief. Why try to stop him from basically doing the same thing?" Abbey asked.

"It's not though, is it? This moves him into areas that could have serious consequences," said Cole.

"I think he can make decisions for himself," she said, looking at Ellis consideringly.

"Abbey, will you be going?" Cole demanded.

"I work on my own," she said evasively.

Cole watched her closely, wondering what her game was.

She laughed, noticing his gaze, and said, "Don't try to figure me out."

"Hmm, you know if I had more data, I might be able to work it out. Would you like to go to the park with me for a walk?" Cole said smoothly.

She smiled softly and said, "Only if it's the three of us."

He frowned. He would rather be with her on his own but decided that some time with her was better than none. "Okay, how about the three of us go out this evening?" he suggested.

She said, "Now, that we can do."

They started to go out together, the three of them. They spent all of their time together, walking, talking, and generally enjoying each other's company. It was also the first time in a while that Cole and Ellis could relax, knowing they had a warm place to sleep and food to eat.

As the week progressed, Ellis continued to work with Miss Marjorie. They had the job scheduled for that Friday night, a robbery of a known gangster location. The safe was located inside a large multiroom building. Ellis would manage the door locks and Miss Marjorie would work on the safe.

Cole and Abbey had monitored the location and noted there

were external guards day and night, with a shift change at 9pm. They were also able to confirm that no one entered or exited the building after that time. Miss Marjorie used this information to set her schedule for the heist. She went the night before to test the time and to loosen a spot in the roof to drop into the area where the safe was located.

Friday night, Ellis and Miss Marjorie left for the job. Cole and Abbey waited for them to return. They were dozing on the chairs in the sitting room when they heard a banging at the door. Abbey ran to the door to let them in; Ellis was supporting Miss Marjorie and moved her to the couch.

"What happened!" Abbey demanded as she followed them.

Ellis was looking at Miss Marjorie, concerned. "I'm fine. She saved my life. She stepped in front of me and took the bullet. I was standing like a statue, not moving. She tried to get me to move but I just froze." He looked over at Cole and said, "Looks like you were right. I shouldn't have gone."

Cole nodded but didn't say anything more. He knew Ellis already felt terrible about the situation.

Abbey saw the blood and tore Miss Marjorie's sleeve off. She looked at it carefully and said in a relieved voice, "She's fine. It's just a scratch. I'll clean it and bandage it."

"Thank goodness," said Cole.

"Ellis, come here," Miss Marjorie called to him as Abbey worked on her arm. He bent down next to her. She said quietly, "None of this is your fault. You were amazing tonight; you got into every door faster than I could have. Without you, we wouldn't have made it inside."

"Without you, we wouldn't have made it out," he said quietly, feeling guilty he hadn't responded better in the high-pressure situation.

"Enough of that. Bed for you both," Abbey told them firmly.

"Yes, I could use some rest," said Miss Marjorie, fatigue making her look older than her years.

Cole called, "What do you want me to do with this?" They looked toward him and saw he was holding bundles of money he had pulled from the bag.

"Wow," said Abbey, rushing over. "That's a good haul."

"Yeah, it'll get us a nicer place," said Miss Marjorie in a tired voice.

Abbey frowned. It was always a nicer place, but only temporarily. She tried to reason with her. "Mom, we could stay here and save money. Not blow it."

"Little girl, that's my money and a cut of it belongs to Ellis. You have no stake in this."

"And no say in where we end up," she said bitterly.

Miss Marjorie frowned at her, not answering.

Ellis stepped in before they could argue further. "You need some rest. Let's get you to bed."

"Thank you, *Ellis*," Miss Marjorie said, looking pointedly at Abbey.

Ellis and Cole watched the interaction between Miss Marjorie and Abbey over the next week. Abbey had voiced her opinion about how the money should be spent and didn't bring it up again. Miss Marjorie made all of the arrangements and announced the date of the move.

After they moved to a larger place, Abbey grew moodier with every week. "Hey, what's wrong?" asked Ellis.

"This," she said, waving her hand, indicating the stylish, fully furnished room around them. "It's just temporary. She gets a score and spends it immediately."

"She likes to live this way," he said in a calm voice.

"Well, I don't," she said and stomped off.

Miss Marjorie started planning another job. The nicer apartment was a priority for her. She looked over at Ellis; he was good in the field but had said a definite no when she tried to get him involved. Backup would be needed. Her eyes found Abbey and she said in a firm voice, "Abbey, I need you on this job."

"I thought you said my skills weren't good enough," she answered in the same tone.

"Well, it's time to test you in the field," Miss Marjorie commented.

"I prefer to work alone," she said forcefully.

"If you want to stay here, you need to work with me. I need help. I need someone I can trust."

Abbey felt forced and she didn't like it, but she had nowhere else to go and finally said reluctantly, "All right."

The job was located at a local department store. The safe was a large one in the manager's office. They also had onsite security staff. Miss Marjorie set up the job so they would enter a weak point in the roof structure. She had weakened it herself over the past two weeks. She had Cole and Ellis case the location at night to check for security schedules.

The final plans were set for that Thursday at 1am. Miss Marjorie and Abbey set off, dressed in black. Cole and Ellis would wait up for them.

The evening wore on slowly for Cole and Ellis, each watching the clock.

When it got past the hour they should have returned, they decided to go to the job. At that moment, Miss Marjorie crashed opened the door, and said, "Abbey's caught." She threw her bag down and sat.

The boys looked at one another, their worst fears coming true. "What happened?" asked Cole. "Who got her? Was it the security guards?"

"Yes," she muttered, not explaining further.

Ellis insisted, "We need to try to get her out."

"No," she said. "We lay low. They'll know someone else is involved and arrest whoever shows up."

"We can't just leave her there!" said Cole forcefully. Ellis agreed.

Miss Marjorie had gone quiet.

They sat there, watching her for the next hour, whispering back and forth, trying to work out how to get Abbey home.

A loud knock was heard from the door. Miss Marjorie reacted violently and almost fell out of her chair. "Hide! I have to hide!" she said as she ran into the bedroom.

The knocking grew louder.

Ellis looked at the door and asked in a low voice, "Should I get it?"

Cole replied in the same tone, "Yes."

Ellis got up to answer it. It was Abbey. "How did you get away?" he asked.

She didn't answer. Instead, she narrowed her eyes and asked, "Where is she?"

Miss Marjorie stood in the doorway of her bedroom and said with false bravado, "See, I knew you'd make it out. How did you get away?"

Abbey looked in disgust at her mother. "Did she tell you what she did? Did she tell you she left me behind?"

The boys looked at her in disbelief. Miss Marjorie had saved Ellis' life and helped them so much, but had left her daughter behind at a job?

"You're like a cat, always landing on your feet. I knew I didn't have to worry about you. You got back here, didn't you?" Miss Marjorie said defensively.

"What happened?" asked Ellis, taking Abbey's hands in his.

Abbey swallowed the lump in her throat and started. "We had emptied the safe and were making our way back out, through the roof. I thought we had time before the next security rounds, but we got spotted. I lost my footing on the roof and slid down the shingles. When I called for help from this one," indicating her mom with her head, "she just left me."

"What happened next?" asked Cole, caught up in the story.

"The guards rescued me and took me into custody. They put me in cuffs and placed me in a room until the police were notified. I got out of the cuffs and crawled through the window," she explained.

"Well, you're home now and safe. You'll just need to keep a low profile for a while, maybe change your appearance," Miss Marjorie said consideringly.

Abbey looked at her incredulously and said in a loud voice, so no one could mistake her meaning, "I'm done! Done with you and done with this life!" Her mom was not as careful as she used to be, and she would get caught sooner or later. Abbey didn't want to go down with her.

"If you're done, then I think you should plan on living elsewhere," said Miss Marjorie in a voice ringing with anger.

"I plan to. I want my cut from tonight's heist," Abbey insisted.

Miss Marjorie pulled out a bundle of bills and tossed it at her.

Abbey counted it quickly and said, "Hey, there was much more than just this."

"Think about it as a finder's fee. I have expenses," muttered Miss Marjorie.

Abbey stomped off to her room. Cole and Ellis followed and watched her pack.

"Where are you going?" asked Cole.

"As far from her as possible. I can't stay here; they'll be looking for me. I'm heading to New York City, then to Europe."

Both boys frowned at that statement.

"Would you like to come with me?" she asked, not looking up.

"Who are you talking to?" asked Ellis.

"Both of you."

"You can't have both of us," said Cole and looked at Ellis. "Right?" Ellis nodded in agreement; he didn't want to share either. All three of them were so young, trying to make a decision like this. Cole wanted her all for himself and Abbey had always shared her time between them.

"I don't see why there should be a decision. Can't we just continue as we are?" she said, looking at them. She was happy with things as they were.

"No," said Cole resolutely. He wanted this worked out.

Ellis spoke up and said in a kind voice, "Abbey, it isn't fair to any of us. The one you don't choose can still be your friend."

With tears in her eyes, she looked directly at him and asked, "What if I said Cole, instead of you?"

"Then I would have two best friends," he said resolutely, not willing to lose either of them. They were his family and he would do anything for them.

Abbey looked at him and said in a low voice, "Ellis, can't you fight for me? Show some emotion?"

Even at that time, Ellis was more removed and not as emotional as his peers. He lived a lot of his life in his head. His response to her was just to shake his head.

She stomped her food and said, "I won't do it. I won't choose."

They went down to the train station with her, keeping a lookout for any persons who might be following them. "Abbey."

"Yes, Ellis?"

"I have something for you." He handed her a large portion of the money from the heist he had been involved in.

"Oh," she said with tears in her eyes. "I can't take all of your money."

"It isn't all of it," he assured her, but it was most of it. "Take it and be safe."

"I will." She kissed both boys' cheeks and boarded the train for New York.

That was the last time Ellis had seen her.

〜

He continued to watch the dancers, absently trying to place Abbey's head on each of the women. He seemed to have achieved this and saw her dancing by him. He shook his head to clear the memory, but when he looked again, he could have sworn that was her. *My imagination is getting away from me.*

"What was that?" asked Cole.

Ellis started when he realized Cole was still beside him, that he'd muttered his thought out loud. "Nothing," he said absently. "I just thought I saw someone." He continued to watch the dancers intently to see if he would see her again. They twirled past and the music came to a stop. The woman he was watching turned toward him and strode deliberately over to where he and Cole stood. Cole was not facing the dance floor and had not noticed her walking up to them.

"Abbey," said Ellis in a faint voice, "is it really you?"

"It is," she said as he moved to hug her. She returned it warmly. He stepped back but kept her hand in his. She looked happy to let her hand stay where it was.

Cole had turned to speak with an associate, but immediately turned back when he heard her voice. He watched as Ellis stepped back after hugging her.

His voice was hard when he said, "Abigail, why are you here?"

Ellis turned and gave him a long look. He hadn't seen Abbey since that day she refused to choose between them. He narrowed his eyes at Cole, wondering if *he* had seen Abbey since then.

Before she could answer, Jeremy and Emma strolled up. "Hey, Pops," said Jeremy as he put his arm around Cole's shoulders. "Are you having a nice time?"

"Yes, you need to dance," he said in a firm voice to Jeremy.

"I believe my card is open if you would like to dance with me," suggested Emma in a teasing voice.

"I'm not sure I want to let you go," Jeremy teased her.

Emma laughed, but no one else in their small group did. Emma noticed they were very quiet and nudged Jeremy, nodding toward them.

Jeremy looked curiously at the woman standing with Cole and Ellis. She had not turned toward them. He noticed Cole and Ellis were also preoccupied.

Cole looked over at Jeremy and said with a smile, "Why don't you take the next one with Emma and save one later for me?"

Jeremy raised a brow at him, but took the hint and said to Emma, "Shall we?"

"We shall," she said with a smile, but concern lit her eyes. They went to the dance floor and, as Jeremy twirled her into his arms, she asked, "Should we be concerned?"

He looked over her shoulder toward their two fathers and finally said, "No, I don't think so. I'll check with them later."

Cole looked harder at Abigail and asked again, "Why are you here?"

She smiled innocently. "What, I can't attend a charity dance? I paid for my ticket."

He looked around for a place where he could speak to her privately. "This way." He turned away from them and strode out of the room, expecting them to follow.

Ellis shrugged and offered his elbow to her; she took it moving at a slower pace behind him. As they entered, Cole's calm demeanor vanished as he slammed the door behind them. He turned to her and said, "What are your plans?"

"I plan to meet my son," she said simply.

"Here? Tonight?" he asked loudly.

"Yes, I don't want to waste a moment," she said, using the same loud voice.

"No!" Cole shouted.

Ellis stepped in, "I feel like I have started to read a book in the middle. I assume the two of you were…"

"Married," supplied Abbey.

"When?" Ellis asked, confused that his two closest friends had been married... meaning Abbey was Jeremy's mother.

Cole sat on the long leather couch, leaned his head back, and closed his eyes. "It was after you and Mary had married, and Dora was on the way."

Abbey sat slowly and said, "I was in New York and I was headed to see you both here in Chicago."

"Why didn't I see you?" Ellis asked.

"I never made it there. I ran into Cole in New York," she said quietly. She didn't say that she had told Cole she had finally made her decision about who she wanted, and she was on her way to Chicago to tell Ellis she loved him.

~

New York 1865

Cole watched as the rain fell. It was hard and cold on his face that early morning, but at least the gale-force winds and fog had abated. He was on a whaleboat that belonged to the U.S. Revenue Cutter Richard Rush. They were chasing a steamer; they had information that indicated it was carrying a large amount of opium.

Cole stood on the side of the whaleboat with his men, waiting for the steamer to give up the chase. It tried to outrun them but it was no use; the winds were with them.

They had caught up and boarded the mostly empty ship steamer. One of his men called from down in the hold, "Opium!"

"How much?" Cole shouted back.

"More than 500lbs of opium packed in 1/2lb tins."

Drug use had increased in the U.S. with large amounts of Chinese-made opium being smuggled in on ships. The U.S.

Treasury had hired the Pinkertons to help out with the case. Cole was already a lead investigator, making a name for himself within the agency.

The drug smugglers were taken into custody and moved to the whaleboat. They left several sailors from the whaleboat to bring in the steamer. The smugglers were escorted off and given into the custody of the U.S. Treasury Department.

As Cole and his men started to exit the boat, the Treasury representative thanked him for their assistance in taking down the steamer and recovering the opium. They shook hands and he departed with the smugglers and drugs. Cole stood on the boardwalk and watched as they moved the carriages and wagons away.

"Always involved in something, aren't you?" asked a female voice.

Cole stilled immediately when he recognized that voice. He said without looking back, "Abigail."

"Yes. Did you get bored waiting for me?" she teased him.

He turned slowly; it had been so long since he had seen her. She was the same girl he remembered, but now she had a polished look. "I didn't know you were back in the country."

"I just got back," she said lightly. "I'm on my way to Chicago."

"You are?" he teased back. "On the way to see me?"

"Why don't you give me a ride to my hotel, maybe dinner tonight? I can explain things then," she said quietly.

"I can do that," he said, looking at her for answers he wasn't sure he wanted to hear.

The trip to her hotel was full of conversation. They had been friends a long time and they had plenty to catch up on. They were laughing about a story involving Ellis, Cole, and Abigail as they pulled up to the hotel. "I'll pick you up at 7 for dinner?" he suggested.

"That would be lovely," she said. The stories brought her back in time when they were all friends. When they tried to get her to decide between them, she had opted not to make one and left. Now she was older, she felt she could make that choice. They said goodbye and agreed to meet in the lobby later that evening. She rested in her room and then picked out an outfit to see an old friend.

She felt a bit nervous as she walked down the stairs to the lobby. The decision she was planning to share might hurt Cole. Pausing, she looked around and saw him sitting on one of the settees. He was taking in the whole room, observing everything. *He hasn't changed through the years*, she thought.

He turned, as though he had felt her gaze. She could feel the heat across the room. *Wow*, she thought, *this will be harder than I thought.*

He stood and walked over to greet her. "Abigail," he said and leaned down to kiss her on the cheek.

"Cole," she replied.

He offered her his elbow, which she accepted, and they departed for the restaurant. The carriage ride was silent and once they reached the restaurant, it continued. Cole reached across the table and took her hand in his. "Abigail, is there something you want to tell me?"

She took a deep breath and said, "You could always see to the heart of things. I'm here because I wanted to see you and Ellis."

"And," he prompted.

"I finally made a decision," she said decisively.

He didn't have to inquire what she was talking about; he knew. He looked at her for a long time and said, "You didn't choose me."

"No," she said softly. "I chose Ellis."

He shook his head and said with a twisted smile, "It would have been better if you had chosen me."

She frowned and said, "I don't understand."

"Abigail, you waited too long," he started.

"Why has he forgotten about me?" she asked coyly.

That made him laugh; no one could forget Abigail. "No, he never forgot you."

"Then why did you say I waited too long?" She was feeling bewildered by the turn of the conversation.

His face went solemn. "He's married."

She felt her stomach drop and asked in a casual voice, "Do you think it will last?"

"I do," he said. "He's very happy and they have a baby on the way."

"Happy and a baby. I guess there's nowhere to go from there," she said, feeling down. *All that way and to not even see him.*

"Aren't I a good substitute?" he asked, trying to lighten up the atmosphere.

"Yes," she said, letting him lighten her mood. "I don't know why I thought he would wait for me."

Cole didn't tell her that Ellis did wait, far longer than he should have. He looked at her and knew he wanted the opportunity to win her himself. "Let's enjoy our dinner."

"Yes," she said, picking up her fork.

"And a stroll after," he tempted her.

"That would be lovely," she commented.

The next few weeks were a whirlwind. Cole applied himself to entertaining her. As they got to know each other again, she remembered why the choice had been so hard. Cole was wonderful company and they got along so well. She watched him as much as he watched her. Studying him, she came to a conclusion and it was Cole. They had similar backgrounds and wanted similar things.

So, when he stopped her on their stroll a few weeks later to ask her to marry him, she said, "Yes."

Back to present-day Chicago

"We decided to get married. Jeremy came about a year after that," Abigail explained to Ellis, without mentioning she thought she would end up married to him and not Cole.

"Why have I never heard about this?" asked Ellis, feeling hurt that his two closest friends had kept something so vital from him.

"We weren't exactly close during that time," Cole muttered.

"That's true," admitted Ellis, acknowledging that he'd had a part in their separation. He asked the obvious question, "So, why aren't you together now?"

Instead of answering, Cole stared at Abigail. She stood, agitated. "Fine, I admit it. I screwed up."

And when she didn't continue, Cole said quietly, "She was on the run when we married."

She walked toward the fireplace and turned back to them, saying, "I was in prison in France. I took a necklace. I didn't think it would be missed."

"Not missed! It had an emerald and was surrounded by diamonds," Cole said in disbelief.

"I returned it," she said defensively.

"Yes, after you were caught," he said, still bitter about the event that destroyed their family.

"Yes," she said, not adding more.

Cole looked at Ellis and said, "She escaped prison in Europe and went on the run. When the men showed up to take her, I had to stay to look after Jeremy. He was just a little guy and he needed me."

"And left me to fend for myself," she said, bitterness now coloring her voice. "Just like *she* did."

That statement almost broke Cole's heart. He wanted to defend his actions but didn't think he could. He sighed and said, "I'll talk to Jeremy tomorrow." He looked at Ellis. "I'll include Emma, also. Jeremy will need the support."

"Emma?" asked Abbey, clearly bewildered at this person's name being introduced into a private family matter.

"Yes," said Ellis. "She's my daughter. She and Jeremy have been together for a while."

"Are they married?" she asked, curious about her son's life.

"No, but fully committed to one another," said Cole.

"Whose idea was it to not get married?" asked Abigail, studying Ellis.

"I believe it was a joint decision," Cole answered smoothly. He knew it was Emma's request, but Jeremy supported her.

She let that go, for now, knowing she would want to hear more about this commitment. "You'll make sure that I see him tomorrow?" she asked Cole.

"If I can work it out, plan on dinner at our house," he said, looking at Ellis.

She looked at both and laughed out loud. "You're living together?"

"We are. The kids have Ellis' house for their business ventures. We get along well together," said Cole. He decided that was enough for one night and stood. "I would prefer that you left now."

"Now, Cole," she chided him, "I would like to dance with Ellis. After all, I paid for my ticket."

He leaned forward, placing his hands on his thighs, and said, "As long as you don't approach Jeremy and no funny business."

"You mean like this?" she asked as she pulled his watch from her bosom.

"That's my watch," said Cole. She handed it to him with a coy smile. Cole took it from her and shook his head, thinking, *She's the same person she has always been, a charming thief.*

"Don't worry, I'll be on my best behavior," she assured them.

Cole quickly checked his pocket and Abigail noticed, saying in a wry voice, "Don't worry, Cole. Your wallet is safe." She watched as he slowly dropped his hands. She turned away from him and asked Ellis, "Shall we?" He happily obliged and offered her his elbow.

As they were walking back, Ellis noticed she had to wipe her eyes. "That scene affected you more than you let on," he said quietly.

"Yes, I just didn't want him to see," she said. "He always thinks the worst of me."

Ellis changed the subject and asked, "How about that dance?"

She smiled gratefully and said, "I would love that, dear Ellis." He showed a debonair side to his personality by twirling her onto the dance floor. They danced three more dances together.

Ellis was captivated. Outside of Mary, Abbey was the only other woman he had loved. He murmured in her ear, "You didn't come back to see me like you did Cole."

She shivered as she felt his hot breath on her neck and said, "I had planned to see you, but Cole intercepted me in New York City." That made him stop abruptly on the dance floor as he looked down at her.

Abigail didn't like to call attention to herself and said, "Ellis, we should keep moving."

He stood there a bit longer, then pulled her back to him and started moving again. "You were going to choose me?" he asked hoarsely.

"Yes," she said, softly laying her head on his shoulder. They danced closer, enjoying their time together.

*E*mma looked around as they danced and asked curiously, "Did you see who Papa is dancing with?"

"Hmm, not really," murmured Jeremy, his face in her neck. "I only have eyes for you."

"Really?" she asked with a low laugh, letting her attention be pulled back to her escort.

"Yes," he replied, "and I believe there's a lovely, warm bed at home."

"I'd like that," she said and took his hand to exit the dance floor. Just as they walked past the first table, someone grabbed her arm. She looked back to find Tony standing before her. "Hi, Tony," she said with a smile, one that faded quickly when she realized he'd been drinking.

"You promised me a dance," he reminded her rather forcefully.

"Yes, I did," she said as she turned to Jeremy. She asked lightly, her eyes silently pleading with him to understand, "Jeremy, would you mind?" She didn't want to bring attention to Tony's drinking in his place of work. There were a lot of people there who knew and respected him.

Jeremy nodded, understanding. "I'll be over there." He went to where Dora and Tim were seated and joined them.

"Where's Emma?" asked Dora curiously.

"Tony wanted a dance," he said and his voice betrayed his displeasure.

Dora heard the tone and watched him closely before she commented, "I understand Peggy has been away visiting family. He's probably lonely."

Jeremy nodded but thought to himself, *No, it's just his drinking has shown that he wants Emma back.* He continued to watch them closely.

On the dance floor, Tony tried to pull her in close; Emma placed her elbows between them. "Tony, not so close. Let's enjoy our dance."

"Yes," he said, "let's do that." They continued to dance quietly. He finally burst out in a desperate tone, "Emma, why him and not me?"

"Tony, you know why. We were growing up and apart. It was time," she said in a calming voice.

He seemed to sober abruptly and asked, "What if I want to get back together?"

She answered him in a quiet tone, looking him in the eye. "We aren't going to get back together. We're better friends than anything else. Can't you be okay with that?"

"I'm trying," he muttered.

"Where's Peggy?" she asked, knowing he had real feelings for her.

"She went to visit family," he said shortly.

Emma studied him and asked searchingly, "Was there a reason she left town?"

He turned a bit red and admitted, "She wants to get married."

"And what do you want, Tony?" she asked bluntly.

"I had thought the answer was you. I just wanted to go back to when it was simpler," he said lamely.

"Tony, we've all grown up and moved into our lives. Don't use me as an excuse to delay your future."

He didn't want to talk anymore and requested, "Can we just dance?"

"Yes," she murmured and moved to the music.

When the dance was done, she had him escort her to where Jeremy stood with Tim and Dora. She looked over at Tim and said firmly, "Tim, I think Tony wants to head home."

He glanced from Emma to Tony and said, "Yes, I see that he does." He slapped him on the back, saying cheerfully, "Tony, old man, let's go." He looked over at Dora and asked, "Are you ready?"

She got the message and said quickly, "Yes, I'm tired also. Amy's probably ready to go home, too." She had stayed at the boarding house to babysit the kids. They gathered up their things and, with Tony firmly in hand, headed out. Emma watched them leave and took the chair next to Jeremy.

He was quiet, thinking about Tony. He looked contemplative as he asked, "Anything I need to worry about?"

"No," she said, shaking her head. "I don't think so. I think he just had too much to drink and is missing Peggy."

Jeremy nodded, not voicing his doubts.

Cole walked over to them and said, "Looks like things are breaking up."

Jeremy glanced around and said, "Yes, seems to be a successful night for the Carlyle Foundation."

Emma nodded as she looked around; she wanted to check in and see if they needed to help clean up. "Have you seen Clair?" she inquired.

Cole indicated by nodding his head. "She's just over there."

Emma looked where he gestured and saw Clair speaking intently to a tall man in a suit. *I wonder what that's about,* she thought. Clair didn't seem upset. She continued watching as Thomas approached them; Clair gave him a sweet smile. *He must be a benefactor*, she concluded. Clair and Thomas excused themselves and made their way to Emma's table.

"Did everyone have a nice evening?" Clair asked their small group.

Emma responded with a smile. "The event has been lovely. It also appears to have been successful."

"We were able to fill all of the tables and meet our goals for new projects."

"Wonderful," said Cole, and Jeremy nodded in agreement.

Jeremy asked, "Do you need anything? Would you like us to stay and help clean up?"

"No, no," she assured them, "we have a crew coming in."

Cole said, "Our detectives are in place and will be here through the night. "

Clair said, "I'll get with them and confirm the next steps. Lily will also oversee the closeout." Lilly Edwards had been involved peripherally in another case that the group had solved. She had been caught with stolen merchandise and served some jail time. It was limited because she turned in her boyfriend as the main person behind the thefts. She was truly repentant of her mistakes. After she served her time, she returned and was sent to business school by the foundation. When Clair saw how talented she was, she made Lily her assistant.

At that moment, Lily walked up, wearing a black dress with a white collar. "Clair, we're just about ready to start taking things down."

"Wonderful. Do you think you can handle this cleanup?"

"Yes," she said competently. "I can handle it."

Clair looked at the group and said, "Thank you so much for your support. I'll organize a meeting to review the contributions and suggestions for new projects." She looked back at Lily and said, "Let's move to the office and confirm the details." Lilly nodded and followed her.

Jeremy noticed Cole looked like something was bothering him. "Pops, are you okay?"

"Yes," he said and took a deep breath to steady himself. "Jeremy, can you and Emma stop by tomorrow? I need to discuss something with you."

Jeremy frowned as he watched him, growing more concerned by the minute. "Pops, do you want to talk to us tonight? We can come by the house."

Cole shook his head. "No, it can wait until tomorrow." *It has waited this long*, he thought. *One night won't make a difference.*

"We will come by the house in the morning," confirmed Jeremy.

"I will see you then."

Emma stood up decisively and said, "I'm ready to head home. What about you?"

Jeremy stood up as well and said, "I am. Pops, would you like to ride with us?"

"Yes," he said laconically, knowing his ride had left without him.

Their hired carriage was waiting outside to take them home. They dropped off Cole on their way. Once they arrived home, Jeremy helped Emma down and they walked into the house, talking softly.

Voices sounded from the sitting room as they took off their coats in the foyer. Dora called out, "Emma, Jeremy, come in, sit down."

They joined the other couple, winding down for the evening. Emma looked at Tim and asked, "Did Tony get home okay?"

Tim grimaced, and said, "Yeah, I think he'll be nursing his head tomorrow morning."

Dora couldn't wait any longer and said, "Emma, did you get a chance to see who was dancing with Papa?"

"What?" Emma asked, distracted.

Dora continued, "The lady dancing with Papa. I saw them together, then they were gone."

Emma frowned at that. "He didn't tell you he was leaving?"

"No," Dora said.

"That is odd," she murmured.

"Yes, he was gone, and I noticed that woman with him was also gone."

"Are we already calling her 'that woman'?" Emma teased.

Dora frowned, thinking Emma wasn't taking this seriously enough.

Emma yawned and said, "We can ask him tomorrow. Cole wants us to stop by in the morning."

Jeremy said, looking at his watch, "I hope we can get some sleep before that."

Emma leaned over and murmured suggestively in his ear, "Maybe."

He laughed in a low voice and said to Tim and Dora, "We'll see you in the morning." Tim's laugh followed them up to their rooms.

Jeremy and Emma had an enjoyable interlude and slept in the next day. "We need to get up," Jeremy said softly into her hair.

Emma moaned and said into his chest, without looking up, "I guess we have to. Why did we make a morning date with your father?"

"He needs us, and I think it might be important," he reminded her.

"You're right," she said as she turned over and stretched. "Up we go." They both rose, with Jeremy exiting through the secret entrance to his room to prepare for the day. Emma finished getting ready and tucked her white tailored shirt into her green skirt. She put a red tie around her collar. Rather than her bowler, she picked up a straw hat with a matching green ribbon.

Strapping her clutch knife to her leg, she heard Jeremy call through the door, "Ready?"

She went and opened it, seeing him. "Let me grab my bag and notebook."

"Thinking of investigating something today?" he teased.

"No, just habit," she commented absently as she placed it in her pocket.

He took her hand as they made their way downstairs. It was about 9am on Sunday; everyone was free to get breakfast for themselves, so the family could usually attend church. As they reached the bottom of the steps, Emma heard the sound of children laughing. She turned toward it and saw Dora, Tim, and the children. They had mentioned they'd decided to skip church and spend the morning with the kids. Tim was chasing Patrick around the room.

Emma watched Patrick with Tim and thought, *He's so much a part of our family.* Dora was enjoying their antics, holding baby Lottie and laughing. She was such a beautiful baby girl, with strawberry blond hair, a mix of colors from Dora and Tim.

Lottie was struggling to get down; she wanted to join in on the fun with the boys. Dora finally gave in but said, "Careful, she wants to play also." Patrick and Tim slowed a bit to include her in their chase.

Dora noticed them in the hallway and called out, "There's some pastry and fruit in the kitchen if you're hungry."

"I am," said Emma. "We have to eat quickly; we're on our way to see Cole."

"Hmm. While you are there, could you see if you can figure out who Papa was dancing with last night?" she asked nonchalantly.

Emma grinned wickedly. "I can do that."

"Food?" asked Jeremy, wanting to get their day started.

"Yes," she said and walked with him to the kitchen. Once

there, they put together a quick breakfast. Emma noticed Jeremy was quieter than normal and inquired, "Are you okay?"

"Yes. I'm just worried about Pops. He seemed troubled last night," he explained.

They finished their breakfast and passed the sitting room to let Dora and Tim know they were heading out. "Let us know if he needs anything," Dora said over the noise of Lottie's happy screams as Tim tossed her into the air.

Jeremy said, "We will." He looked at Emma and asked, "Carriage or trolly?"

"Let's take the trolly, get some wind in our faces," she suggested.

"Sounds like a plan," he said as they headed to catch it.

They got off the trolly and walked the two blocks to Cole and Papa's house. Jeremy opened the door and called out for Cole.

They heard him say, "I'm in here, my boy." They walked through the foyer and saw him standing in the sitting room, holding a coffee cup. "Come in. come in. Would you like something to drink? Eat?"

"No, but thank you," Jeremy answered for them. "We ate before we came over."

"Good. Well, sit," he said.

As they sat, they looked at Cole expectantly.

He placed his coffee cup on the side table and sat on the chair opposite them. He appeared at a loss for words as he stared at Jeremy.

Jeremy burst out, "Pops, you're scaring me. Out with it. What's wrong?"

Cole thought the best way was to say it straight out. He leaned toward Jeremy and said, "Your mother is back."

That took Jeremy a moment to process, and he closed his eyes. He felt Emma's hand squeeze his. When he didn't say anything, Emma inquired softly, "How long has it been since you have seen her?"

"I'm not sure," commented Jeremy in a hoarse voice, opening his eyes.

"I am," commented Cole in a bitter tone. "She went away when he was about two."

Jeremy could barely take it in and asked, "Pops, where's she been all this time?"

Cole exhaled deeply. "I'm afraid she'll have to answer that. I only know why she left initially but not why she stayed away."

"Pops, you never told me why she left. You just said she had to go," Jeremy said.

Cole didn't answer. Instead, he asked him a question. "Did I ever tell you how we met?"

"No, I don't think so."

"It was back when we were homeless and making money by pickpocketing and doing odd jobs. Kids tended to stay in groups to survive. You know how close Ellis and I were?" Cole asked, lost in his thoughts.

They nodded for him to go on.

He continued, "We were about fifteen when we met Abigail. She had been on the streets longer than us and had graduated from pickpocketing to actual theft. She was excellent at stealing things and not getting caught. When we were taken in by the Giblers, she had already left for Europe."

"What happened then? How did you get together?" asked Jeremy, eager to hear more about her.

There was no reason to disclose that he and Ellis had asked her to choose between them before she left. "All three of us made our way forward, Ellis here, me in New York, and Abigail in Europe."

"When did you see her again?"

"I was in New York working for Pinkerton and I was waiting at the ship dock. I had a case that was wrapping up. Then I heard her voice. She looked so elegant," he reminisced. "We started to see each other and decided to marry and settle down. That's when we had you."

"Were you happy?" asked Jeremy, curious about their life together.

"Yes, very much so. We were together for about a year before we knew you were on the way. We were still in New York at that time. I was working for Pinkerton and Abbey was setting up the house for us. It was a busy time,"

They sounded happy. How did things get so bad that they separated? Jeremy wondered. He asked, "Pops, what happened? Why did she leave?"

"I told you she did well in Europe, and she was heading home to settle down?" They nodded as he continued. "What she did well, what she was good at, was being a thief. She was very good at it and could get in and out of a building with no one noticing."

"Thief!" exclaimed Jeremy.

Something occurred to Emma. She had come across the name of a lady thief in Europe. "Was she called Mistress K?"

"She was," he acknowledged with a twist of his mouth. "She liked the romance of it."

Jeremy had heard of her also. "She's famous, or rather, infamous."

Cole nodded.

"So, what happened?" Emma asked. Abbey had managed to have a very adventurous life.

"She got caught and went to a Paris prison. She escaped and managed to get enough money to get a boat to New York," he continued.

So, maybe I shouldn't model my life after her, Emma thought with a wry smile.

"Did you have any idea?" asked Jeremy, wondering if Pops had shielded her from the police.

"None. It wasn't until you were about two that there was a knock on our door. It was a Saturday. We were home, relaxing, playing with you. I got up to answer the door and it was the local authorities standing there. They asked for Abigail and said they were working with the Paris police. I remember she just stood there, looking poleaxed, holding you so tightly." Cole seemed lost in his memories.

"How did they know she was there?" asked Emma, gently trying to pull him into the present.

"There had been a local jewel robbery that matched her modus operandi. They tracked her there; she had been selling small loose jewels in local pawn shops," he explained.

"Was she arrested?" asked Jeremy, bewildered.

Emma watched Jeremy's reaction and realized this wasn't an exciting story about a stranger, but a story of why Jeremy's mom had chosen that life over him.

"Yes, they took her immediately," Cole said.

"Did you ask her if she did it?" Jeremy asked, still hoping she was not guilty.

"They found a necklace when they searched the house," Cole said, shaking his head. "I confronted her and she admitted it. I asked her why she did it, and why she jeopardized everything we had. All she said was she enjoyed it."

"Enjoyed?" Jeremy echoed.

"Yes, the thrill, the chase," Cole said and stopped talking for a moment. "I thought, when she settled with us, that she had changed. I was wrong. She had not."

"Did you help her?" Jeremy asked, unsure what to say, not wanting to take sides in the family drama that had happened so long ago.

"I did."

~

Cole paced around the small interrogation room.

"It won't do any good to wear yourself out. You might as well sit down," Abbey commented.

"Sit! How can I sit? They're sending you to Paris," he said.

She cuddled the baby to her chest, not wanting to let him go. She brushed the curls off of his head and kissed him. He was content to lay with his mom.

Cole watched and thought, *She is so good with him.* He sat down and placed his head in his hands, mumbling, "What are we going to do?"

"It looks like I'm going back to Paris. I'm not sure how long I'll be there," she teased.

"You escaped once before. Do you plan to do it again?"

"Cole, we can get through this—" she started to say.

He interrupted her. "Why didn't you tell me you were on the run? We could have tried to work it out."

"Really?" she said incredulously. "So, had I stepped off the boat and said, *By the way, I'm on the run,* would you have married me?"

Cole just looked at her, not speaking.

"You really went all the way to the other side, didn't you? You never asked me why I took the necklace here or why I was in prison in Paris. All you have cared about is that I was in the wrong."

"No, that's not true," he protested, knowing he was losing something special.

She heard the doubt in his voice. She continued to hug Jeremy close as an officer came to the door and said, "It's time."

She stood slowly and looked at the now sleeping baby. *How can I leave him?* she thought as she carried him with her to the door.

"You'll need to come alone," said the officer kindly.

"Yes." She kept her tear-filled eyes directed away from Cole as she handed him the baby. She said in a low voice, "Take care of him."

Cole took Jeremy and held him close, watching her leave.

"I got her a lawyer and even traveled to Paris to make sure she was okay. But it was no use. She was guilty," he said quietly. "I went to find out if she stayed with us as a cover or if it was genuine."

"What did she say?" Jeremy asked, wanting to know the answer.

"She said she loved us," he admitted.

"Did you just leave her there?" asked Jeremy, not wanting to believe he would do that.

"No! No," he said rather loudly. "I did not. I went to see her in Paris, but Jeremy, I had to get back to you. I left you in New York with friends. I also had responsibilities with my job. I saw her that last time at the prison and told her that I would write, and we would wait for her to get out."

The trip to Paris was long and difficult. When Cole finally made it there, they had already pronounced Abigail guilty of a jail-break and added more time to her sentence. He was able to get the French police to let him see her.

There was no big reunion. He entered the room and saw her, wearing a gray cotton dress, standing near a table. She didn't rush over to him. He got the message and stayed away.

She asked, without looking at him, "You didn't bring Jeremy?"

"No," he said as he frowned. "It wasn't possible."

"Who is he with?"

"I have him with the Martins. They'll take care of him until I return."

"You return," she said slowly.

"Yes, I can't stay here. My life and Jeremy's are there," he said bluntly.

"What about me, Cole? Am I just to be left behind as a bad mistake?"

"I don't know what else to do. I have an attorney for you. I'd like you to meet him and see if he can get your sentence reduced."

"I'll see him, not for you, but Jeremy."

"I'll…" he started.

"No," she said shortly, "you'll not do anything. I don't want you to see me again."

"Why?" he asked, bewildered.

"I never should have chosen you, Cole. It wasn't right for us when we were teenagers, and it isn't right now."

"What about Jeremy?"

"I don't know. I hope to come back and be with him someday."

"Did you leave her there?" Jeremy asked, somewhat accusingly.

"You think I would leave your mother alone in a foreign country?" he asked, wondering if his son thought so little of him.

"I don't know what to think."

"I sent letters letting her know about you. I went over several times, but she refused to see me. When I heard she was finally getting out, I made my way back to Paris to pick her up, but she was already gone. That was the last time I heard from her."

Emma spoke up. "This is your first contact since then?"

Something occurred to her and she asked, "Are you still married?"

Jeremy had wondered that as well.

"No," said Cole. "I waited the mandatory time and filed for a divorce. You don't need the other spouse present if you wait."

"Do you think she's still stealing things?" asked Jeremy.

"I don't know," he said honestly, "but her fingers are nimble as ever." He told them about the watch.

Emma burst out laughing. "Got you, did she?"

"Yes, it looks like it's my lot in life to be bested by intelligent women." He smiled for the first time that morning.

That made Jeremy smile, too. "It must be hereditary." Emma nudged him playfully.

"You'll have to ask her when you see her," Cole said. He closed his eyes and took a deep breath. "Would you like me to set up a meeting?"

"Could we do it today?" Jeremy looked over at Emma. "I don't think I can stand the wait."

Cole looked serious as he said, "I'll arrange it for you, Emma and Abbey. Is this afternoon at 4pm, all right?" At Emma's nod, he continued. "She's staying at the Palmer Hotel."

Jeremy and Emma stood to go. Cole looked hesitant when he walked over, looking him directly in the eye. "My boy, I never meant to keep her from you."

"I know, Pops." He reached over to hug him tight.

Cole returned the hug in full measure. When he pulled away, he had to wipe his eyes. Jeremy's were also shining bright.

"Let me know how things go if you want to come by after. I'll be home all evening," he stated gruffly, patting Jeremy's arms.

Jeremy could tell that was important to him. "Yes, Pops, I'll come by after."

Emma hugged Cole, and they exited the building. Jeremy took her hand in his as they descended. He paused at the bottom and faced her. "I didn't expect that would be the topic."

"No, that was a surprise. Do you remember her at all?" she asked.

"Just vague memories. A song, a voice," he said musingly.

"Nothing else?" she inquired.

"No."

"Did he tell you anything about her over the years?"

"He told me she was lovely."

"Did he say why she left?"

"I don't think I ever asked."

"Weren't you curious?"

"No, I don't think so. It was always just Pops and me. We were—*are*—happy. There didn't seem to be a gap needing to be filled."

"Yes, I can see that." She knew how close they were in their personal and professional lives.

"Let's head home." They turned and continued holding hands as they walked. Taking their time, each lost in their thoughts.

They reached the house and entered through the kitchen. It was just about time for lunch. Amy and Ethyl didn't work on Sunday and Dora liked to put together a later lunch for the family. They found her working efficiently. She called over to them, saying, "Great timing, could you grab the trays and move them to the table?"

"Of course. Sorry, we weren't here sooner," Emma said, moving to the table to help.

"That's okay, I understand family stuff," said Dora as she put together the bread tray.

They grabbed the roast chicken and assorted vegetables to move to the table. "Patrick, Tim, bring Lottie in," called Dora. Jake was already at the table.

Emma asked, "Is Savannah going to be on the road for a while?"

"Yes, that show she's working will be out for another six weeks," said Dora.

Tim came into the dining room carrying Lottie under one arm and Patrick under his other. He asked, "Were you looking for two packages?" They were giggling as he put them in their seats. Patrick sat by Jake; Emma and Jeremy sat down near Tim and Dora.

Dora had baby Lottie in a chair that placed her higher at the table. Papa had built guards around it so she couldn't fall. Dora started to cut the chicken and mushed the veggies up a small mound and placed them in front of Lottie.

Once the family said prayers and started eating, Dora asked, "Well, what was up with Cole this morning?"

Emma looked at Jeremy, leaving the answer up to him.

Jeremy looked around, realizing this was his family and he could tell them. "My mother has come back," he said simply.

Dora dropped her fork in surprise. She knew he hadn't had contact with her in a long while. "Have you seen her?" she asked.

"No, not until this afternoon. Pops is sending over a confirmation as soon as he speaks to her," he explained.

"Emma, are you going to accompany him?" Tim asked curiously, buttering his bread.

"She is," Jeremy stated firmly, taking her hand in his. She squeezed it in response.

Dora said sincerely, "Jeremy, I know everything's going to be okay."

"Thanks, Dora. I hope so," he replied, still feeling out of sorts about the situation.

Dinner continued and conversation flowed around them. Jeremy ate quietly, lost in his thoughts. They helped clear the table and cleaned up. Jake headed to his lab, and the rest of the family moved to the sitting room. Emma asked Jeremy quietly, "Do you want to talk?"

"No, no, I just want to sit here and try not to think about it."

Emma got a book from the side table and started to read. After a while, they heard a knock on the door. She looked around and said, "I'll get it. You stay here."

She went to the door to retrieve the note from the courier and carried it unsealed to Jeremy. He opened it. "It says she would like us to go to the hotel at 4pm."

"We can do that," said Emma.

"I'll arrange a carriage," said Tim and excused himself. Patrick had gotten his toys and was playing on the floor, while Dora continued to entertain Lottie.

Emma picked up a book to distract her mind until it was time to leave.

Tim returned and said, "The carriage is arranged for 3:30."

"Thanks," said Jeremy gratefully.

"No problem," he said and settled down on the floor to play cards with Patrick.

The time came around quickly and they heard a knock on the door. Emma glanced at Jeremy and asked, "Ready?"

He took a deep breath. "Yes." He stood and offered her his hand, saying to Tim and Dora, "We'll be on our way."

Dora grabbed his hand as he moved by her. "Jeremy, we're here for you if you need anything."

"Thanks, Dora," he said sincerely, leaning down to kiss her cheek.

In the foyer, they put on their jackets, opened the door, and found the carriage driver there waiting. "I have a pickup?" the driver said.

Jeremy nodded and indicated, "That's us. We need to go to the Palmer Hotel. On second thought, drop us two blocks from there." He looked over at Emma and she nodded in agreement.

"Yes, sir," the driver said and waited for them to climb into the carriage. Emma stood on the box and Jeremy swung her in, entering behind her. He left them off as instructed; they paid him and walked the last two blocks to the hotel.

They arrived there and took a moment outside. He couldn't make himself go in. Emma asked tentatively, "Jeremy?" When he didn't reply, she said, "Jeremy, we don't have to go in. We can leave a note."

"No," he said. "I need to see her." He took her hand and they went in, making their way through the dramatic lobby, with glittering chandeliers and a painted ceiling. Emma had not been in this hotel before and was looking everywhere as she walked. Jeremy didn't see the interior; he was focused on the task at hand.

They approached the front desk and Jeremy said, "We're looking for Abigail Lancaster. She should be expecting us."

The man at the desk was dressed smartly in a blue suit with a blue tie and a white shirt. He nodded and checked his cards. He looked up at Jeremy and asked, "Your name?"

"Jeremy Tilden."

He smiled and said, "Yes, sir, Ms. Lancaster left word that she would like you to join her in her room. It's room 4987." He clicked to the bellman to show them the way. They followed him up the stairs and made their way to her door.

The bellman knocked on the door briskly and a woman answered. She smiled at him and said, "Thank you." He left and went back downstairs.

All three stood very still until Emma realized where she had seen her. "It was you last night! You were dancing with Papa." She looked closer. "The hair, Jeremy has your hair!"

Abbey patted it and said with a nervous laugh, "Yes, with some highlights." Emma noticed the gray threaded through it. She also noticed her eyes, the same shape, and color as Jeremey's.

"Won't you both come in?" Abigail watched them enter and

thought, *I don't get time alone with my son. I also have to have the girlfriend.*

Emma looked around; Abigail had a lovely large room with wood floors, plus a sitting room with couches and side chairs. "Sit, please," Abigail said. "I've ordered some tea and pastries for us."

They sat and removed their hats. Jeremy placed them in a side chair next to him. They sat there for a few moments in silence before Abigail said, "Well, I guess I'll start. What did Cole tell you about me?"

Jeremy straightened. "Pops didn't say much. He just said you were lovely and a great mom."

"He did?" She thought about that statement before she sat up abruptly and said, "He said nothing about my profession?"

"No, not until this morning," said Jeremy, not sure what more to say.

The conversation was making her visibly uncomfortable. She changed the topic and asked, "Can we move to some pleasanter things. I'd like to hear about you."

"I'm twenty-two now, and I'm with Emma," he answered.

"How long have you been together?"

"Four years," he stated, reaching for her hand. Emma placed hers in his and squeezed. Abigail watched that movement.

"Where do you work? What's your profession?"

"I work with Pops at Pinkerton as an investigator."

"Law enforcement, that's nice. Must run in the family. You live on your own?"

"We both live in Emma's family boarding house," he said, looking over at Emma.

"Hmm," Abbey said.

Emma spoke up then. "We'd like to have you over for dinner sometime while you're in town."

"That would be nice," she said noncommittally. She still wasn't sure about this young lady. She did notice Emma had looked around the room carefully as they sat down. Almost like she would if she were casing the place. *That can't be right. I must be mistaken.*

"Mom, may I call you that?" he asked tentatively.

His question brought all of her interest back to him. Her eyes welled up. "I would love that."

"Mom, how long are you back for?" he asked with hope in his voice.

"I'd figured to be here at least six months. I have something I'm working on that will take some time," she said.

That verbiage made Emma uneasy and she frowned, clearing her face before Abbey could see it.

Jeremey asked a hard question. "Mom, I have to ask. Are you on the run from something or someone? We can help."

"No, that won't be necessary. I'm okay. I won't need any help," she answered. Again, the way she said it gave Emma pause.

Turning her eyes to Emma, she asked, "What do you do?" Implying that she didn't do much.

There isn't anything friendly here for me, she thought.

Jeremy started to talk, but Emma stopped him by giving his hand a slight squeeze. "Really, nothing much. I design lace patterns and work at the family bakery occasionally, things like that." She didn't want to share that she was also an investigator, especially at that moment. Her current case involved the diamond merchants and improving their security measures.

Jeremy got the message and said, "My favorite is her strudel."

"Oh, I have that here," Abigail indicated as she uncovered the pastry tray. She was happy she had gotten him something he liked.

Jeremy and Emma smiled, recognizing the pastry. Emma said, "You got that from my family bakery."

"How do you know that?" she asked, puzzled.

Emma explained, "The design is specific to us, how the pastry is folded."

"Oh, that's interesting." She didn't think it was. The silly girl with no other ambitions, they were not going to get together at all. She must be like her mother, not like Ellis.

They each took a piece of pastry to eat. Jeremy finished his, took a sip of tea, and said, "I'd like to hear more about where you were during our time apart."

She smiled graciously. "I think we'll have time for that later. And I would like to be alone with you to discuss that."

Emma smiled genuinely and said, "I think that's a wonderful idea. I'll be busy for a while; that will give you both some time alone."

Abbey looked at her in surprise and said without thinking, "An important lace appointment perhaps or pastry emergency?"

Emma heard the tone and understood it as being protective of Jeremy. She laughed and said, "Something like that."

Abigail gave her a considering look. She had thought Emma would be pushy and intrusive into her time with her son. Instead, she volunteered to be absent and allowed them time together. She looked at Jeremy and said, "Lunch in a few days?"

"How about dinner instead?" he suggested.

She countered with, "How about dinner out and then back here to talk."

Jeremy nodded his agreement.

Emma watched them talk, glad they were making plans to meet again. He looked over at her and said, "Ready to go?"

She nodded and they stood. Jeremy said, "Mom, I'll see you in a few days. Would you like me to pick you up?"

"Please, I'll meet you in the lobby."

"I'll be here at seven."

CHAPTER 6

They were quiet and contemplative as they left the room and exited down the stairs. "Jeremy?" asked Emma.

"After we leave the building," he requested. She nodded and walked with him through the lobby and outside. They walked down the block when he stopped and turned her to him. "Emma, what did you think of her?"

She reached over and brushed his hair off of his forehead. "Well, I did love her hair and her eyes," she teased.

"No, really, what did you think?" He wanted to hear her honest impression.

She looked into his eyes for a long moment before saying, with a sigh, "I don't know her."

"But you saw something." He could see it in her eyes.

"I saw what you saw, a woman trying to reconnect with her son." She hesitated before saying, "Though I do feel she's keeping something back about why she's here."

"Emma, you did see something. Is that why you didn't let me tell her you're an investigator?"

"I don't know exactly. Part of it was playing into the role she assumed for me."

"And what role was that?" asked Jeremy, not seeing what she had.

Emma laughed. "She thinks I'm after you for nefarious reasons."

He chuckled and said suggestively, "But you are, aren't you?" He grew serious and asked, "Why the subterfuge?"

"I do have a case right now that's private. It just seemed easier, if she wasn't going to be around very long, to have her think I'm just a bit of light fluff."

He nodded. "You're right. If she stays, things will unfold naturally. Are you sure you don't want to come with me when I meet with her?"

"I would like to be there and hear more about her life. But I realize she wants to do this in private." She touched his face before warning him softly, "Just be cautious, Jeremy. We don't know her and what she's involved in."

"Yes, I'll take that to heart. We promised to go by Pop's place. Would you like to head over there?" he asked. She nodded and he lowered his head to kiss her slowly. After a long moment, he said, "Let's go." He stepped back and held out his hand; she took it and they headed off together.

CHAPTER 7

They didn't see Ellis pull up in a carriage just as they were leaving. He did see them and told the driver to hold a moment. He noticed they seemed to be wrapped up in an intense conversation. They kissed and walked off in the opposite direction of his carriage.

He paid his driver and climbed down. Straightening his jacket, he looked down at the clothes he had chosen carefully for this meeting. Taking a deep breath, he headed into the hotel. *It's hard,* he thought, *to see someone you haven't seen since you were young.* He was conscious of the gray in his hair and the wrinkles he hadn't noticed until this morning. He hadn't felt like this since Mary. A twinge of guilt spiked at the thought of her; they had something special and two amazing daughters. But Mary had been gone a long time. He shook off any feeling of betrayal and focused his thoughts on Abbey.

He had no delusions about her. They had known each other for a long time. They had slept in the streets and lifted wallets to get food. That last day still haunted him, pushing her to decide between them. But last night, she said she had made a decision all those years ago and was on her way to see him. *I was her choice,* he thought. *What if she had come to Chicago?* He knew what would have happened; he would have stayed with his lovely Mary and his almost born baby. He shook his head, thinking, *It's best it happened this way.*

Ellis thought about that as he walked up to Abbey's room. Cole had kept Jeremy's mother a secret from him all of these years. *But did he or did I just choose not to ask? In all of our time together, rebuilding a friendship, and living together, I never brought it up. Had I seen her in Jeremy, but ignored it?*

He headed up the stairs, knowing he was expected. He strolled to the door and knocked briskly. She opened it immediately. "Ellis," she said warmly. "Please, come in."

He looked at her a long time and thought, *I knew who his mother was all along.* He went in and closed the door quietly behind him.

CHAPTER 8

$\mathcal{E}$mma and Jeremy walked up the steps to Cole and Ellis' house. They entered and called out, "Pops!"

"In here." They followed his voice into the study. He was sitting at the desk going through several files and looked up as they entered. "Come in, have a seat. You weren't there long," he observed.

"No, it was more of just an initial meeting," explained Jeremy.

"I don't think she liked me there," commented Emma, sitting down in one of the dark leather chairs. She took off her hat and tossed it onto the desk.

"Really?" said Cole, eyeing her. He swung his gaze to Jeremy. "Did something happen?"

Jeremy sat in the chair opposite Emma's and said, "No, I think she wanted to see me alone. I don't think she felt she could talk openly with Emma there. She kept everything to short answers."

"Will you be seeing her again?" he asked.

"Yes, in a few days," Jeremy confirmed.

He nodded and asked them both, "Do we think she's involved in something here?"

Jeremy answered first, saying, "I hope not. I'd like to get to know her."

"Emma?" asked Cole, clearly valuing her thoughts.

"I have some hesitation about her," she admitted, "but I think Jeremy needs to have his time with her."

"Thanks, Em," said Jeremy, his love for her shining in his eyes.

"Just don't mention our current project," Cole warned her softly.

"I won't. She doesn't know I'm working for you. We told her about my other jobs instead," she said ambiguously.

"I'm just covering us in case she's here for something other than a family reunion. Keep your eyes open and don't get pulled into anything." He frowned at Jeremy. "I prefer to have Emma accompany you on these meetings with your mother and have her give you a rational view."

Jeremy was getting a bit exasperated. "What if," he asked, "she's actually here to see me and doesn't have an ulterior motive?"

Emma and Cole looked at one another and nodded. "We'll give her the benefit of the doubt," Cole said.

"Yes, we will," echoed Emma.

"All right then," he said, gratified at their response. Something occurred to him and he asked, "Just what is this current case you're both involved in?"

"That, we have to keep private," Cole said smoothly. "We'll bring you in when we are further along."

That seemed to satisfy Jeremy and he nodded in understanding. Cases were usually kept to minimal staffing for privacy and he was not involved in all of Emma's assignments.

Cole switched topics and said, "Would you both like to stay for dinner?"

"Will Papa be here," asked Emma.

"No, I believe he has other plans," he said quietly.

Emma frowned but didn't ask any more questions. She looked over to make sure Jeremy was okay with staying. "We would love to," he said. They sent a note over to Dora, letting her know they wouldn't be there for dinner.

They got off the topic of Jeremy's mother and discussed current cases and books. It was a pleasant evening. On their way out, Cole asked, "Emma, could you stop by in the morning to review the case?"

"I'll be there," she confirmed.

As they left, Jeremy said, "Do you think she's here for something nefarious?"

"I'd just caution you to remember she's quite famous in her field. She's also a very clever woman."

Jeremy considered her words. "I'll keep it personal. I may never have another opportunity to get to know her." He put his arm across her shoulders, pulling her in close.

CHAPTER 9

The next morning, Emma accompanied Jeremy to the Pinkerton office. "Are you okay with going on your own?" she asked him, concerned about this new person in their lives.

"To see Mom? Yeah, I'm fine. I think she'll share more if we are alone," he explained.

"Yes," she agreed. She also knew that, if Abbey tried to involve him in something, he could handle it. And if he couldn't, she would be there.

They entered the building and said a quick goodbye as she continued down to Cole's office. She knocked on his door and heard him call her in. As she entered, she saw him at the desk. He looked up with a smile. "Good morning, Emma. Thanks for coming to see me this morning."

She sat down in the chair and pulled out her notebook. "Ready?" he asked.

"I am," she said firmly.

He started his review, "The couriers are on their way with the diamonds." Diamonds were considered a rare item and were associated with the aristocracy in the 19th century. The discovery in the 1870s of diamond deposits in South Africa changed diamonds from a rare gem to one that could be available to all who could afford them.

Emma was curious about something. "Cole, how did Tiffany & Co. get the diamonds from the French Government?"

Cole looked down at the file in front of him and pulled out a newspaper article. "The Crown Jewels were auctioned in France after the fall of Napoleon III in 1871. The Third Republic of France was uncomfortable with what the jewels stood for. Tiffany & Co. was there to bid and managed to buy more than two-thirds of the merchandise and a place in history."

"And all of these are on the way here. Why did they choose Chicago as the beginning of their tour?"

"Philip Johnson, the museum curator, has a fine reputation for protecting works of art. That case you worked with him in Paris?" Emma nodded and he continued. "He came highly recommended as the first stop."

The case Cole referenced involved Philip, Tony, and Emma working in Paris to recover valuable art.

"Why the tour?" she asked, knowing security would be involved.

"The company wants the jewels seen before they're sold off. I believe it's to raise the price of already priceless jewels. There's also the historical aspect; it'll generate a large amount of press for them."

"What will happen to them eventually? Will they be sold?"

"Yes, and probably for a tidy sum."

Cole went on to the details of the pickup. "We have word they'll be on the Friday train. They will want to keep this as low profile as possible. I'd like you to take delivery at a stop before Chicago. I was also thinking, maybe you should take a friend with you," he suggested.

She frowned. "I'm not sure I want someone along with me. They might get in the way."

Cole tried to explain. "We need it to look like a short trip to shop or such thing. You're getting a reputation as a courier and an investigator."

"Hmm, your right. I have someone I could use. How about Savannah?" she suggested.

He considered that and said, "Not a bad idea. With her acting skills, she can blend in."

"I'll arrange it; she got back from her tour earlier than expected." Emma had seen her at the boarding house that morning.

"Fine, fine. I'll send the train tickets to you. You'll need to stay there a day and return. Of course," he teased, "you'll need to bring things back, to prove you shopped."

"Knowing Savannah, I think I can manage that," she said wryly. She documented the details of who she was meeting in her notebook, continuing to use shorthand to code them.

"I'll leave it to you to figure out the best way to carry them back," Cole said.

Emma thought about that and asked, "Do you have a list of the items?"

"Yes," he said. He reached back into the file and handed it to her.

She evaluated the list and said, "I have an idea that might work." She went on to explain it to him.

He nodded. "I like that. No one will suspect it."

"That wraps us up. I'll be working at the lawyer's office the rest of today if you have anything else to communicate on the case," Emma said.

"Very good. Thanks, Emma. I know this will go well with you involved." With that, she gathered up her belongings, said her goodbyes, and exited the room. She stopped by Jeremy's office to confirm she would meet him here before going home that evening.

On her way out, she grabbed her bike and headed to her

temporary job at the Law office. She had started there a few months ago, working mornings as a typist and file clerk. As she and Mr. Pennington had gotten to know each other, he started to add to her responsibilities. Currently, she was working with him to put together background data for various clients.

The day should be interesting. She would be sitting in on interviews with a client, typing up notes as they worked on her testimony. This was the first time she had done this task.

She entered the office and stored her bike before approaching the secretary's desk. "Good morning, Ethan."

He didn't look up when he responded, "Conference room. Mr. Pennington is there and the client should be here soon."

"On my way in," she said and took out her notebook before knocking on the door.

Mr. Pennington called her to enter. Emma went in to be briefed about the client they would be interviewing that day.

CHAPTER 10

At the end of her day, Emma met Jeremy at the Pinkerton office. When she arrived, he was talking to one of the secretaries. He looked up when he heard the door, smiled, and asked, "Ready to go?"

"I am. Can I leave my bike here?" she asked.

The secretary, Stan Ellington, said, "Emma, I can drop it by on my way home." He lived a few houses down from them.

She smiled at him and said, "I would appreciate that."

"Anything you can share on the new case?" Jeremy asked as they were leaving.

"Not yet, but soon," she promised. They headed home, holding hands and talking quietly, enjoying their evening together. They had planned a dinner out, alone.

It was late when they arrived home, but Dora was waiting up for them, holding a sleeping Lottie. "Hi," she said softly. "I waited up to see how it went with your mom. I didn't get a chance to ask yesterday."

They sat with her in the sitting room and, speaking in the same tone as Dora, he said, "It went okay."

Emma looked at Dora and said, "Dora, she looks like Jeremy."

"How do you mean?" she asked curiously.

Emma explained. "She has his curly auburn hair and his eyes."

"Really?" said Dora, and the description stirred a memory. She looked at Jeremy and asked, "Was she at the gala?"

"I didn't see her, but Pops said she was," he confirmed.

"Emma!" she said, louder than expected. The baby stirred and she lowered her voice. "Emma, that's who Papa was dancing with."

"Pops did say they grew up together." Jeremy yawned the last words. "I'm going up to bed." He looked at Emma and asked, "Coming?"

"I'll be up in a while," she said as he leaned down to kiss her. She returned it warmly.

Emma and Dora watched as he strolled up the stairs. Dora leaned closer to Emma and asked, "Should we worry about Papa?"

She smiled slowly. "I don't think we have to worry about that. Papa knows how to take care of himself. Also, I think he'll tire of the excitement and go back to his basement."

Dora mulled that over before saying, "I'm not so sure about that. I remember how he was when Mama was alive. He wasn't always like he is now."

Emma hadn't expected that answer and responded in a serious tone, "I'll keep an eye on the situation."

CHAPTER 11

The next morning, Emma and Jeremy were readying for their day. She had just slipped her dress over her head, pulled it down, and asked, "Jeremy, will you help me with this?" She indicated the buttons on the back of her dress.

"Sure," he said, moving over to her.

As he handled the buttons, she asked, "What are you working on today?"

"I'm clearing up some casework and organizing some mug books. We're applying the method you reviewed in Paris: signaletics. We are adding in the measurements for the of head and body, shape formation of the ear, eyebrow, mouth, and eye."

"And that will also include such marking such as tattoos, scars, and personality characteristics?"

"Yes." As he finished the last button, he said, "All done." He gave her a pat on the back.

"Too bad we can't just get everyone's information on file to be able to access."

"Yes, but what file room could handle that?" he asked with a laugh.

She returned his laugh and asked, "Have you approached Jake about taking pictures to add to your books?"

"Yes, he's interested. I'm also thinking we should utilize Dora's skills at drawing when we have a description but a photo isn't available." He looked at his watch and asked, "Where are you today?"

"I'm still working at the lawyer's office—mornings this week and courier stuff in the afternoons. One of the jobs will have me at the museum later today."

"Tell Tony hello for me," he commented, watching her reaction.

"Oops," she said with a grimace, pausing while putting on her jacket. "I forgot about the last time we saw each other."

Jeremy saw her expression and said," I wouldn't worry. He just got a bit too far into his cups. I'm sure he didn't mean the things he said." He hoped he was right.

She straightened her shoulders, pulled her jacket down, and said, "It'll be fine." She put that out of her mind and looked at Jeremy. "Any thought on the questions you might ask your mother tonight?"

"No, not really. I mean, the hard question is: why haven't you come back before this?"

"Will you ask it?"

"I'm not sure. I'm wondering if I should just enjoy the time with her and let the past go."

"Can you do that?" asked Emma, knowing she would have to ask the hard questions.

"I'll see how it plays out," he said noncommittally.

She put her hand on his. "Jeremy, will you let me know if something comes up that you need my help on?"

He frowned and sat down slowly on the bed. "That's the same tone you and Pops had last night. Was there something you saw in her that I didn't?"

She sat next to him, took his hand, and said, "We're naturally cautious and we care deeply for you. Jeremy, I just don't want you to get hurt."

He squeezed her hand and sat mulling over what she'd said. He sighed. "I'll be going into this with my eyes opened."

"Good, that's all we ask."

"I would ask that you also give her a chance if she does turn out to be genuine."

"Deal," she said as she stood. She picked up her blue belt and clipped it around her waist. Her knife was strapped to her thigh and she started to gather her notebook and pens.

He stood to finish dressing and said, "Hey, Em, one more thing before you leave." He pulled her into a long embrace, then pulled back and said, "Off to work."

"Will you be coming home before going to dinner?"

"Yes," he said absently as he got his jacket. He slipped it on and departed to his room through the secret entrance. He called, "See you on the other side." He closed the door and bookshelf.

She waved her hand at him with a smile, then moved to the door and opened it. She saw Jeremy exit his room and said in a singsong voice, "Good morning, Jeremy."

He said in a similar tone, "Good morning, Emma," and held out his hand to her. She took it and walked with him downstairs. They ate breakfast with the family and headed out to their jobs. Emma got her bike out and walked Jeremy to the trolley. She kissed him, saying, "Goodbye. See you this evening."

"Yes," he said softly and rubbed his finger across her furrowed brow. "Don't worry about me."

"I'll try not to." She looked over his shoulder and saw the trolley arrive. "You need to get going."

He looked quickly over his shoulder and said, "I have to go," and grabbed her up for a fast kiss. He pulled back abruptly and grinned before running for the trolley.

She pulled in a shaky breath and watched him jump onto the

moving car. Getting on her bike, she headed to the law office. As she arrived, she got off the bike and placed it on her shoulder to climb the stoop to enter the building. The job allowed her to learn more about the law, knowing that a better understanding could be beneficial in her investigations.

Making her way in, she could see Ethan was in place, already reviewing files on his desk. After she stored her bike, she walked up and said, "Ethan, what's on the calendar today?"

Without looking up, he reached for his bound black book. He opened it and said, "Full day. Mr. Pennington is in court all day on the Banks case."

Emma knew that case well. She had written briefs, sat in on interviews, pulled files, and double-checked the background of the witnesses. "What would you like me to work on today?" she asked, knowing she reported to him when Mr. Pennington was not there.

He finally met her eyes and said, "Mr. Pennington thought you might enjoy observing voir dire today." Emma knew from working with them that voir dire is a time prior to the trial when the lawyers can ask questions to determine the competency of a witness or juror.

She knew Ethan didn't like small talk, so she gathered up her materials and bike and headed to the courthouse. She hid the bike behind some bushes and walked in. Following the long hallway, she made her way to the courtrooms. She knew what court Mr. Pennington was assigned to and found the right location, confirming with a glance that he was in the room. He sat with his client at the table to the left of the judge, and she walked swiftly up to him. The client saw her approach and tapped his shoulder. He turned to see who it was.

"Emma," he said. "Thank you for coming up to the court today. We will be doing voir dire, questioning the jury. I would like you to sit behind me and watch how it works."

"Of course," she said. She leaned closer and asked in a low voice, "What if I see something that might help?"

He had seen her observation skills in the office and her background checks contained more than just data, they included an in-depth analysis of character. He wanted to see if she could use that skill to help him with the voir dire. "If you see something, get my attention. Tap your pencil on your notebook, but don't be obvious about it."

"Okay, but what if I don't see any concerns?" she asked, looking forward to observing the process.

"Then I will use my best judgment." He stopped talking as the judge entered and took his place.

Emma thought about the interview she'd sat in on yesterday. It involved the case she was here to observe; the plaintiff was being charged with bigamy. Mr. Pennington had reviewed it with her before meeting the client for the first time.

"Bigamy?" Emma asked Mr. Pennington as they waited for their client to arrive.

Mr. Pennington explained that bigamy was when a person was married to more than one spouse at a time. It was a federal enactment of the United States Congress that was signed into law on July 8, 1862, by President Abraham Lincoln.

"Our client, as you know, is Elle Gilmore/Banks, and her husband, Mr. Banks, contends she knowingly married a second man—Mr. Gilmore—after he went away for business," he explained.

Emma had completed the background check and asked, "Wasn't her husband gone more than fourteen years? Isn't only a year required for her to claim abandonment as grounds for a divorce?"

"Well, it might be," he allowed, "except she didn't wait the mandatory year and she never filed for divorce. He will also try to prove that he sent money in that first year and, when she did remarry, she did so without a divorce."

"Why is the money important?" she asked.

"Unfortunately, it's that one thing, that money in the first year, could meet the provision of necessary support and prove he didn't abandon her."

"He was contending that his sending letters and some money were necessary support? That would be so little. Also, why come back now?" she asked, bewildered by his intent. *What is he trying to accomplish with all of this?*

"That is what we need to find out. We need to know his motivation for coming forward after all this time."

"Is he staying at a local hotel?" asked Emma, thinking ahead.

"We have information from his lawyer that he's at the Smith Tower," he commented, watching her take notes.

"I'll check to see if he has talked to anyone. Can I talk to your client's husband, er... her current husband?" she asked with a slight smile.

He chuckled in return. "Well, yes."

She checked her watch attached to her blouse and said, "I have an appointment this afternoon. I'll follow up."

"We have some time; our court date is set for next month."

Back to the present day in court

Emma sat in the gallery behind Mr. Pennington, evaluating the jury pool as they waited for the judge to enter. The rows had been marked so the public would not accidentally sit with jury members. *Who we want on the jury are people who have an understanding of our client's plight.* She watched as the court officer escorted the first twelve people into the jury box. Emma knew that, once one juror was removed, another from the individuals gathered would replace them.

She wanted to tell Mr. Pennington something before they started, so she dropped her notebook to get his attention. When he leaned over to pick it up for her, she leaned in and said, "We don't want strong personalities. We need ones that understand the woman's role."

The judge looked at Mr. Pennington and said, "You may begin." He nodded, stood up, and approached the jury box to start his questioning.

As he walked up, Emma studied the jurors. *No women,* she thought with a shake of her head. *One day, we'll be better represented.*

He asked a few general questions of the group. "First, how many of you are married?"

An easy question to start, Emma thought as she continued to watch. Hands were raised quickly and most were married.

He continued. "How many of you have been divorced?" A few hands came up slower. He started with those men first. He pointed to one, saying, "You, sir, are you happier since your divorce?"

"Well, yes," he said loudly. Laughter could be heard in the courtroom. The judge sent a warning glance toward them. They quieted down in response.

"Why is that, sir?" asked Mr. Pennington.

"Well, she wasn't nice and she wouldn't fix my dinner," he answered candidly. More laughter from the court.

The judge had enough and lowered his gavel, demanding, "Silence." The court quieted again.

Mr. Pennington looked around the room and didn't see Emma's pencil move. He asked similar questions of the other divorced persons. He kept all three.

He started questioning the married men. "Sir, are you happily married?" The man he was asking squirmed in his chair and avoided eye contact. At this point, it didn't matter what his answer was. Mr. Pennington saw Emma's pencil going. He said, "That is all right, you don't have to answer. We would like to thank this juror and dismiss him." He continued; they had gotten four that might be more willing to listen to the reasons why their client decided to move on with her life without getting a divorce.

Mr. Pennington completed his questions and strolled over to his desk. He murmured so only Emma could hear him. "Any others you want to strike?"

She dropped her notebook and, as she picked it up, murmured, "The preacher and the schoolteacher."

He nodded, pretending to look at his notes before signaling to the judge. "I would like to remove two people." He listed their names.

The judge nodded and dismissed the jurors, thanking them for their time. Two others took their place and Mr. Pennington sat down with no further objections. The State, who was prosecuting the matter, went next. His examination of the jury was more perfunctory. Emma could see he felt confident and didn't make any changes. The judge set the trial date, locked in the jury, and dismissed everyone.

Emma rose with the others and went out ahead of Mr. Pennington. As she exited the court, she looked to her left and saw Mr. Banks, the defendant's first husband, the man who had started this. She was curious about him. The background check she had completed indicated he didn't live in the area but instead lived in Cleveland, Ohio. *Judging by the cut of his clothes, it looks like he is doing quite well.*

She continued watching him and saw him staring down the hall behind her. She turned, following his gaze to Mr. Gilmore, the defendant's second husband. His anger seemed focused on Mr. Gilmore and not on his wife. *Was it because he'd married his wife or was it something else?* Emma pulled out her notebook to refresh her memory on the relationship between the husbands. Their interview indicated the two men were close friends before the marriage and Mr. Gilmore was the best man at the wedding.

She continued to watch the scene play out. At that moment, Mrs. Gilmore exited the courtroom with Mr. Pennington. She immediately went over to Mr. Gilmore and was drawn into his arms. Emma glanced at Mr. Banks to see his reaction. His face darkened, his expression meaner, and he started toward them. Emma reached into her pocket for her clutch knife, ready to step in if needed. He took two steps toward them and noticed the policeman in the hallway. Turning abruptly, he left the building.

Hmm, she thought, *we may need to schedule some protection for Mr. and Mrs. Gilmore. I'll mention it to Mr. Pennington.* Once the threat was gone, she gave one last glance toward Mr. Pennington and the Gilmores before heading out.

She would meet Mr. Pennington back at the office. As she left, she noticed the sun was up and bright. *It's a lovely day,* she thought. She retrieved her bike from the bushes and rode it back to the office.

As she was storing it in the office, she heard Ethan say, "Back already?"

"Yes, jury selection went fast," she said brightly.

He commented, not looking up, "That's good."

Mr. Pennington heard them as he walked into the building. "It was excellent. Emma, step into my office, please."

Ethan did look up when this request was made and seemed surprised. Most of Emma's instructions came through him. She would like to have stuck her tongue out at him, but thought better of it and followed Mr. Pennington instead.

Emma entered his office and watched as he set his briefcase on the desk. He sat quickly and leaned forward. "Emma, sit down," he said briskly. She sat in a heavy chair in front of the desk. "I was very impressed with your performance at the courthouse today."

"Thank you," she said, waiting for him to continue.

"Emma, I think we can work together more. Would you be interested in helping with future voir dire's?"

She tried to stay calm as she answered, "I'd like to help with that."

"I think we could be a good team."

She liked the idea of further involvement in this and other cases. Something occurred to her, and she said, "I'm thinking we might find something that could, hopefully, get this case closed before the trial date. The background we put together was based on information we have here in town and some telegrams we used to confirm his business address."

"What are you thinking?" he asked expectantly.

"I've been thinking about Hugo Banks and his long absence. We've taken him at his word about his life outside of Chicago. I'd like to go there and look more into his background. Has he been alone all of this time? Why hasn't he come back before now? Why did he stop sending money that first year? I'm thinking it's odd that he married her and left town immediately. He's accusing her of bigamy, but was *he* the perfect husband?"

"You make a good point," he said contemplatively. "Do you have an idea?"

"Yes," she said, pulling out her notebook, "what is the business address?" She took it down and said, "I have another project that will put me in that area in the next few days. I'd like to go to his house and see if there's anything out of the ordinary."

"You might find nothing," he suggested.

"Or I might find something," she countered.

"Let's take a chance and have you go there to investigate. I have something that might help; in speaking to the client, I learned she was dating Mr. Gilmore before her marriage to Mr. Banks."

"Really? Why the switch-up?"

"It happens that Mr. Gilmore and Mrs. Gilmore were quite serious and then something happened to have him leave town abruptly. During the following period, Mr. Banks started spending a large amount of time with her."

"She was lonely," Emma guessed.

"It looks that way, and he took advantage. They were married on the day Mr. Gilmore returned."

Emma frowned. "I'll need to interview the husband when I return."

"I think that would be a good idea."

CHAPTER 12

She was mulling over her ideas for the trip and how to tie both cases together as she rode over to the museum. Once there she stopped her bike and placed it on her shoulder and headed up the marble staircase leading up to the entrance. The pickup would be packages that needed to go to the rail station. Entering the museum; the guards took the bike from her to store it and directed her to Tony's office.

Casual, she thought. She didn't want to add to his worries, but she needed to check in with him. Placing her hand on the door, she raised it and knocked. When his voice called out for her to enter, she opened the door and saw him busy at his desk.

He looked up and said, "Good afternoon, Emma. I appreciate your taking this package to the train station for me."

"It's no problem." He was trying to rush her out without talking, but she wasn't going to let him off the hook that easily. She was always one to ask the hard question. "Tony, do you have a minute?"

He looked resigned. He knew she would want to talk, even if he didn't want to. "Yes."

She shut the door and moved farther into the room. "Tony, are you okay? I was worried about you."

He didn't pretend to misunderstand and said, "I'm fine. Truly. I think you were right; I missed Peggy and drank too much."

"Do you want to talk about it?"

He looked at her, smiled, and said, "I love that you care about me."

"You know I always will."

"I know. I sent Peggy a letter this morning, telling her I'm an idiot and want her to come back."

"That's wonderful, not that you're an idiot." She laughed. "She's a lovely person."

"Yes, and probably too good for me."

"It looks like I don't need to involve myself further."

"No," he agreed.

"I'll take the package and head out."

"See you soon."

"You, too."

CHAPTER 13

That evening after dinner, Emma covered the information with the team on the bigamy case. "Why would anyone want more than one spouse? Isn't one plenty?" asked Tim, wondering about people.

Dora laughed and teased, "I agree, I wouldn't want to have to manage two of you."

"Oh, I don't know," teased Tim. "You could have an army and still manage."

"That is true. When will you leave, Emma?" asked Dora, changing the subject.

"I expect by the weekend."

Savannah was there and spoke up. "I'll be accompanying her. I understand there's some excellent shopping in that area." Emma had reviewed the other case with her and she knew not to mention it to anyone.

Dora didn't change her expression but thought something else was going on. *Emma wouldn't just take someone with her on a case, even Savannah.* Dora knew the rules and wouldn't ask in front of the group.

"It'll be nice to have the company on the trip," Emma said warmly.

Cole asked, "How long do you expect the case to take?"

She knew he was asking when she would be back with the jewels. "Oh," she said casually, "just two-to-three days. It shouldn't be long."

Emma looked at Jake and said, "I will need to borrow your camera."

"Will you take care of it?" he asked seriously.

"Of course," she responded in the same tone.

"I will have it ready and loaded with film."

"Thank you."

As they finished their meeting, Dora mentioned, "We filled another room at the boarding house. A Mr. and Mrs. Miller. He's a war veteran and he and his wife are newlyweds."

"That's nice," commented Emma, "that they found each other."

"They're due here in two or three days."

"I'd like to meet them," Emma said sincerely.

"Emma," said Cole, "can you walk me out?"

"I can." She looked over at Jeremy and said, "I'll join you in the sitting room."

Jeremy said, "Bye, Pops. See you at the office." He watched them leave. *It must involve the other case; I wonder how this connects to the trip Emma is about to take?*

Cole and Emma walked out the front door; he slipped his hand into his pocket and pulled out an envelope. "These are your and Savannah's tickets. Your rooms are also arranged and paid for. You'll be there under your names; it's less trouble that way."

"Agreed," she said as she took the envelope and checked its contents.

"Emma," he said, his voice lowering with his concern, "be

careful. The people who want these jewels will be watching closely."

"We'll take every precaution and return safely," she promised.

"Okay then." He kissed her on the cheek and headed down the stoop toward home.

Watching him closely, she acknowledged she had been worried about him as of late. Ellis was spending more and more time with Abbey. She would have to keep an eye on Cole.

CHAPTER 14

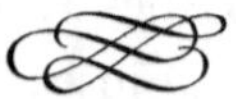

The next day, Emma was getting organized for her afternoon meeting. She looked at her list and confirmed she had everything she needed. She grabbed her hat and headed down to get her bike for her appointment at the museum.

A lunch date had been arranged with Tony to confirm the plans for picking up the jewels. She made her way there and placed her bike on her shoulder to enter the museum. The guards took it from her and told her Tony was waiting in his office. She smiled as she took her lunch pail and headed that way. Knocking lightly, Tony's voice called, "Come in."

She entered and saw both Philip and Tony were present. Philip said, "Emma, thank you for making time for us today."

She sent a quick smile to Tony as she handed him her lunch pail and sat down. Philip said, "Business first."

Emma nodded and looked toward Tony, who also nodded. She pulled out her notebook to read the details the Pinkertons had provided. She started with, "We have confirmed that Tiffany & Co. is sending a selection of the French Crown Jewels to the Museum from New York City. They've already set out to the predetermined location."

"How are they protected?" asked Philip.

"They'll have two guards accompanying the courier. The plan is for me to go by rail and meet them halfway. I'll meet the courier and take it over from there."

"By yourself?" asked Tony.

"No, we've approached Savannah. The cover story is that we're shopping and will be there overnight." She went into detail on how it would work.

CHAPTER 15

Friday morning came quickly; Savannah and Emma would be taking the early train. "I can take you and Savannah to the station," said Jeremy, yawning and sitting up in the bed.

"No, we're good. I've arranged a carriage for us." She closed her bag with a snap and walked over to the bed. She leaned down to kiss him and said, "I appreciate the thought."

When she got close, he pulled her to him and said, "I'll miss you."

"I'll miss you also." She kissed him softly. She leaned into him for a moment and asked, "How is your visit going with your mom?"

He pulled her closer to him and laid his chin on her head. "She's talking but she's used to hiding parts of herself. I think it'll take some time. I just hope I have it."

"Do you expect her to leave soon?"

"No, just a feeling."

She kissed him again and got up to finish getting dressed.

He stayed in bed, watching her close her bag and place her

knives in her hat and on her thigh. "Do you need help with the bag?"

"No, don't get up. It's early. You stay in bed," she said in a low voice. She heard someone going by the door. "Sounds like Savannah's moving downstairs. I have to go," she said, picking up her bag and heading to the door.

Smiling at him, she left the room and headed downstairs. She saw Savannah ready and waiting by the door She asked expectantly, holding her bag and a hand on the door knob, "Ready to go?"

Emma nodded and slipped on her hat, motioning for Savannah to exit ahead of her. Their carriage was waiting on the street for them. They handed the driver their bags and waited for him to help them inside. "Train station, please," indicated Emma.

They were silent as they made their way. The driver helped them down from the carriage, and they paid him before walking toward their train. Emma said, "We should go straight to our car."

They found their sleeper and settled in. Emma asked, "Do you want to go over the plans for both cases?"

"Yes, please. I like to be prepared."

"First, we arrive and check-in at the hotel. From there, we will go to the Cramer Paper Company. I'll be going in alone, dressed as a courier, and you'll wait for me outside."

CHAPTER 16

CRAMER PAPER COMPANY

*E*mma entered the office dressed in pants, a loose shirt with a vest, and a slightly worn jacket. Her hair was braided and tucked into her hat, giving her a boyish appearance. Savannah waited for her outside, as Emma directed.

Emma approached the reception desk and indicated the envelope she was carrying. "I have a package for Mr. Hugo Banks."

"I can take that," said the man sitting there.

Emma pulled it back. "No, this has to be given directly to Mr. Banks."

"Well, he isn't in the office just now," he said, sounding exasperated. He tried again to take it.

She kept it from him and countered with, "Do you have a home address? This has to be delivered today."

He gave her a long look, pushed his chair back, and said, "Yes, just a moment." He pulled open the file drawer beside his desk, flipped through the files, and pulled out a card. "That's interesting, I hadn't noticed that before."

Emma waited for him to continue his thoughts.

"There are two addresses. One for here in Cleveland and one for Cleveland Heights—ten minutes away."

Two, Emma thought. *That is interesting.* She pulled out her notebook and asked, "Could you let me see them?" He handed her the cards. She copied the addresses and handed them back, saying, "I'll check both. Thank you so much for your time."

He put the cards back up and returned to work.

She exited the office building and found Savannah. She held up her notebook and said, with a grin, "Got it."

Savannah grinned back and said, "Where to now?"

Emma looked down at her clothes. "First, I think I need to change." She linked arms with Savannah to stroll back to the hotel. "You won't believe what I found out. He has two addresses."

"Two? Why two?" asked Savannah, bewildered.

"I think it might be two different wives."

CHAPTER 17

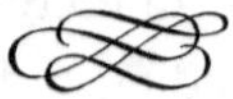

The trip to the hotel was made in silence, with Emma and Savannah lost in their thoughts about what they'd learned

When they were alone in their hotel room, Savannah said in amazement, "Two?"

"And the first one is in Chicago," she reminded her.

"Three," said Savannah as she collapsed on the bed, looking very confused.

Emma watched with a slight smile as she changed into a light blue skirt and fitted high neck white lace blouse. "Don't try to make sense of it. People are motivated by things that others wouldn't understand."

"Yes, I guess so," she said, pulling herself into a sitting position. "All right, what's the plan?"

Emma finished packing her camera and other supplies as she explained her plans and Savannah's role in them. After the briefing, they picked up their things and headed to the front of the hotel where carriages stood waiting. They gave the first address to the driver, it was time to meet the second Mrs. Banks.

As they pulled up, they noted the house was a lovely green Victorian style with white trim and flower boxes in the windows. Emma looked at Savannah, and Savannah commented softly, "Just believe what you're saying."

Emma nodded and climbed down with the help of the driver. After they paid him, they walked up the wide steps to the porch. They saw two girls of about eight and ten sitting on the porch swing. Emma glanced over at them and asked, "Is your mother home?"

The older girl looked up from her drawing pad and said, "Mama's inside. Do you want me to call her?"

"I would appreciate that, thank you," Emma said.

The older girl walked to the door, opened it, and called, "Mama!" She went back to pick up her drawing pad and, before starting her sketch, said, "She should be out momentarily."

"Thank you," said Emma with a smile.

"You're welcome," she replied.

Emma looked at Savannah and mouthed, "Polite."

Savannah nodded.

A lovely woman came to the door. She didn't notice the ladies waiting for her. "Patrice, did you call me?"

"Yes, Mama. These ladies wanted to see you," she said, indicating Savannah and Emma.

As Mrs. Banks turned toward them, Emma watched her closely. She appeared to be in her early thirties, pretty and elegant, with her dark brown hair worn in a chignon. Her clothes also seemed well made.

She looked at the two strangers curiously and said, "I'm Mrs. Banks; can I help you?"

Emma took the lead. "I'm Emma Evans and this is Savannah Woods. We're with a new women's group here in town. We're doing an article for our magazine on important women in the area."

"Really?" she asked. "And I was selected?" Her cheeks flushed and her smile went wider. She believed them, it would make the subterfuge easier to carry off.

"Yes," said Savannah, assuming her role as interviewer and distracting her so Emma could look around. "We have some questions for you and then we would like to take some pictures of you and the house."

"Oh, that is lovely. Would you like to come inside?" she said graciously as she backed up and held the door open for them.

"Thank you," said Savannah. She kept talking while Emma took in her surroundings. She got an idea of the layout of the house. The foyer was lovely; it was a light blue and white trim. A small table and chair sat in the corner. To her right was a large opening revealing a dining room with a large brown table. To her left, there was a sitting room, done in the same white and light blue tones as the foyer. The mantle was visible from the doorway and had pictures on it. Emma nudged Savannah; she got the message and said motioning to the sitting room, "Such a lovely room. Can we start here?"

"Yes, of course."

Emma stepped over to the mantel to see the pictures. It was definitely Mr. Banks. "Can I take some pictures of the room?" Emma asked, holding up the camera she had brought with her.

"For the article?" Mrs. Banks asked, delighted. "That would be wonderful."

Emma pulled out her camera and started taking pictures. She made sure to get more than just the mantle.

Savannah continued with her questions and asked about the mantel. "Is that your husband in that picture?"

"Well, yes!" She laughed. "He's a wonderful man. We've been married for close to fourteen years."

Fourteen years, Emma thought, continuing to take pictures. *That's very close to the number the defendant has been married. So, who is the bigamist here?*

"Can we have one of you?" Emma inquired.

"That would be lovely. How would you like me? By the chair?" she suggested.

"That would be just fine," said Emma. She steadied her camera and took several pictures.

Savannah inquired, "Can we see the rest of the house?"

"Of course." They finished their tour and assured her that the article would be coming out soon. Savannah waited until they had walked about a block away before she asked, "Do you think she knows?"

"About her husband? No, she was too open. Allowing us in the house was not expected."

"What about that second address?" asked Savannah.

She checked her watch and said, "Lunch first?"

"Yes, please." They hailed a carriage and inquired about the next address located in Cleveland Heights.

"It will be about twenty minutes from here," the driver commented.

"Do you know if there are any local restaurants near there?" Emma asked.

"I do. I can take you to one."

They agreed and had a nice carriage ride to the restaurant. As he helped them down, he inquired, "Should I come back for you?"

Emma handed him the money and said, "No, we'll walk there. Thank you." They watched as he drove off.

CHAPTER 18

They finished lunch and strolled to Mr. Banks' second address. "Same as before?" asked Savannah.

"Yes. It worked last time, Let's give it a try," commented Emma.

The house was very similar on the outside to the other house, even the colors—green and white. Kids were playing in the yard, two girls about the same age as the first two from this morning. She and Savannah continued to the door and knocked. As they waited, the sound of heels clicking on the floor reached them. A woman opened the door, perhaps a little older than the other Mrs. Banks. She smiled, though Emma thought her face was more guarded than the first wife. She asked, "May I help you?"

Savannah spoke up and said, "Are you, Mrs. Banks?"

"I am, and you are?" she inquired, her tone pleasant.

"I'm Savannah Woods and this is Emma Evans." She gave the same story as before about the women's organization interviewing important women in town.

This Mrs. Banks gave them a look through narrowed eyes, the pleasant expression fading. "Won't you come in?"

She stepped back and they entered the house. The second house was set up eerily the same as the other one. They went to a similar sitting room, with a similar mantel picture. *Two wives; no, three wives. Why?* Emma was itching to take her pictures but would have to wait for the questions. She glanced at the wife, seeing the distrust in her eyes and the set expression on her face. *This conversation is going to go differently than the last one.*

This Mrs. Banks didn't wait for them to start. She stated, "Caught on to him, have you?"

"I'm sorry, I don't understand," said Savannah, trying to stay on script.

Mrs. Banks looked at both of them. "I know why you're here. You found out about my husband's other wives."

Emma knew their cover had been blown. "May we sit down?"

She nodded and indicated the settee.

They sat and Emma started. "Okay, yes, we are investigating him. He's turning over evidence against another wife."

"The first one? The one in Chicago?" she inquired.

"Yes," Emma confirmed.

"I should have known. He had a thing about her." She stood, went to a box sitting next to the couch, and pulled out a newspaper. It was folded to the one article and she handed it to Emma.

Emma took the paper and read it out loud. "Mr. and Mrs. Gilmore are celebrating their fourteenth wedding anniversary and a great success in their business."

"He fixated on that story; he would pull it out and read it over and over again," Mrs. Banks said with a sigh.

"But he left her. Why do that if he wanted her?" asked Emma with a frown.

"He never really wanted her, you see. He just didn't want Mr. Gilmore to have her."

"This was about Mr. Gilmore, the man she married after

him?" Emma asked, wondering if they had found a key puzzle piece.

"Yes, he had everything a little better than Hugo. He had the better grades in school and always got first place in contests. Hugo just felt he couldn't win, but after Mr. Gilmore left town, he pursued Lily, doing whatever he could to get her to agree to marry him."

"But if she loved Mr. Gilmore, why did she say yes to Mr. Banks?" asked Savannah.

"Hugo let slip that, a few years ago, he lied and told her Mr. Gilmore had met someone else on his trip and didn't want her anymore."

"She believed him?" Savannah asked in disbelief.

"She was young and very naïve," she said with a shrug. "He not only lied; he also hid something from her."

"What was that?" Emma asked curiously.

"Mr. Gilmore planned to ask her to marry him as soon as he returned."

"So, all of this was so Mr. Gilmore couldn't have her as his wife," Emma said contemplatively. "But they got together anyway."

"Yes. He thought she wouldn't have done that without trying to divorce him. Too proper, he figured."

"You knew about the other two wives. Why did you stay with him?" Emma asked, curious about the circumstance this Mrs. Banks found herself in.

She got up and went to look at Hugo's picture on the mantel; she turned slowly back to them and explained. "I didn't know initially. I was young when we met and my parents had passed away. I wanted a family and I knew he could take care of me financially. We had been married for over 10 years when I found out. We had the girls and I didn't want to break up the family. He splits his time between the houses."

She looked at them both and asked, "What will you do with this information? Will you turn us in?"

"I won't do anything without giving you fair warning," Emma stated.

She squinted her eyes, not sure she believed her.

"I give you, my word."

She took a moment to consider Emma and said, "Okay, then. I trust you."

"Thank you."

"If you need a place to go… if this situation doesn't work out for you, I have an address for people who can help with the next steps." Emma quickly wrote out the Carlyle Foundation's address and Clair's name. She handed it to Mrs. Banks.

"Thank you," she said graciously, taking the information.

"Would you mind if I take a few pictures for my files?" asked Emma.

"As long as you keep them private," Mrs. Banks cautioned.

"I will," she promised.

Emma took pictures, identical to those of the other house, and Mrs. Banks graciously allowed one of her. They finished and said their goodbyes.

After they left the house and were out of hearing range, Savannah asked, "Will you keep your word?"

She looked at her and said, "Yes. I think this will give us a bargaining position."

Savannah nodded and asked, "Where to now?"

She checked her watch. "I think dress shopping is next."

Savannah grinned. "That sounds like a great idea."

They spotted a carriage and waved for it. It pulled up, and they asked to be taken to their appointment at the dressmakers. They had seen some previous designs they thought would suit them.

CHAPTER 19

$\mathscr{A}$t the dress shop, Savannah twirled in her blue jewel-toned suit dress. It had a full bustle in the back. "I haven't had a dress with a bustle before. I always thought they looked a bit ridiculous. But honestly, I kind of like it." Their measurements had been sent over when the plans for the trip were first put together, so only minimal changes had been necessary.

Emma came out a lovely vision in pink, a suit dress similar to Savannah's.

"Oh, lovely," the seamstress said as she saw them together.

"The measurements are perfect," said Emma admiringly.

"Yes. It was short notice, but we were able to get them completed."

"The adjustments we mentioned?"

The seamstress nodded and showed her how to access them.

"Good."

"I have something else for you." She went to the next room and brought out two large boxes, saying, "I have some lovely hats for you to try."

She pulled them out and Emma said, "I like those." Savannah

agreed and they tried on the hats and Emma said, "These are perfect. We'll wear these out."

They thanked her for the clothes and the fast service. Emma gave her the envelope Cole had sent to pay for the dresses. The seamstress' eyes widened at the amount. "Thank you!"

As they exited the shop, Emma said, "I believe we have a bit of time before we are due back to pick up our bags. Would you like to shop some more?"

"That would be nice." They browsed a few more stores and boutiques before returning to the hotel. They entered and went to the desk to confirm their train tickets and their luggage pickup. As they were finishing the details, Emma felt a tap on her arm. She turned toward it and saw a boy of about ten.

"Miss," he inquired. He waved to her to bend down, so he could speak into her ear. "They want to see you over there."

She glanced over and said, "I'll be there," and slipped him some coins. He grinned brightly and left.

Emma looked at Savannah and said casually, "Let's stroll around the hotel a bit before heading out."

Savannah got the silent message and said, "Lovely idea." She took Emma's arm and they walked around the lobby and into the area where the conference rooms were located.

"I heard there's some art this way," indicated Emma.

They headed away from the lobby and entered the conference room on their right. As they did so, Emma shut the door softly behind her and said, "Mr. Morgan, I presume." She studied at the average-looking man with one bodyguard.

"Miss Evans," he said.

She nodded and said, "This is Savannah Woods. She's helping out on this case."

"Miss Woods and Miss Evans, we appreciate your help with this transport." He took his briefcase and placed it on the table. As he opened it up the brilliance of the diamonds took their breath away.

"How will you transport this safely?" he asked.

Emma smiled and looked at Savannah. "Could you turn around?"

The man looked confused at her directions to Savannah. She turned and Emma reached into her bustle and opened a slot. "We have several of these made and lined to house the jewels."

He smiled. "Ingenious." He removed them and handed them to her to place in the hiding place. Emma turned to allow them to do the same to her.

Once the jewels were safely hidden away, Mr. Morgan said in a satisfied voice, "It has been a pleasure doing business with you ladies. You'll be heading to the train directly?"

"Yes. We'll wire you when we have made the delivery to the museum."

"Very good. We'll be staying in the hotel for a few more days."

Emma nodded. "That will help with our cover. We'll head out now. Please wait a while before exiting."

"We will. Thank you, Miss Evans and Miss Woods."

CHAPTER 20

They made their way to the rail station and entered their sleeper car. As they opened the door, they saw the bags were already there. The hotel had arranged for them to be delivered to the train ahead of them.

Emma opened her bag and said, "I've been searched. Check your bag."

Savannah opened her bag and said, "Yes, mine was searched also. So, you think they know why we were here?"

Emma said, "Possibly. They may have checked as a precaution. We only have a two-day trip to get home. We will need to be on guard," As she saw the porter passing, she opened the door and waved him over saying, "We're tired and would like some privacy." She gave him a tip.

He took the money and nodded. "I'll take care of it."

She went back into the room and closed the door. "That should give us our privacy. We should be left alone."

"Good," Savannah said as she fluffed the bustle and sat down.

The train moved forward with a jerk. Once the motion smoothed out, they took off their hats. The day moved slowly into the evening. Emma kept her bag close to her; she had Jake's camera in there and she knew there would be dire consequences if she did not return with it. *Both from Mr. Pennington and Jake,* she thought.

As the evening progressed, she thought, *Maybe this will be a quiet trip.* At that moment, there was a knock on the door.

"Odd, I told him we wanted to be left alone," said Emma.

"It might be the dinner we ordered earlier," suggested Savannah.

"Yes, that's true," said Emma absently.

"I'll get it," said Savannah, standing up to approach the door.

Emma was beginning to unbutton her jacket when she noticed something odd about the porter's shadow. The figure was much taller than the porter she had spoken with earlier, and he appeared to have two other people with him. Savannah was reaching for the door when Emma shouted, "Stop!"

The door swung open before Savannah could reach it. Three men pointed guns at them. "Hands up, please." Emma did not have access to either of her knives. She and Savannah were pressed to the windows in the car.

The smallest of the three spoke, "Let's move out."

"Move?" asked Emma. "Where to?"

"Just follow directions," the little man said, waving his gun at her.

Emma grabbed her bag and left the sleeper at their direction. There was no one in the hallways at this late hour. They pushed them to the end of the car, toward the outer door. One man pried it open while the others watched. They were traveling at a fast clip and would soon be approaching a river.

The man, apparently their leader, said, "The jewels. We know you have them."

Emma frowned. "Who are you?"

He replied his voice harsh, "That's none of your business! Now, give us those jewels!"

She looked at them, knowing arguments wear futile. There

was only one way out and she said to no one in particular, "Jump wide, slide, then barrel roll."

Savannah got the message as Emma reached for her arm with one hand, the other clutching her bag, before pulling them both through the door that had been opened. As Emma planned, there was a grassy incline before they started over water. Both she and Savannah slid, then tumbled down the hill. Gunfire sounded from the train and, as they rolled to a stop, she shouted, "Stay down!"

They stayed crouched for a few moments as the train went by before Savannah inquired, "Is anyone coming after us?"

"I don't think so," said Emma, straightening slowly watching the departing train. "I expect they'll try again in Chicago." They sat for another moment and she asked, "Are you okay? Stand up and let's see if we have any injuries to deal with."

Savannah stood slowly and said, "Yes, I think I'm okay."

"Me, too," Emma said. "Train travel has been exciting lately."

"Well, at least no crash this time," said Savannah wryly.

"Agreed," said Emma. "Turn around, let me check the jewels." They were still in their compartments and appeared to be unharmed.

"I will check yours." Savannah checked Emma, and again, no problems. "So, what now?" she asked.

Emma looked around, recognizing the area. "I think I know someone who lives nearby. We'll head that way." She grabbed her bag and they helped each other up the incline.

As they got onto firmer footing, Savannah asked, "So, who do you know in the area?"

"You know Clair's safe house, the one where we move women who need protection? This is one of those ladies we helped."

"When was the last time you saw her? Will she remember you?"

"I think so. I saw her at her wedding about a year ago. She was very happy."

Savannah gave her a look. "Did you investigate her new husband?"

"I did. It was my wedding present to her," she said with a laugh.

"Was she upset that you looked into his background?"

"No, I think she was relieved. Marriage is such a gamble and so much is taken at someone's word." They walked and walked. "Not much further now," said Emma. A large house appeared ahead and to the right. The area was lush and green. They walked up to the house and Emma knocked on the door.

A few moments later, it opened and a little maid asked, "Yes, how may I help you?"

"I would like to see Mrs. Landry, please."

They heard a woman's voice behind the maid. "Who is it, Betsy?" Emma knew that voice and smiled.

Betsy moved out of the way and they saw Mrs. Landry. "Emma! How wonderful to see you. Betsy, let her in." The maid was still hesitant to let the disheveled women into the door but backed away.

Emma and Savannah entered the large foyer; dark wood gleamed from a recent cleaning. "Alison, this is Savannah Woods."

"It is nice to meet you," commented Savannah.

Alison got a good look at them and said, "Goodness! Were you in an accident? Please follow me into the sitting room. Betsy, please bring us some tea and cakes and some cookies."

"That does sound good," said Savannah with a sigh and she sat down on one of the sofas.

Emma pulled her up before she hit the chair, "Wait a moment."

"Oh, yes," remembered a tired Savannah and turned around with her back to Emma.

She unhooked Savannah's bustle and turned to have Savannah due her own.

"That is an odd thing, a removable bustle. It would make it more comfortable to sit down," Alison said, examining the back of the dresses.

Emma folded up the bustles and put them into her bag.

"Now, tell me what happened."

"Well," Emma started.

Savannah interrupted in an excited voice, "We jumped from a train!"

"Really?" Alison asked, fascinated. "Why on earth would you do that?"

Emma looked at her and smirked. "We didn't plan it."

"So, tell me!" exclaimed Alison.

"Not much to tell. Some men were trying to get something from us." She cut her eyes to Savannah, who got the message.

"And you jumped out of a moving train? What did they want?"

At that moment, Betsy came in pushing a tea table. They waited until she set it up and left.

Savannah had already made her way to the cart and was pouring tea for everyone.

"Oh, it's a case," Alison said knowingly.

Emma leaned forward and said in earnest, "You must not tell anyone."

Alison assured her, "I would never say anything. I owe you my life." They clasped hands for a long moment. Savannah brought over their tea and as they finished Alison said, "We need to get you both into some clean clothes."

Emma said, "We would appreciate that. Also, is there any way we can get some transportation to Chicago?"

Alison looked thoughtful and said," I'll ask my husband. Jim should know what to do."

"When will he be home?"

She checked her watch and said, "Soon. Let's get you both cleaned up."

Emma said, "Just a moment," and opened her notebook, writing quickly. "Could you see that this note is sent by telegram to this address?"

Alison took the note and said, "Of course. Let me step out and get this taken care of."

As she left the room, Emma looked at Savannah and said, "I sent a note to Cole to let him know we're not on the train and to be on the lookout for the three men who tried to rob us."

Alison was back in a few minutes and escorted the ladies upstairs. They went into what must be a guest room. "You both get comfortable and let me get you some clothes to change into." She closed the door quietly behind her, allowing them some privacy.

Savannah looked down at her dress in regret. "It was a lovely dress."

Emma laughed suddenly. "Yes, they were."

Savannah saw the humor in the situation and said, "Well, that just means you owe me another dress."

"That I do." She took off her jacket and held it in front of her. It was shredded down the back. "It was a pretty dress," she said regretfully.

Alison walked in and said, "There's fresh water coming up for you." She laid down the dresses she carried on the bed. "Emma, I think you'll like the dark green and, Savannah, for you I have the dark blue."

"These are lovely. Thank you," said Savannah, touching the dresses.

"Yes, thank you," said Emma. "We'll get these back to you."

"No," she said softly. "Consider them a gift."

"Do you think we'll be able to get transportation to Chicago this evening?" asked Emma.

"I think Jim will provide it," said Alison. "I'll leave you now."

They cleaned up and finished dressing. Emma looked down at her boots and said, "I think it's time for a replacement." The leather was torn, and the heels look beat up.

"Me, too," said Savannah, pulling up her skirt and showing shoes in a similar condition.

"Let's go downstairs and see if Jim has arrived," suggested Emma.

They walked down together and saw a nice-looking man leaning against the molding at the entrance of the sitting room. When he saw Emma, he straightened and came over to them. "Emma! So good to see you again." He was genuinely happy to see her.

Emma felt the same and smiled. She leaned forward and kissed him on his cheek. "It's good to see you also. Jim, this is Savannah. We're traveling together this week, shopping and meeting some people." It was all the truth; when working a case, you needed to keep certain items private. Alison wouldn't disclose what she had learned.

He understood her ambiguity and said, "Alison says you need transportation to Chicago. I have my carriage set up for you. I would just ask that you house and feed the horses for a few days before sending them back."

"I think we can handle that," Emma said.

Savannah nodded in agreement.

Alison walked in carrying boxes and said, "Betsy put together sandwiches and fruit for you. I assume you want to get back as soon as possible."

"Yes," Emma said gratefully, accepting them.

"Well, let's get you on your way." Jim led them down the front steps, then reached over to take the bag from Emma. She immediately pulled it close to her. "No, no, I will keep it with me."

He looked like he wanted to ask a question, but knew it was not the best time. Alison asked him to help with no questions asked and he had agreed. He knew Emma's approval had moved Alison to accept his proposal. He would do anything for her.

Emma hugged Alison and Jim, saying, "Next time, I'll stay longer. I promise."

"Make sure you do," said Jim. He looked over to Savannah and said, "It was very nice to have met you."

"Thank you, and it was nice to meet you also," said Savannah.

He handed both ladies into the carriage. "Be on your way," he told the driver.

The carriage moved forward, and Savannah said with a sigh, "Off we go again."

"Do you want to try to close your eyes for a while?" She could tell Savannah had been fighting sleep.

Savannah yawned widely and said, "Yes, it just hit me."

"This happens when you go through something traumatic. You either get too much energy or too little."

"What do you get? Too much or too little?"

She shrugged and said, "Probably too much. I'll be awake for a little while."

"Wake me in a bit."

"I will."

"Are you concerned about something happening between here and Chicago?" Savannah asked sleepily as she closed her eyes.

"No, we're in a closed carriage and no one is aware of our movements. I told Cole we'd wait for the next train."

"Oh, in case someone in the telegraph office shares that information," she said intuitively.

"In cases like this, it is best to tell as few people as possible."

"Yes," she said as she laid her head back and went to sleep.

As they bumped along, Emma thought about what to do when they reached Chicago. After a while, she let the carriage rock her to sleep. A few hours into the trip, she was jostled awake when they slowed. As they stopped, she stuck her head out of the door and called, "Is everything okay?"

The driver called back, "I need to let the horses rest."

"Of course. We have some sandwiches if you'd like to have one with us," she offered.

"Betsy made me a box," he called back down.

"I'll wake Savannah and we can eat while we are stopped." She pulled herself back into the carriage and nudged Savannah. "We need to eat."

She nodded as she sat up and yawned broadly. Emma handed Savannah her box. She opened it and took out her sandwich and an apple. She bit into the sandwich enthusiastically, saying, "I didn't realize I was so hungry."

"Me either," said Emma, eating at a similar speed.

When they finished eating, they stepped down from the carriage and looked around. "Where's the driver?" asked Savannah.

"He's tending the horses and, once they've rested, we'll be on our way," said Emma. Savannah nodded.

They sat talking quietly and heard the horses being hooked back up.

When they didn't hear anything else, Emma called, "Everything okay?" She looked around for the driver and noticed his box lunch on the ground, unopened. Stepping back against the carriage, she retrieved her clutch knife.

She said in a low voice to Savannah, "Stay with the carriage and stay down." A crunch of branches directed her to the right; she turned and threw her knife toward the sound. The blade made contact and she saw a man stumble into view, the knife sticking out of his shoulder.

"You bitch. Why don't you just give us what we want?" he snapped, holding a gun on her.

We, she thought, looking to her left and then right.

"Oh, it's just me. I was following up on a hunch that you'd survive and, as a bonus, I'd get the jewels."

"Where are your partners?"

"They're on their way to Chicago, waiting for you or me to show up."

"It sounds like you don't plan to meet them."

"Why should I?" he groused. "I'm the one who jumped off a train and got a knife stuck in my shoulder. "

Emma kept him talking to distract him while Savannah swung a very large tree branch against his head, taking him unawares. He fell to his knees, dropping the gun.

"Ow," he said, grabbing his head. He saw who hit him and said, "I didn't figure you as a threat." He also realized he no longer had his gun in his hand.

"Are you looking for this?" said Emma. She had retrieved the gun during the confusion and was pointing it at him.

"You'd never shoot me."

"Oh?" She pulled the trigger, sending a bullet close to his ear.

"Hey, that almost hit me!" he said, outraged.

"Next time, it will," she promised. "Where's the driver?"

He indicated to the right with his head. Emma said, "Savannah, go check on him and see if he's okay. Also, check the seat for rope or something to tie him up."

Savannah nodded and did as ask. She soon returned, supporting the driver. He appeared to have a head injury.

Emma asked, "Are you okay?"

"I'm dizzy, but I think okay. I just need to sit down," the driver responded.

Savannah helped him into the carriage and tossed the rope to Emma.

Emma called back, "Hey, bring me the wine."

Weird time to drink, thought Savannah, but she brought it out of the carriage and over to her.

Emma took it and, surprisingly, handed her the gun and said, "Shoot him if he tries anything."

The man jumped when he heard this direction.

Emma turned around and reached down to rip some of her petticoats off. She took the wine and rope with her and headed toward the man.

"Hey, what are you up to now?" he asked, not trusting her.

She reached up and removed her knife from his shoulder. "I need to bandage you before we tie you up." He barely heard her answer due to the pain washing over him. She examined the wound and said, "It doesn't appear to be too serious. You need to sit down." When he looked like he might argue, Savannah cocked the gun.

"Okay, where do you want me?"

"Here is fine. Now, can you remove your jacket?"

He was able to get it off and knelt for her so she could dress the wound. He watched her and said, begrudgingly, "Thank you for helping me."

She looked at him out of the corner of her eye and said, "If you had killed the driver, I wouldn't be."

He shut up after that and let her work on his shoulder. She lifted the bottle and poured it on the wound without warning him. "Ahh!" he screamed and raised an arm to hit her.

Savannah said, "I wouldn't do that." She had moved closer and had the gun trained on his head.

He calmed himself and tried to keep still. Emma completed tending to the wound and told him, "Move to the tree and sit down." He did as he was told. Winding the rope around the tree, she tied it securely around him.

"Hey, you're not just going to leave me here?"

"I'll send a telegram and have someone come get you in a few hours."

He didn't say anything in response. Emma thought, *He thinks he can get away.* She shrugged. *That's a chance we have to take.*

She walked toward Savannah and took the gun from her. "Let's get going."

They headed back to the carriage. "The driver can't drive," protested Savannah.

Emma smiled. "I can drive it." She leaned over into the carriage and asked, "How are you feeling?"

"Yes, I'm fine. Are you sure you can handle it?" the driver asked.

"I can," she said firmly. "Savannah, grab my bag." She did so and they secured the door.

The driver leaned out the window to give the last instructions. "Miss, just continue west. We're about two hours out of Chicago."

"Thank you," said Emma.

"Can I ride up with you?" asked Savannah, excited at the idea.

"Of course." They both climbed up and Emma took the reins. She looked over at Savannah and asked, "Ready?"

"Yes!"

Emma clicked at the horses and got them moving.

Savannah sat quietly as they moved along. She finally asked, "Why did you help him?"

Emma was silent for a long moment and said, "I don't know, except that I saw he had spared the driver. I felt I could do the same for him."

Savannah considered that as they road through the evening. The horses were rested, and they made good time to the city. "Where to first?" she asked.

"Hospital," she said firmly. "We need to take the driver to the Sisters; they'll take care of him." They headed there and when they arrived, Emma said, "Wait here. I'll go in and get help."

She hopped down and made her way into the hospital. A few moments later, she returned, accompanied by a Sister and two orderlies. She went to the door of the carriage and opened it. "He's in here."

The Sister climbed in to check his status. She said to the orderlies, "Take him inside. We need to give him a full evaluation."

Emma stood by as she watched them move him. "Sister, I'll stop by to check on him in the morning. I'll also alert his employer of what happened."

The Sister agreed and headed in with her patient.

Savannah leaned over and said, "Where next?"

"Next, we get the horses fed and settled for the night."

They headed to the Cousin's stable and Emma unlocked the door with her hairpin while Savannah unhooked the horses. The doors were pulled wide and each walked a horse into an empty stall. They got them water and food and brushed them down.

When they finished, Emma said, "We need to get to Cole's house."

"Do you expect to find him there?"

Emma thought about that and said, "You're right. They might be at the rail station. Rather than run all over the city, let's go to Tony's. We need to get the items to a safe location."

They made their way on foot to Tony's apartment. As his career had moved forward at the museum, he began doing well enough to get an apartment of his own. He had been there since their return from Paris. They made their way up to the third floor and Savannah said, "It's late." It was after 10pm and she was worried they would disturb him.

"We'll knock until he wakes up," Emma said simply.

They stood in front of his door and knocked; Emma leaned on the door, hearing more than one voice. She raised her eyebrow at Savannah, who shrugged.

"Who is it?" Tony asked through the door.

Emma called, "Tony, it's Emma and Savannah. We're back and need to speak with you as soon as possible."

Tony opened the door immediately and was shrugging into his jacket.

Emma looked behind him and saw Peggy standing there. She appeared to be trying to fix her hair. What got Emma's attention wasn't her hair; it was the ring on her finger. She made a mental note to ask about that.

"Emma, you were expected back on the train," Tony said.

"We had to find some alternate transportation," she said dryly.

"You could say that," said Savannah in the same tone.

Emma was all business. "Tony, we need to get these items to the museum and contact Cole."

"Cole is at the train station investigating. We will need to contact him."

"Tony," Peggy said quietly. "Should I leave?"

"You might need to," he said regretfully and went over to take her hand. "Would you mind if I tell them?"

She blushed prettily and said, "Yes."

They turned toward Emma and Savannah and said with a wide grin, "We're getting married."

Emma looked closely and thought, *He looks happy.* She smiled back and said sincerely, "Congratulations! That's a lovely ring."

"Congratulations!" said Savannah.

"Thank you. We're so happy," Peggy said.

"I can tell," Emma said. She grew serious. "Tony, you might want to have Peggy accompany us until we get these items safely to the museum."

"Do you think someone followed you?" he asked, concerned for Peggy's safety.

"No, I think we took care of that, but I want to be sure."

He nodded and said, "I agree." He looked over at his fiancé. "Would you mind coming with us?"

She answered quickly, "No, of course not."

Tony and Peggy finished getting organized and all four went downstairs. They made their way on foot to the museum. The group climbed the front stoop and saw the guards outside. Tony spoke to them. "William, I will need you to go get Mr. Johnson."

"Yes, sir. There are three other guards inside. I'll have one replace me here."

Emma had written the note for Philip and handed it to William.

Tony said, "And after you confirm with Mr. Johnson, please also get Mr. Tilden at the rail station. He's needed also."

He nodded and went inside to brief his replacement before leaving.

Emma spoke with the guards outside. "Be vigilant about any visitors to the museum that were not cleared by Mr. Johnson or Tony. Do not let anyone in."

They agreed and watched as the group entered the doors of the museum.

Cole and Philip arrived in the next half hour. They found the group in Tony's office. Emma had waited to reveal the jewels until they arrived.

Cole immediately went to Emma and Savannah and asked, "Are you both all right?"

"We are," said Emma, speaking for them both. "Though we did leave an injured man tied to a tree about two hours from here by carriage."

Cole smiled wryly and said, "I'll have someone pick him up."

Emma asked, "Were you able to get the other two?" The room went quiet as everyone waited for that answer

Cole looked around and said, "Can I trust you not to let this go outside of this room?"

"Yes," everyone agreed.

Cole looked at each one and nodded. He started, "We knew you were on the 8pm train and three men were involved. I received your wire and we were waiting when it arrived." The room was on the edge of their seat, wondering what happened next. "They weren't there."

"Not there? Did they get mixed up with the other people disembarking?" asked Emma, confused at the information.

"No, we had the train stopped and allowed no one off. They may have jumped before it got to Chicago."

"Really, isn't that dangerous?" asked Emma sarcastically.

Cole smiled slightly and asked her, "Can you give us a description?"

"Yes, I can get with Dora and have her put together some sketches as soon as possible."

"We'll get them," Cole promised.

Philip said, a bit impatiently, "I would like to see the jewels."

Emma looked at him and said, "Yes, I'm sure you do." She opened her bag and pulled out the bustles. Philip gave her an odd look. She explained as she opened each pocket. "I had these made to transport the jewels, in case we were intercepted."

"Clever," he said in approval.

When she started to pull them out, he said, "Wait a minute," and cleared off his desk, laying a cloth liner over it. Emma waited for him to set up and then started removing the jewels. Everyone went quiet as she pulled each one out.

"The queen's jewels," murmured Peggy, recognizing them. Her family had, in part, come from France.

"Yes," commented Philip, admiring them. "We are the first stop to display them to the public. These will show beautifully."

Emma was tired and wanted these items secured. She said, "Where do we store these tonight? And how many men are in place to protect them?"

"For that, I'll need to reduce the number of people in the room. Sorry, ladies," Cole said to Savannah and Peggy.

Tony said, "Let me escort you to the photography exhibit while they work out the security details."

Emma watched the door close, and Philip took over from there. "We'll have normal security, but we'll be adding two men outside and one to the display."

"Will you lock the jewels up each night?"

"Yes, they will be moved to the safe each night."

"Who has the combination to the lock?" asked Emma.

"Just me," said Philip.

"We need to keep it that way," said Cole.

"We will," he said firmly.

They completed their review and Emma said, "If we're good, I'd like to go home. It's been a long day."

Cole said, "I'll take you and Savannah home."

"I would appreciate it," she said, grateful for the transportation.

They watched as Philip relocated the jewels to the wall safe. Tony's office had no windows and was the best location to secure them. Cole waved one of his men to the room and said, "You'll need to stay in here and make sure no one has access to that safe except for this gentleman."

He nodded and sat down at the desk.

Cole asked, "Ready?"

They stepped out of the office and Emma said, "Savannah, let's go home. Goodnight, Peggy, and Tony."

Cole had a carriage waiting and helped the ladies inside. "Savannah, we were able to get your bag. It's in the carriage."

"Good, thank you," Savannah said, relieved.

As they headed home, Cole looked at Emma, stroked his goatee, and said, "We need to talk about what all happened."

"Cole, I agree, but could I please get some sleep first?"

"Okay then. I'll come by in the morning."

"If you could come early, I'd appreciate it. I have to get some information over to Mr. Pennington's office. I also need to check in with Jake on some photos I need to be developed."

He agreed. They made it over to the boarding house and he helped them down. "Do you need any help inside?" he asked as he handed their bags down.

"No, we're fine," Emma said, her voice sounding tired. He nodded and watched until they made it safely inside.

Savannah said quietly as they entered the house, "Well, that was exciting, but I'll need some time before the next one."

"Agreed," said Emma. "Do you need anything to eat?"

"What I need is a bed."

"Me, too. Up we go."

Emma made her way upstairs and into the dark bedroom. She heard a rustling of sheets and Jeremy asked, "Finally home?"

"Yes," she said softly, making her way in the dark. She leaned down and kissed him. "Let me get cleaned up and I'll join you."

"I'll be waiting," he said softly back. He had missed her and wanted to just hold her to him.

She took her robe and nightdress and made her way to the bathroom to wash up and brush her teeth. As she completed her task, she gathered up her items and headed back to her bedroom in the silent house. The door closed behind her with a click and she reached to lock it before laying her clothes on the chair. Jeremy held the covers for her and she walked swiftly over, sliding in beside him. "Mmmm," she said as he folded her into his arms, her back against his chest.

"Welcome back."

"Thank you."

"Would you like to talk or..." He looked down and saw she was already asleep. *I think that means we'll talk in the morning.* He closed his eyes, thankful she was back.

CHAPTER 21

Emma slept hard and didn't wake until the next day. When she awoke, the sun was streaming into the room. She turned over and saw Jeremy watching her.

"Good morning."

"Good morning," he said, pulling her to him. They spent some time enjoying each other's company. After the quiet interlude, they both got out of bed to begin their day. He noticed her back as the sheet fell away; it was black and blue with bruises. "Hey, what happened? Are you okay?"

"I'm fine, just sore. I'll put on some compresses today. I'll explain later, I promise," she said.

He took her at her word and said, "Meet you in the hallway?"

"Yes, I need to clean up and get dressed," she commented.

"Me, too," he confirmed and moved to open the bookcase. He looked over his shoulder and called to her softly.

"I'm glad you are back," he said.

Her gaze softened. "Me, too."

"Can we talk this morning?" he asked.

She shook her head regretfully. "I may not have a lot of time."

"Let's grab breakfast and see if we can have some time alone in the kitchen."

The bookcase closed and she moved around, grimacing as she felt every bruise. Her body had tightened up overnight. It would be slow going this morning.

They dressed and met in the hallway to walk downstairs, holding hands. It was early and there were few people up at this hour. "Should you have gotten some more sleep?" He noticed she was moving a bit slower than normal.

"No, too much going on today."

"Do I get to hear about the assignment?"

"Not yet, but soon," she promised. "I can tell you about the other case I was there for. It became interesting quickly."

"Then I want to hear about it."

Emma stopped and said, "Dear-one, I didn't ask. How did the dinner go with your mom?"

"Again, a topic that will take some time," he said softly.

"Tonight? Just the two of us."

"I think that can be worked out." He leaned over to kiss her.

They entered the kitchen and the first person Emma saw was Cole talking to Dora. When he saw her, he set down his coffee cup. "You did say early," he reminded her.

"I did, but can I get some breakfast?"

"Yes, I think we have time."

Dora had given them space to talk before she said to Emma, "I'm glad your back," and hugged her tightly.

"Oh!" Emma moaned in surprise.

"What? Did I hurt you?" she asked, pulling back quickly.

"No, just an event last night that I had to deal with," she assured her. "Let Savannah sleep in this morning. She'll also be a bit tired."

Dora got them some breakfast and Emma ate without talking. She had been very hungry even before going to bed. When she finally looked up from her food, she saw that the group was watching her with a look of awe on their faces. She looked down and realized the quantity of food she had eaten. Smiling ruefully. "Well, I was hungry."

Ethyl came over to take her plate to the sink. She had been hired as a kitchen helper when Amy got promoted to cook. "Thank you." Ethyl smiled and continued with her work.

When Emma finished, Cole said, "Ready to talk?"

"Yes," she said decisively. She kissed Jeremy and smoothed the worry lines on his forehead. She looked over at Tim and asked, "Can we use the study?" He had been using it as an office since Papa moved in with Cole.

"Sure," he said. "I can stay in here and torture Patrick," he teased. He made a lunge for the boy and Patrick ran around the table.

Dora and Lottie were laughing, watching their antics. Emma followed Cole and sat carefully as he shut the door. He joined her on the couch. "Okay, tell me about the pickup."

She pulled out her notebook. "We arrived and worked my other case. We then went to our appointment to get our dresses with hidden pockets. After we went straight to the hotel to meet with the courier; he had one armed guard."

"Was there anything out of the ordinary about him?"

"No, I felt he was honest. We took custody of the jewels and caught the later afternoon train The couriers indicated they would be staying at the hotel for a few days waiting for confirmation that we arrived safely. Could you send a telegraph to the hotel to confirm our safe arrival?"

"I can do that," he said, making a note. He continued, "Did the thieves try immediately?"

"No, but our bags were searched, we noticed that on the train. It was a few hours into the trip when they appeared."

"Why do you think that was?"

"At the time, I didn't think. I just reacted."

"But now?"

"I think they meant to get the jewels and toss us off the bridge."

"But you jumped before they could push you?"

She acknowledged the statement with a nod. "I knew where we were on the trip. I've taken that route many times and knew we were coming up on the bridge. I figured the best way out was to jump where we could slide down the embankment. We slid and then rolled. Oh, and by the way, we owe Savannah a new dress and a pair of boots."

"We'll take care of that," he assured her. "What happened next?"

"I remembered that Alison and Jim Landry live nearby, so we walked and were able to get a carriage from her and her husband to take us to Chicago. "

"The rest I know. We had the man picked up last night."

"Did he give up the two other would-be jewel thieves?" she asked, thinking they might get a notice out to have them picked up.

Cole shook his head. "He was dead."

"Dead? But how can that be? I patched him up and I didn't hit anything vital," she exclaimed.

"It wasn't the knife wound. He was shot."

"Shot? So, he wasn't alone. They must have dropped off the train also."

"They must have been separated somehow, and he found you first."

"I didn't expect that news," she mused.

"Yes, so the identifications of the two other men are more important than we thought."

"I'll work with Dora this morning and get the drawings over to you."

"Great." He stood and waited for her. When she didn't stand, he said, "Is there more to discuss?"

"Cole, please, sit back down," she said, looking serious.

He sat.

"Cole, what about Abbey? Do we have a concern with her showing up in town at this particular time?"

He sat silent for a long moment before saying, "I want to believe she's here for Jeremy, but my experience says she's here for the jewels."

"Is she using him as an excuse?"

He just shook his head. "I don't think so."

"But you are still suspicious of her?"

"How can I not be?"

"Should we talk to Jeremy, come clean about everything?"

"We'll have to tell him soon, before the museum opening this weekend."

"Agreed. Do we mention our concern?"

"That's tricky. We don't have any evidence against Abigail."

"Cole, this is Jeremy. He's a trained investigator. I think we should tell him our concerns."

"Could we get the drawings done first and bring them to the office?"

"Yes, I'll tell Jeremy I'm working."

She followed him out to the hallway and into the dining room. They found Jeremy and Tim talking while Patrick ran around the table, making the baby laugh.

Jeremy held out his hand to Emma, and she went forward to take it. "Have you seen Jake yet this morning?"

"Yes, he's in talking to Ethyl. They get along rather well."

"Let me step in quickly. I need some film developed from my trip."

He nodded and watched her leave. He turned to Cole and asked, "Everything all right?"

"Yes, just wrapping up a case. Jeremy, we'd like to brief you on it today at lunch." Jeremy looked surprised because the case had been kept very quiet.

Jeremy shook his head. "I told Mom that I would meet her for lunch and show her some sites."

"Oh," Cole said casually, "what are you taking her to see?"

He listed some buildings around town and then said, "Oh, and the museum. She wants to see what types of art they have on display there."

Cole didn't know what to say. It seemed awfully coincidental. "I'd like you to be read in on this today. Could you delay?"

Jeremy heard his tone and said, "I'll be there. I'll send a note as soon as we get to the office and ask her to reschedule."

"Thanks."

"Pops?"

"Yes?"

"I appreciate you giving me room to get to know her. I know this can't be easy for you."

He sighed. "I am trying, but know you can come to me no matter what."

"I know, Pops, but I just want to spend time with her while I can."

"Is she planning on leaving soon?" he asked quietly.

"Not yet, but I'm not sure she's here permanently."

"Has she said anything?"

"No." He didn't continue.

"Would you like to go into the office with me?" Cole asked

"Sure, I'll get my jacket and tell Emma we're headed out."

The door swung open from the kitchen and Emma walked out talking to Jake.

"We have to head to the office," Jeremy said. Nodding she accompanied them both out and kissed Jeremy goodbye.

Once they were gone, she went in search of Dora, she had a question for her "Dora," she called.

"We are still in the dining room."

Emma entered and saw her feeding the baby small cut-up bites. "I need a favor after breakfast."

Dora looked up and said, "Sure, anything for you."

"Let me know when you're ready." She sat and watched them finish their meal.

Dora wiped Lottie's face and called to Tim, "Tim, I need you to watch Lottie."

Tim came out of the study and said, "Of course, come to Papa. Would you like to spend time with me?" She giggled as he took her out of the room.

"Where's Patrick?" Emma asked, looking around for him.

"He's in the study with Tim. Papa has started him on a school program, so he's working on his letters and his numbers. Okay, what can I do for you?"

Emma got up and retrieve Dora's sketchpad from the buffet. She handed it to her.

Dora frowned, taking it, and said, "What do you need to be sketched?"

"Three men tried to take the items I was delivering to the museum last night." Dora's face reflected her concern. Emma immediately said, "Not to worry, we were able to evade them. One was picked up last night. I told Cole we'd get him some sketches of the other two this morning."

Dora opened up her pad and held her pencil ready. "Okay, let's get started. Tell me about the first gentleman."

"Kind of a large square face. Smallish eyes." Emma watched her draw and said, "Like that, but a bit further apart. A strong nose, looks like it might have been broken. There is a bump here," she said, pointing to her nose.

She made the adjustment and asked, "Hairline?"

"Not yet receded, full head of brown hair, probably late 30s. Some lines around his eyes."

"Ears?"

"Nothing outstanding."

Dora turned the sketch pad toward Emma, revealing the drawing. "That's him," she confirmed.

Dora turned it back around, flipped to the next page, and said, "You mentioned a second person?"

"He was significantly smaller than the two big guys. Angular face, long nose." Emma looked at her drawings and said, "Narrower in the chin."

Dora made the change. "The eyes?" she asked.

"Larger."

"Like this?"

"No, a bit more."

"Ears?"

"Larger."

"A real looker this one," Dora commented. She turned the finished product toward Emma, who nodded. Dora carefully tore the pages out of the sketchbook and handed them to her. "Is Jake developing some pictures for you?"

Emma was looking at the sketches and said, "Yes, he said they should be ready later today."

"Did he mind helping?"

Emma smiled and said, "He finds the subject matter boring, but he'll get them printed."

CHAPTER 22

LAWYER'S OFFICE

"Emma, you're back!" Ethan was so surprised, that he looked up at her.

"I am. Is he in?" she asked.

"He is, and he's with our very worried client."

"Well, I think I have some helpful information."

"Then go right in."

She nodded and headed to the conference room. Knocking lightly on the door, she called, "Mr. Pennington. "

She waited for his response and was surprised when he opened the door and stepped out. "Emma, I hope you have good news for me."

"I do."

He looked contemplative, trying to determine if he should review the information with her first. He came to a decision. "Emma, I'm going to bring you in and let you discuss what you found. I'll let you know if you need to stop."

Emma nodded understanding; this was his business and she needed to follow his direction. "Let's go in." She entered the office and saw Mrs. Gilmore weeping into her handkerchief. Mr. Gilmore was patting her back.

"Mr. and Mrs. Gilmore, you remember my assistant Emma."

Mrs. Gilmore took a deep shuttering breath and said, "Yes, you were in my interview and also in court with us?"

"Yes, I was," Emma confirmed.

"Emma has found out some information that may be beneficial to our case. Emma," he prompted.

She pulled out her notebook and started, "I went to Cleveland where your..." she hesitated a moment and then said, "where Mr. Banks lives. I first went to his business address. You were correct; he has worked there since you were first married. Have you ever been there?" she asked Mrs. Gilmore.

"No, he wouldn't allow it," she said quietly.

Emma nodded. "I went to the personnel office and got his home addresses." She let that sink in for a moment.

Mr. Gilmore caught it first. He frowned and asked, "Addresses, as in plural?"

"Yes," she confirmed. "It was baffling to me also, so I decided to investigate further. I went to the first one and I found a lovely woman there. She's been married to him as long as you've been married to Mr. Gilmore."

All three were shocked and just stared at her. She continued. "I spoke to her for a long period and I got pictures."

Mr. Pennington jumped on that statement. "Where are they?"

"Being developed, so you'll have them tomorrow morning." She looked at her notes and said, "They have two little girls. They seem to be doing well." She looked up and saw the mention of children had made Mrs. Gilmore start crying again.

Her husband explained, "We waited, you see, to make sure we wouldn't harm the child."

Emma nodded understanding that a violation of that particular societal rule could be bad. She waited for the client to calm again. "Then I went to the second address."

"Was it in the same town?" Mr. Pennington asked.

"No, but only about 20 minutes away in Cleveland Heights."

He nodded for her to continue.

"I got to the second address and found a very similar house. So similar that there were even identical pictures on the mantel."

"Was it…" Mrs. Gilmore asked.

"Another wife? Yes," Emma confirmed.

"Children?" Mr. Gilmore asked, not really wanting to hear the answer.

"Two," she confirmed. "And they have been married about the same amount of time."

Mr. Gilmore looked at Mr. Pennington and asked pleadingly, "I hope that, at last, there's a way out of this mess. He has two more wives; can't we use that to help us?"

"We shall see," said the lawyer. "Emma, what else did you find?" He figured there was additional information.

"Yes, the wife in Cleveland Heights is aware of his other marriages."

"She went along with this?" asked Mrs. Gilmore in amazement.

"Yes. She lost her family at a young age and she also seems to have genuine affection for him," she said by way of explanation.

"Then why would he do this to me?" she asked, bewildered, remembering the young man who wanted to marry her so badly, they'd married the day he asked her.

Emma stood with that question and paced a bit, then looked over and said, "I believe it's a long-standing grudge against Mr. Gilmore. As I understand it, the three of you were close growing up."

"Best friends in fact," Mr. Gilmore confirmed. "We were both in love with Elle." She smiled and squeezed his hands. "We were also involved in the same activities and the same classes in school."

"You weren't just in the same activities; you were competitors," Emma guessed.

"Friendly competitors. At least, I thought we were."

His wife touched his arm and said, "You were always first in every competition."

"And he was always second. I guess I just never thought about it before."

"Did the competition extend to Mrs. Gilmore?" asked Emma.

He looked at Elle and said, "Yes, we were always trying to one-up each other."

"How did he end up marrying her, instead of you?" Emma asked curiously.

"Well, I had to leave for a few months; my father needed help at home."

"That was when Hugo started pressuring me," stated Mrs. Gilmore.

"Had you told him something before you left?" Emma asked Mr. Gilmore.

"How did you know?" he asked in amazement, not looking at his wife.

"The second Mrs. Banks mentioned he lied to Mrs. Gilmore."

"What did you tell him?" asked Elle, making him look her in the eyes.

"I had planned to ask you to marry me when I returned," he said quietly.

"And he knew that? When you left?" asked Elle.

"Yes, he took the opportunity and convinced you to marry him instead."

The tears dried up, replaced by anger. "He took advantage and treated us like pieces in his very own chess game."

Mr. Pennington spoke up and tried to diffuse the emotion

starting to envelop the room. "Did you marry Mr. Banks while Mr. Gilmore was gone?"

"No. Hugo wanted to wait for Gerald to return. He wanted him there, as our witness," said Elle.

"What happened after the ceremony?" Mr. Pennington asked.

"Hugo seemed so happy about the marriage," said Elle, remembering that day.

"What he looked was satisfied," Mr. Gilmore commented. He was also thinking about that day and the misery he'd felt.

She nodded in agreement. "He left a few days later for his new job and said he would send for me."

"But he didn't," Mr. Pennington confirmed.

"No, there were occasional letters with promises that he would come get me, but I never saw him until now," she said.

"Why didn't you just divorce him? Call it abandonment?" Emma pressed.

"It's hard to prove it because he would send a note a few times a year, acting like we never were apart. Gerald and I decided we would take the chance of being together. We got married in a local town and told people we eloped."

"How did you think this would end?" Emma inquired.

"We didn't know. We just knew we wanted to be together," Mrs. Gilmore said simply.

"So, what are our next steps?" asked Mr. Gilmore.

Mr. Pennington looked at Emma and said, "Once we have the pictures, we'll have a private meeting with Mr. Banks and talk about a nice quiet divorce."

They looked so relieved; Emma nearly smiled.

"I'll set up a meeting with him for tomorrow. Emma, can you have the pictures here in time?" asked Mr. Pennington.

"I'll have them ready," she promised.

"I'll set up the appointment. You two will not have any

contact with Mr. Banks." He went as far as shaking his hand at them to make his point.

They understood that they shouldn't let their emotions ruin their plans to resolve the situation. They stood and approached Emma. Mrs. Gilmore said, "Thank you so much for helping us. We didn't think there was a way out of this mess."

"You're welcome," she said sincerely.

Mr. Pennington showed them out and came back into the room. He looked at Emma and said, "Very good work. Did you manage to get a copy of the marriage licenses?"

"You mean these?" she asked as she pulled the papers out of her purse. "They had copies in the file."

He chortled and rubbed his hands together. He reached out for them and said, "Emma, I will be putting you on permanent retainer after this."

Emma blushed; she liked the idea of working for him in a more permanent manner. "Thank you, Mr. Pennington, I would enjoy that." She glanced at her watch and said, "If you don't have anything else for me, I need to type up some letters before lunch."

"That's fine," he said as he sat down, taking notes to prepare for the next day. Emma headed to her office.

Finishing up her letters, she called goodbye to Ethan as she was leaving. She jumped on her bike and headed to the Pinkerton office to talk about the jewels with Cole and Jeremy. Jeremy would be there and they would have to discuss the possibility his mom was in town for the jewels. She and Cole would have to tread carefully.

It was sunny and a bit chilly, but she enjoyed the ride. She stopped at the office and put her bike on her shoulder to walk up the stoop. As she entered, the man at the desk said, "Emma, they're in Cole's office."

"Thanks, Joseph." She handed off her bike to him, adjusted her jacket, and patted her hair before she knocked on the door.

Her hand was shaking as she reached for the knob, taking a deep breath, she entered.

Jeremy and Cole sat with a tea service at the small dining table in the office. She walked toward it and leaned down to kiss Jeremy. He smiled and said, "Active morning?"

"Yes, we made significant headway on the case I was researching. I still have some follow-up to do in the next few days." He nodded, standing to hold her chair for her to take a seat.

Cole had a file opened in front of him and pulled out pictures. Emma knew what it contained. He started by looking over at them, saying, "Let's get started. Emma was assigned a case to work on a delivery for the museum." Jeremy listened intently but did not understand their apparent tension. "She went to pick up the items and, on the way back, she and Savannah were attacked and had to jump from the train to get away."

"Emma!" Looking at her quickly, he said, "Is this the reason for the bruises? Did you or Savannah break anything?"

"No, we're okay," she assured him. "Though I'm sure Savannah would disagree."

He frowned in question.

"Her dress was ruined when we tumbled out," she explained.

He would have to get more data from her on that jump from the train. "What was so important about the package? I assume it was something you could carry."

"Yes." She nodded at Cole, and he handed out the pictures.

"These are the Crown Jewels from France. Tiffany & Co. has purchased this lot." He laid out the pictures in front of Jeremy.

Emma didn't need to look at them; she had seen the beautiful gems in person.

"Emma and Savannah got alternate transportation to get back here." He left out the henchman who had been executed. "They delivered them to the museum last night."

"I understand the secrecy on something like this. Why do you both appear nervous about reading me in on this case?" Jeremy asked. He had seen Cole's tell; he was tapping his foot. Emma was sitting still, too still.

"We're concerned about the jewels and a theft that may occur at the museum," stated Cole.

"Yes, I would expect so. These are amazing," he said, picking up the pictures, looking at each one. "Did you want my help with the design of the security at the museum?"

"Yes. But we also want to speak with you about your mother," Cole said bluntly.

"My mother?" he said, astonished. "Why bring her into this?"

"Well," Cole said wryly, "she is the queen of crime." A name that had been given to her in France.

Jeremy shot him a glance and said, "That was who she used to be; she's changed. You haven't spent any time with her."

"No," Cole said consideringly, "I haven't. I guess I should change that."

Jeremy didn't know what to say about that statement.

"Jeremy," Emma said gently, placing her hand on his. "We're concerned about the timing of her arrival." She held up her hand when he would have interrupted. "We understand she came directly here from France as the jewels were moved to the States."

"If that's true, why didn't she just steal them in transit? It would have been easier," commented Jeremy, still angry at their assumptions.

"I don't know," she said honestly. "She may not have had an opportunity."

"Or," he suggested forcefully, "it's a coincidence and she's here to see me."

Cole said, "We trust you and want you to be involved in the protection detail for the exhibition." He knew he didn't have to say that this job was confidential and no details should be shared outside of the Pinkerton staff.

"I would ask that you give her the benefit of the doubt," Jeremy stated.

Cole sat back and watched him for a long moment. "I will."

Jeremy glanced at Emma, who nodded and said, "I will."

"But that doesn't mean we are not going to work very hard to make sure the collection isn't stolen," stated Emma.

"Agreed," Jeremy said.

"You mentioned you were going to show Abigail around today?" asked Cole.

"Yes," he said hesitantly.

"One of the locations you mentioned was the museum."

Jeremy frowned. "It's a world-renowned museum and is very popular."

"That is correct. Plan on being there tonight. We will be working to set up the security and display cases. The publicity will go out tomorrow to the papers; crowd control will be an issue during the day. There is also a very private party, invitation only."

"Is this the event we are attending tomorrow night?" asked Jeremy, looking at Emma.

"Yes, the invitation said it would be a special limited-time exhibit. Also, Tim and Dora will be there. I think Papa also," Emma said.

"Hmm, I didn't realize," said Cole, frowning. "Ellis is seeing Abigail," he admitted to them.

Jeremy looked shocked. "He is?"

"Yes, they always had a close relationship, and I haven't seen him much since she got back into town."

"She hasn't mentioned him," Jeremy said awkwardly.

"No, they're keeping it private and uncomplicated."

"Do you think it is serious?" asked Emma.

"For Ellis, I think it probably is," Cole commented.

"And Mom?" asked Jeremy.

"I don't know for sure. When she came back, before we got married, she came back for him. Not me." Cole sounded a bit bitter about the situation.

"Pops?" Jeremy asked, worried about him.

"I just felt she only married me because Ellis was settled with Mary."

Emma tried to pull them out of the past and asked, "Do you think he will bring her to the event?"

"Yes," he said simply. "I haven't seen him this happy since your mama."

Emma sat back and said weakly, "But it's only been a week."

"Their shared history creates shortcuts."

"I'll need to mention this to Dora. Should we be worried about him?" asked Emma.

"No," Cole said emphatically before Jeremy could. Jeremy looked a bit surprised at the strength of the comment. "No, Ellis is the one she really wanted."

Jeremy sat and absorbed that but didn't say anything.

Cole realized how that might sound to Jeremy and said, "I was the second choice, Jeremy, not you."

"I know that." The time he'd spent with Abbey had proven that she loved him and bitterly regretted her time away. He looked at Emma and Cole and asked, "Are we going to the museum?"

Cole stared at Jeremy, realizing the time Jeremy had spent with Abigail had been good for him. He smiled. "We need to cover some details here first."

"How long will the exhibit be here?" asked Jeremy.

"Two weeks," replied Cole.

"Do we have enough men to be on the day and night shifts?" Jeremy pulled out a notebook to catalog the details.

"Yes, I've brought in ten men from around the greater Chicago area. Five will work nights and five will work days.

They won't be dressed as Pinkertons during the day; they'll be assigned to walk around. Our men will have their normal roles, looking like nothing out of the ordinary has changed in the normal security."

"Speaking of the event, I do have a dress to finish the details on," stated Emma, standing up.

"Quick lunch first?" suggested Jeremy.

"Yes," she said softly, knowing he would want to talk. "Park?"

Cole stood, too. "I also have a lunch to attend, so I'll leave you both." They said their goodbyes and watched him leave the room.

"Let me get my lunch pail. I see you have yours," said Jeremy. They headed to his office and then down the stoop toward the park. It was a quiet walk.

"Eat first," she suggested as they sat down.

He nodded and they ate. When they finished, Emma asked, "You wanted to talk?"

He wiped his mouth slowly. "I don't think we've ever fought before."

"Are we going to now?" she questioned.

"I'm not sure. Emma, I need you to give her a chance. I need you to spend some time with her. You're usually fairer with people than you have been with her. You and Clair allowed Lily Edwards to come back after she went to jail. You took her at her word that she had changed."

She thought about it and said, "Yes, I'm normally more open about second chances, but I'm concerned about you being taken advantage of."

"You think I went into this with my eyes closed?"

"Yes, at least partially," she admitted.

He looked at her for a long moment and acknowledged, "You're right, but I wouldn't be a party to any kind of theft."

"Have you seen anything that might lead you to believe she's here for anything other than to see you?"

"Honestly, no. When we talk, it's usually about me," he said and reached for her hand, "or about you."

"Oh," she said.

"Oh," he mocked back. "Will you come to dinner with us tonight and give her a chance?"

She tilted her head and considered what he said. "I will, but," she cautioned him, "I'll also be looking to make sure she isn't up to any shenanigans."

"I wouldn't expect anything less," he teased.

"So, is our fight over?"

"I think so."

"Okay," she said, laying her head on his shoulder. "What's this about Papa spending so much time with Abbey?"

"I don't know," he admitted. "We must see her at different times."

She sat up and said determinedly, "Well, I think we should surprise the happy couple."

"Now?" he asked, surprised at the request.

"Sure, I have a few things I can put off."

"But she isn't expecting me for a while."

"No better time to go," she said, drumming her fingers on her lips.

He saw the move and thought, *Planning*. "Emma, I'm not so sure about this."

"Why not?" She laughed, putting her hand down. "You want me to get to know her, right?"

He laughed back, realizing she had decided to investigate the mystery of her dad and his mom. He held out his hand. "Okay, here we go."

She took it and headed out of the park. They waved for a carriage and had it take them to his mom's hotel. If he had any nerves, they were dispelled by the look of mischief in her eyes. "Come on, let's not give them a chance to hide," she said.

Together, they made their way to the stairs. Jeremy stopped her. "I think we should take the elevator."

Her back was stiff, she smiled and said, "Yes, please." The elevator opened and they approached the door, Jeremy was having some doubts, but this was how Emma worked. If his mom wanted to know who she was, this was probably a good start.

Emma knocked and called out, "Housekeeping."

"Housekeeping?" mouthed Jeremy.

"Surprise," she mouthed back, silently laughing.

She leaned her head on the door and heard a muffled man's voice requesting a moment. The door opened a few seconds later, and Emma came face-to-face with her papa.

"Emma!" he said in surprise.

"Papa!" Emma said, feigning surprise.

"What are you doing here?" he asked.

"I could ask the same," she said, looking at him pointedly. "We haven't seen much of you lately. And, as I understand it, neither has Cole."

Before they could get into further conversation, Abbey came up behind him and said, "Why don't you let the children come in?"

Papa turned around and Emma could see his eyes soften. "You're sure?"

"I am." He moved back and waved his hand for them to enter.

"Good to see you, Jeremy," he said, greeting him warmly.

"Hi, Ellis, how are you?" he asked.

"Oh, I'm good," he said, looking at Emma thoughtfully.

They moved into the living room. Abbey said, "Sit down. What made you want to pay me a visit today?" She watched Emma as closely as she watched her. She worried about Jeremy being with this girl because she seemed to have no drive or want to be anything. *Nothing like me,* she thought again.

"Oh," said Emma, "I heard Papa might be here and I wanted to see him."

Abbey and Emma kept staring at each other. Ellis had said Emma was part of a temporary business, mostly office work. *Is there more to her than that?* she wondered. "I understand you were out of town for a few days."

Okay, she is getting directly to it, thought Emma. "Yes, I went shopping with a friend."

"Shopping, you say. What did you find on your shopping spree?"

"We found some lovely dresses," Emma said truthfully.

"Oh, really? I would like to see them."

That won't be possible, thought Emma, *the dresses were a total loss.* She commented, "Maybe one day."

Hmm, Abbey thought, wondering about this girl.

Emma turned the question back and asked, "How long have you and Papa been spending time together?"

Papa started, "Now, Emma, that isn't any of your business."

"No, it's okay," Abbey interrupted. "We're old friends who are getting reacquainted."

"I think it's more than that. Do you plan on sticking around?" Emma asked bluntly.

Abbey looked her in the eyes and said simply, "Yes."

"All right then," said Emma, coming to a silent decision. "Would you like to come for dinner tonight at the boarding house? You and Papa?" she asked, eyeing them both.

Papa glanced at Abbey, looking for her response. She nodded, and he said, "What time should we arrive?"

"How's 6:30pm?" replied Emma.

"We'll be there," he said.

Jeremy looked surprised and happy. He said to Abbey, "I'm sorry I canceled our afternoon. Would you like to go out now?"

"No, I think we'll wait until a later date."

They talked a bit longer, and Emma indicated she needed to head out.

Jeremy said, "I'll go with Emma. We'll reschedule your tour."

They said their goodbyes and left. Jeremy started to put his arm around her shoulder and remembered her back. He took her hand instead and pulled her close to him. "Thank you for that."

"Anything for you," she said, leaning into him. They stayed close together as they went outside. Jeremy waved down a carriage and as they waited for it, he noticed she looked upset. "What's the matter?" he asked.

"I just invited two more people for dinner and didn't tell Dora or her staff first," she groaned. "I promised to be more considerate."

"I can drop you by there and head back to the Pinkerton office."

She said in a low voice, "Yes, that will be for the best."

"Not to worry," he said. "She won't be too mad. Distract her with Ellis and Mom's romance."

She brightened and said, "You're right. She'll want to see that in person."

As they pulled up in front of the boarding house, she kissed him quickly and said, "Wish me luck."

"I'll see you tonight. Wait I will help you down. You need to put compresses on your back," he reminded her. "Yes," she said, grateful for the help.

He escorted her to the door and returned to his waiting carriage. "Can you take me to the Pinkerton office?" Jeremy asked the driver.

"Yes, sir."

"Thank you."

CHAPTER 23

"*D*ora!" Emma called as she entered the boarding house. She could hear Lottie laughing and followed the sound. She found Dora sitting on the floor with the baby and Patrick. He was using the dancing man to make her laugh.

Lottie wobbled over to her.

Emma laughed and started to bend down to pick her up. She groaned instead.

"It's your back, you need to have compresses applied." She got up to retrieve them.

"Dora, I wanted to tell you something," she called as she eased herself down to the floor next to Patrick, giving his hair a quick tousle.

"Just a minute."

"Hey, Emma," said Patrick. "Can I ride your bike?"

"Well, you're still a bit short. How about when you get taller?"

"Okay." He went back to entertaining the baby.

Dora came back in with ice wrapped in a cloth. "Lay on your

stomach," she directed. Emma did as she was told and the ice was placed on her back.

Lottie patted her head. "Thank you, baby," said Emma. "Is Tim working in the study?" asked Emma as she tried to let the ice work.

"Yes." Dora noticed Emma was drumming her fingers on her lips. "What aren't you telling me?"

"Well, a few things," she admitted. "First, I invited Jeremy's mom over for dinner."

"Emma! We talked about this. We need to let the staff know ahead of time. But," she said begrudgingly, "it is family, so I'll let them know."

"Oh, and Papa will be here also," she said nonchalantly.

"So, two more. Watch the baby, I'll go tell Amy and Ethyl that two extra people will be here for dinner." She was almost to the kitchen when she realized what Emma said. She turned back without telling them about the additional people and rushed back. "Emma, did you say Papa and Jeremy's mom would be here? They're still seeing each other?"

"I'll tell you all about it, but you might go ahead and mention the additional people to Amy and Ethyl."

"Yes," Dora said distractedly. "I'll be right back." As she walked back into the room, she called, "Tim, come play catch with Patrick."

Tim came out and said, "I would love to. Patrick, get your ball." He ran to get it, always wanting to spend more time with Tim. They went outside.

Dora sat back on the floor and gave the baby some blocks and dolls to play with. She leaned back against the settee and said, "Okay, what's going on with Papa and this woman? Is it serious?"

Emma looked over and said, "Very."

"Is she still a thief?" Dora knew about her background.

"I can't tell."

"You can always tell," Dora scoffed.

"Not this time. She's good."

"So, why invite her over?"

"Because we need to get to know her. And, if Papa's serious, we need to know if she's manipulating him."

Dora saw something else in her expression. "Emma, do you have something else to tell me?"

Emma laughed suddenly. "She is fascinating. She's done so much."

"Emma, she's spent time in prison for some of those fascinating activities."

"I know," she admitted, "but I'd like to speak with her frankly about some of them."

"Just watch how you do it," Dora cautioned.

"I will," Emma said, drumming her fingers on her lips once again.

CHAPTER 24

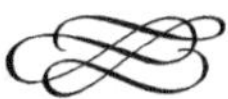

DINNER THAT NIGHT

The ice had helped with Emma's back and Dora had allowed her into the dining room. She watched Dora fuss with the table setup.

"Does it look all right?" she asked, worried.

"It looks lovely," Emma assured her.

"I will need help serving. I asked Amy to help out with the baby tonight," Dora said.

"I am sure we will have lots of willing hands."

Jake came in at that time and said to Emma, "I have your pictures ready if you want to come to the basement and view them."

Emma looked a bit distracted and said, "Jake, put them away for now; we'll review them after dinner." He nodded and moved to the basement to clean his workspace. "Oh, Jake, please don't mention the pictures at dinner."

"Why would I?"

"You're right. I'm sorry," she replied.

Dora asked, "Are we ready for dinner?"

"Everyone's here. We're just waiting for Jeremy, Papa, and Abbey," said Emma.

They heard the door open and Jeremy's voice call out, "Em, we're here!"

"Ready," said Dora, taking a deep breath. Their papa had not been serious about anyone but their mama.

Emma offered her hand to Dora. "Let's go." Dora took it and they made their way to the foyer.

As they entered, they saw Papa was more put together than they normally used to seeing him. His shirt had been pressed and his vest was buttoned under his jacket. His hair had also been meticulously combed. Emma's mouth quirked up and she sent a wink toward Dora as they greeted them.

Tim entered from the study with Patrick. "I'm Tim, this is Dora and Patrick, and I believe you already know Emma," he said to Abbey.

Emma watched as Abbey was introduced. She was dressed very elegantly, wearing a dark skirt and a lovely blue blouse. She also appeared nervous. Emma saw the smallest shake of her hand. She knew she had to make good on her promise to Jeremy and stepped forward. "Yes, we got to spend some time together this afternoon. Welcome, Abbey, to our home."

Papa looked over at Emma and smiled, happy she was making an effort.

Abbey nodded graciously. "Thank you for inviting me."

Dora said, "Why don't we move into the dining room? Dinner is ready, and we can finish the introductions there."

Their group followed her direction. Savannah was coming down the stairs as they made their way there. Jake was already in his seat, waiting for dinner to begin.

"Where is Lottie?" asked Papa.

"Amy has her upstairs. You can go up later and see her," suggested Dora.

"That would be nice." He looked over at Patrick and said, "Would you like to spend the day with me tomorrow? I'm looking at several job sites." He saw Dora's expression and said, "Not to worry. He will stay with me."

Tim said, "It's okay, Dora. Didn't he take you to these types of sites when you were little?"

Dora had the grace to turn red. "You're right. Patrick, would you like to go with your grandpapa? Tomorrow?"

"Yes, please," said Patrick. He loved spending time with his Papa Ellis.

"Okay, now that's settled, can we sit?" asked Emma.

Everyone took their seats. Emma completed the introductions and food started being passed around the table. The food was amazing and the platters emptied fast.

Abbey said, "That was wonderful. Thanks for including me."

Dora said, "Thank you. Amy is our cook and she did a wonderful job. I'll let her know how much you appreciated it. Okay, everyone up and grab something to move into the kitchen."

Abbey looked a bit surprised at the demand but noticed the others doing as directed. *I guess I'll help,* she thought and picked up the nearest tray and followed them into the kitchen. Emma picked up a pitcher and Jeremy took it from her with a shake of his head.

He saw noticed Abbey watching them and said, "Emma pulled her back earlier and needs to take it easy."

Abbey wondered about that as she entered and placed the tray on the kitchen table. The area was well done and very professional. Dora organized everyone to their workstations for cleaning and putting up dishes.

As they completed their task, Dora spoke up. "Tim, why don't you take Papa, Jeremy, and Jake into the sitting room with you?"

Tim knew that tone and didn't hesitate to say, "Let's move into the sitting room."

Abbey started to move with Papa, but Dora said, "Why don't

you stay here with us?"

Emma said, "Yes, please."

Papa looked like he was going to say no.

Abbey looked at them and said, "Yes, I'd like to stay."

Savannah smiled." I have a late date. Don't wait up."

"Sounds like fun," said Emma. Savannah headed to the foyer and then they heard the door open and close

"Would you like some dessert, Abbey? It's a Kuchen."

They didn't talk right away. Dora cut slices of the desert and placed them on a tray for the men. She opened the kitchen and called, "Tim, please come get the dessert." He came to take the tray and thanked her for the treat. He kissed her on the cheek, picked up the tray she'd prepared, and went back into the sitting room.

Cutting additional slices for Emma, Abbey, and herself, she sat down with them. She gave Emma a long look.

"Okay," Emma mouthed, "I will."

"Abbey," Emma started, "we wanted to meet with you by ourselves. We understand you and Papa knew each other a long time ago."

"We did," she confirmed.

"We also understand that it was Papa you were coming back for, but you ended up marrying Cole."

"Also true," she confirmed, wondering where this was going.

"We want to know if you plan to stay and if you are serious about him."

She looked at both of them and said coolly," I wouldn't normally share my plans, but yes, I do plan to stay. At least, as long as Ellis will have me."

"You realize our hesitation in believing what you're saying. You made a similar commitment with Cole, and you ended up returning to your previous field."

Abbey frowned. "Now, that is overstepping. What happened at that time is between Cole and me."

"And Jeremy," Emma reminded her.

"Yes," she acknowledged," and when *he* asks, I'll tell him. "

"That's fair," Emma said. "But I do have to ask the hard question. Are you out of the thievery business?"

Abbey gave her a long hard look. "I'm definitely out of the business."

Emma watched her closely, looking for any tells that would give away a lie. Abbey's gaze was steady, her voice even and her manner a bit defensive. But that last one was to be expected.

Emma nodded and said to Dora, "I think we should give her a chance."

Dora reached over to touch Abbey's hand and said, "Please, forgive us. We're very protective of our papa."

Abbey released the breath she didn't realize she was holding. Ellis' girls were fierce and she wanted them to know she wouldn't do anything to hurt him. She also wanted to be with Ellis for a long time.

"I hope we can move forward from here," said Abbey.

"As do we," said Dora, answering for them both.

"Emma," Abbey said, moving them on to another topic, "Is that an example of your lacework?" She nodded at Dora's lace overlay.

"It is," she confirmed.

Dora fingered the lace. "Isn't it lovely? I have several that she has made me."

"Really? Could I see them?" Abbey asked, a real interest in her voice.

"I don't see why not. I have them in a room upstairs," Emma said.

"I don't want to disturb your baby," Abbey said, looking at Dora.

"Oh, you won't. I have them in another room. Emma uses the attic for her final lacework. Would you like to follow us up?" Dora asked, pushing back her chair in anticipation of standing.

"Yes, very much so," Abbey said sincerely.

They headed upstairs and, as they passed the men in the sitting room, Dora said, "We're heading up to look at some of Emma's lace designs." Papa looked happy that his girls were getting along with Abbey.

They walked up to the fourth floor and entered the attic. It contained twin beds, a desk, and an area where drawings were displayed, showing intricate lace designs. Abbey immediately went to the drawings. "These are just lovely. Have you started them yet?"

"The one on the left is the one lying on the bed."

Abbey went over to examine it and picked it up. "This is so intricate; it must take a huge amount of time to get the detail right."

"It does. I work on it between jobs and in the evenings," explained Emma.

"Ellis mentioned you were a temporary worker," she said absently.

"Well, not exactly. We own a temporary business and I also work jobs for our company," explained Emma.

"That sounds interesting," she said. "I do wish I had seen these before. I would have loved to have some lace additions to the dress I'm wearing to the event at the museum."

"Oh," said Emma nonchalantly, "are you and Papa attending?"

"Yes, we're looking forward to it. As I understand, a new exhibit is the reason for the event." She said, just as casually, "Will you be there?"

"Yes," said Emma. "We're going also."

"I had hoped to see the museum before the event. I understand there are some wonderful paintings and photographs."

"There are," said Dora, not realizing she was telling more than Emma wanted. "A close friend is the assistant curator. He's in charge of the new exhibits."

"Well, that is interesting. You must introduce me."

"We will," murmured Emma.

Abbey continued to study the lace and said, "I would love for you to design something for me. Can we get together next week and talk about it?"

"I would like that," said Emma honestly. She did enjoy her lacework.

"Well, I must be going; I'll see you both at the event."

"We'll walk you down," offered Dora.

As they left, Emma said to Abbey, "I was thinking, I would love to hear about your past adventures."

Abbey paused and said with a faint smile, "I might just do that." She eyed Emma contemplatively and turned to continue walking down the stairs. Emma seemed the opposite of her. *Why would she want to hear those old stories?* She shrugged and put it out of her mind.

They heard the men talking as they entered the foyer. The ladies entered the sitting room, and Papa looked up. "Hello, dear. Are you about ready to go?"

"I am," she said and turned toward Dora and Emma. "Dora, thank you for the lovely meal. I look forward to seeing you both soon."

Jeremy was watching the interaction closely and decided it had gone well. "Mom, would you like to tour tomorrow?"

"I'd love to see you for lunch, but I think we can wait on the tour until after the event."

"Okay," he said and leaned over to kiss her on the cheek.

Papa and Abbey said their goodbyes and left.

"Where's Jake?" asked Emma, looking around.

Tim said, "He went down to his basement workroom to check on some things. Dora I am going upstairs to check on the kids."

"I should be up soon," she said watching him go up the stairs.

"I need to check with Jake," said Emma starting to head

toward the basement.

"Hey, wait a moment," said Jeremy, stopping her before she could leave the room. "I'd like to hear your and Dora's impressions of Mom."

Emma hesitated. She wanted to look at those pictures, but she allowed herself to be pulled to the settee. She sat down and watched as Dora joined them

Jeremy didn't wait and asked abruptly, "Did you like her? It looked like you got along okay."

Emma answered, "We got along surprisingly well."

Dora said, "She's a very interesting woman. I think I could like her." She glanced upstairs again and said, "I need to go help Tim."

"Thanks for staying a moment," said Jeremy.

She smiled and headed upstairs.

Jeremy turned his gaze to Emma. "Well?"

"I like her."

"Do you trust her?"

"Trust needs to be earned," she said cautiously, "but I'm giving her a chance." He nodded. She glanced into the foyer and said, "Would you like to accompany me downstairs to check with Jake?"

"No," he said. "I think I'll go up and read for a while before bed."

"Okay, I'll see you soon." She kissed him warmly.

He escorted her out and headed upstairs as she approached the door to the basement. She descended the stairs and called out, "Jake!"

When she didn't get a response, she called again, "Jake!"

He stepped out of his photography room and saw her. "Yes, come down. We need to review your photos."

"On my way." He had the gas lights turned up in his lab and her pictures laid out on the table. He had grouped them by family.

"These are excellent," she murmured as she picked them up to examine them. "They're so clear."

"You did a good job taking the pictures," he acknowledged.

"Thanks!" She smiled and asked, "Can I take these with me?"

"Yes, they are dry. Will you be using them tomorrow?"

"Yes, the lawyer and client will be very happy with these." She gathered them up and said, "Thank you so much."

"Just let me know when you might need the camera next."

"I will." She leaned over and kissed him on his cheek. He didn't change his expression as he looked back at his table, gathering up supplies to put away.

She headed upstairs, looking at the pictures. She knew Jake would make one last sweep through the house and turn off the gas lights that remained lit.

She opened up her door and saw Jeremy already settled in the bed reading. "The pictures came out amazing," she said, jumping onto the bed.

"Let me see." He laid his book down next to him.

She set them out for him to review. As he looked at them, he saw what she had. "It's odd that the women are so similar and the houses seem to be identical."

"Yes, I saw that also. I would assume it makes it easier to find things." She looked at him and said teasingly, "Do you think he ever forgets which house he is in?"

He nodded and said seriously, "It could be confusing. Will you present these tomorrow?"

"Yes, I think Mr. Pennington is going to use them to put some pressure on the case's star witness."

"Well, enough of that." He moved his book to the nightstand and said, "How about less talking?"

"I'm agreeable to that." She moved the pictures to her desk and returned to the bed. Burying his hands in her hair he pulled her to him. She went willingly, enjoying their time together.

CHAPTER 25

The next morning, Emma was getting ready and could hear Jeremy next door. With her tie in place, she finished lacing up her boots and placed her knives in her leg strap and her hat. She was ready for the day and reached for the portfolio containing the pictures for her meeting that morning. Moving to the door, she opened it and stepped out. Jeremy was waiting and said, offering his elbow, "Ready?"

She nodded and took his elbow.

"Good morning," he murmured as he kissed her cheek.

"Good morning,"

"Headed to the lawyer's office this morning?" he asked, indicating her portfolio.

"I am, what about you?"

"I'm headed to the museum; we're going to be there all day to help with security and setup."

"Good," she said. "We need things to go smoothly. I'll be there this afternoon and evening."

They headed downstairs and had a nice breakfast. Jeremy walked her bike to the cable car. He handed it to her as they saw it approaching. "Have a great day. Send me a note if you won't be there today."

"I will," she promised.

She waved at him as he ran to catch it. She hopped on her bike, holding her portfolio in one hand and steering with the other. She headed over to the lawyer's office, carried her bike in, and stored it in the closet.

"Is he in?" she asked Ethan.

"Not yet, but soon," he responded, not looking up from the files on his desk.

"Do you know how he plans to deliver the evidence?" she asked.

"I think he's set up the meeting for this morning." He heard the door and said, "There he is now."

She turned in response to his statement and watched Mr. Pennington enter the office.

"Hello, Emma. I hope that's my photos," he said, eyeing her portfolio.

"It is," she said with a wide smile. "You'll be happy with the results."

He nodded, thinking it was going to be a good day. "Come in and let me get settled." She followed him into the office and he directed, "Lay them out on the table."

She laid them out, showing the two families. The pictures were eerily similar. He walked over to view them. He was quiet as he took in each house and wife. He straightened and said, "That should do it."

"How will we work this?"

"I have Mr. Banks and his lawyer coming over this morning. I think we'll present this information to him at that time."

"Will we have Mr. and Mrs. Gilmore there as well?"

"I don't think I want them here. It will be less emotional if we present the facts to him this way."

"Agreed. What time?"

He checked his pocket watch. "They should be here within the hour. We need to work on your delivery of the information."

She practiced pulling the files and going over each one and asked questions as she went. He seemed satisfied after a few times through and said, "That should do it. We're ready."

"I'll work on my filing and transcribing until it's time to present these."

He nodded, walked back to his desk, and began pulling out files for another case.

Her mind was on the upcoming meeting as she went to her office and sat at her typewriter. A little while later a knock sounded at her door, she looked up from her typing and called, "Come in."

Ethan stuck his head in. "We're ready for you."

She took a minute to calm herself and checked her clutch knife. The circumstances probably wouldn't call for it, but she wanted to be prepared. People didn't always react as you expected. Feeling more composed, she patted her hair and exited her office to go to the conference room. Ethan nodded encouragingly as she passed him.

She knocked lightly and heard a voice call, "Please, come in."

She pushed on the door and entered the room. Hugo Banks and a man who must have been his lawyer were seated at the round conference table with Mr. Pennington. *Ahh,* she thought to herself, *time for the reveal.*

"I have asked Emma to join us," Mr. Pennington said, "She's done some background work for me on this case. Emma, come in and have a seat." He moved the file to her and said, "Could you start?"

"Mr. Banks, you were married to Elle…" she began.

"We *are* married," Banks interrupted, "not were. *Are.*"

Emma nodded and appeared to agree. She continued, "You can confirm you were married fourteen years ago on this date," she said, showing him the file.

He looked down at it and back up at her. "Yes."

"And after you were married, you immediately left town?"

"I had to leave for work." His lawyer nudged him, and he got the message. "But I stayed in contact and sent money."

Mr. Pennington let that one go by without challenge. They weren't going to argue the small stuff.

Emma continued. "Is this your address in Cleveland?" She set the paper in front of him for review.

"What?" He seemed startled by the question.

"Is this your current address?" she asked again patiently.

"Yes, well…" he said, looking at it. His lawyer looked at Emma, confused about why they were asking.

"My client gave you his current address."

"No, what he gave us was where he worked." She looked at Banks and asked firmly, "Can you confirm that address is yours?"

He finally said, "Yes."

She presented one more and asked, "And this one?"

He went white when he saw the second one.

His lawyer saw his reaction and said, "Maybe we need to stop and let me confer with my client."

"No, we aren't in court," Mr. Pennington said. "We need to continue. Emma," he prompted.

"Yes. To continue, I went to both addresses and met your second and third wives."

Before he could stop himself, his lawyer exclaimed, "His *what?*"

Emma laid out the pictures. "If you will notice, both houses are extremely similar, and there are children."

His lawyer looked like he was going to pull his hair out.

Mr. Pennington took over. "So, what we have here is a situation where I think both sides can help each other."

Mr. Banks' lawyer glared at his client and said, "We're listening."

Mr. Pennington immediately slid a piece of paper in front of Banks. "You sign this letter stating the marriage was never consummated and therefore not valid. We can make this case go away."

"Wait, so they just get a free pass?" Mr. Banks said indignantly.

"I think her living in fear of you returning was punishment enough," Emma commented, wondering how he could be so centric in his logic.

"What do I get out of this?" he asked, shaking off his lawyer's hand on his arm.

Mr. Pennington said smoothly, "We will not disclose the bigamy cases existing in Cleveland and Cleveland Heights."

Emma leaned forward, tapping the pictures, and reminded him, "You have two very nice wives who care for you very much."

He hung his head and his lawyer whispered in his ear. He finally looked up and asked, "Where do I sign?"

"Here." Mr. Pennington pointed to the paper.

Mr. Banks signed and threw down the pen.

Mr. Pennington picked it up smoothly and said, "I'll send this over to the DA. I would assume you will also confirm your mistake with him."

His lawyer prodded him and Mr. Banks grudgingly said, "Yes."

They got up and left. Emma and Mr. Pennington waited for the outer door to close before talking.

He sat back in his chair, looking pleased with himself, and said, "Emma, that was perfect."

"Yes, it went well." She started picking up the pictures and asked, "What will you do with these?"

"Put them in a locked file and, if he ever tries something again, we'll have that to use against him."

"Good idea," she acknowledged.

"Now, I think I'll go see my client and deliver the news in person."

"Would you like me to file that with the court?" she asked, indicating the annulment papers he held. Elle Gilmore had signed them a few days prior in the hopes it would be signed today by Hugo Banks.

"Yes, please," he said.

Emma had done courier work like this before and knew the procedure for delivering papers to the court.

He put them into an envelope. "Directly over, no stops!" he said sternly as he handed it to her.

"Agreed." She took the letter and placed it in her inside jacket pocket. "I'll head there now."

"It's still early. Will you be returning?" Mr. Pennington asked as he checked the time.

"Yes, I have some things to finish up."

"Good, I'd like to let you know how the communication goes with the client."

"I'll be here," she promised and watched him leave. She smiled as she noticed a definite spring in his step.

As she headed out, she told Ethan, "I need to file some papers with the court."

He nodded, acknowledging he'd heard her.

Her bike would be unnecessary, as the court was only a short distance from the office. The filing went smoothly, and she headed out. The day was nice and people were out walking. *Out of the corner of her eye, she saw something, she turned and saw a well-dressed woman with that familiar hair. Abbey.* she thought. Her hotel was located close to the courthouse. She stopped and thought, *That is her. I should say hello.*

Emma started to head over but stopped abruptly when she realized Abbey was speaking with a tall man in a dark suit. She stepped closer and tried to be unobtrusive as she continued to observe them. *I need to be closer to hear them,* and she took a few more steps toward them. She could hear snippets of their conversation and thought, *French*. Though she didn't understand them, she could tell from their posture and facial expression it was an argument. Abbey's head was bowed and her mouth turned downward. She was normally very confident but, in this situation, she appeared to be a bit fearful. The man continued to berate her and Emma watched Abbey wipe a tear as she nodded to the question asked. They seemed to reach some sort of agreement and then departed.

Abbey turned toward the hotel and the Frenchmen went in the opposite direction. Emma decided to follow the man at a distance. His destination was a hotel located about a block down; she continued to follow him discreetly. He went to the front desk and asked for his mail. Emma stood close behind him

"Here it is, sir," said the hotel manager, handing several letters over.

He took them without an acknowledgment, turned away, and headed to the elevator.

"Miss, may I help you?" the manager asked.

"No, I think I have what I need," Emma said and turned to leave. What to make of this? she thought. Is it another piece of Abbey that shows she's not quite out of the business? Is this her partner? Are they here to steal the jewels? She would have to let Cole know about this.

CHAPTER 26

*E*mma went back to the office and start working on transcribing her shorthand notes. She pulled the last paper out of her typewriter and filed it away just as she heard Mr. Pennington in the outer office. Expecting him to return to his office, she was surprised when he came straight to hers.

"Emma! Did you get the papers filed?" he inquired.

"Yes, they said it would be one-to-two days," she confirmed.

"Excellent, that would make it Friday."

"Yes, that seems about right," she confirmed.

"Emma, how would you like to attend a wedding on Friday?"

She looked at him, shocked.

He grinned. "Our clients would like us as witnesses. They also wanted to thank you personally." He had an idea it would be a monetary thank you, but he didn't mention it. "Can you be there?"

"I think so. I have a few things to move around. Will it be in the morning?"

"Yes, I believe there'll be a small tea service provided. We can meet here and take a carriage over."

"That will be nice."

"Good, good." He watched as she started covering her typewriter and pulled out her courier bag. "Afternoon deliveries today?"

"A few and then off to the museum to set up for a special event."

"The one that is tomorrow evening?"

"Yes, will you be attending?"

"Yes, I think I will be. I'm looking forward to it. See you tomorrow, Emma."

She bade him goodbye and headed to retrieve her bike. As she started to exit the building, she heard Ethan say, "Good job, Emma."

She was shocked. Ethan never complimented her on anything. Turning slowly toward him and she said solemnly, "Why, thank you, Ethan."

He nodded and went back to his paperwork.

She smiled as she exited the building, thinking, *It has been a good day.*

She wanted to go to the Pinkerton office to tell Cole about Abbey, but Jeremy was there. Wavering, she finally decided to keep an open mind about his mother *There could be many reasons for a Frenchman to be speaking with Abbey,* she supposed. It was the timing that bothered her.

She continued to think about that as she rode quickly to the boarding house for lunch. Her commission for some lace patterns needed work before she left for the museum.

Riding around the back, she parked her bike by the kitchen door and entered. "Hello, Amy and Ethyl." They said hello back and Emma inhaled. "Amy, what is that I smell baking?"

Amy smiled. "Kuchen."

Emma grabbed one. It was still hot, and she juggled it in her hand until it cooled. She took a bite and said, "Lovely."

Amy grinned. "It's sweet, so I knew you would like it."

"True," she said as she munched on it. "Dora around?"

"Park," commented Amy. "They went out over an hour ago."

"Nice for them," she said, meaning it. Since Dora had gotten help for the boarding house, she was able to spend more time with the kids. She had everything she wanted, and Emma was very happy for her.

Amy asked, "Staying for lunch?"

"Yes, I'll be upstairs until it's ready."

"I'll ring the bell to let you know to come down."

Emma headed upstairs; *lacework*, she thought. She had some details to add to Dora's dress; her own had been completed for a while. Dora's dress hung on a form so she could attach the lace. The event was tomorrow night and she wanted it to be perfect. The lace overlaid a sleek blue dress. It was a bit fashion-forward and would accent Dora's figure. Emma's was similar but, instead of black lace, there was white lace at the cuffs and in layers on the bottom.

She was working steadily and didn't hear anyone come in until someone tapped her on the shoulder. The mirror's reflection showed her who was behind her, she turned and said, "Abbey, I didn't know you were visiting today."

Abbey smiled. "Ellis wanted to stop by and see Lottie while she was awake."

Emma noticed the strained look she had when speaking to the Frenchman had faded away.

"Are they back? Dora had taken the kids to the park."

"Yes, we came upon them as we were entering."

"Papa loves to spend time with the baby. He said she reminds him of us when we were little."

"Yes," she agreed. Abbey looked at the dress and said, "Can I see what you're working on?"

"Yes," Emma said and stepped back.

"I didn't see the full overlay last night. This is nice. Who's it for?"

"Dora, she's wearing it to the event tomorrow night."

"That will be lovely on her." She made a decision. "I'd like one made just like this for me."

Emma looked at her with a measuring eye and said, "I'd have to make some adjustments."

She laughed and said, "Yes well, Dora is a bit curvier."

Emma laughed also and said, "Just don't tell her. She's still concerned about her baby weight."

"She looks lovely, though."

"She does," Emma acknowledged.

"When do you think you could work on it?"

Emma shuffled her schedule in her head and said, "It would take me more than six months to complete."

"That would be fine," she said firmly.

The completion date didn't seem to faze her, and Emma thought, *Does that mean she's staying? Maybe the Frenchmen was just an acquaintance.*

"When would you like to take my measurements?"

"We could schedule some time this weekend."

"After church?"

"We do a family dinner here, and I can measure you after."

Abbey laughed and said, "I'm not sure after is a good idea, with all of the good cooking around here."

"You'll have a treat; Dora still cooks Sunday dinner."

"I heard she's a very talented cook."

"She is."

"I understand you have some talent yourself," Abbey said without mentioning what that talent might be.

Emma frowned, not understanding, and Abbey said, "Baking. I hear there are several desserts you make that could hurt my waistline."

Emma smiled. "I have several you might like."

"Excellent." She sat on the bed and said, "You can finish your work."

"You don't mind?" Emma asked, knowing she had a short window of time to work on it.

"I'd love to watch."

Emma went back to the dress and kneeled at the bottom to confirm the proper length. She finished the final work and stepped back, saying, "I'm finished. I'll do a final check when Dora puts it on. That way, if there are any pulls, I can fix them."

"I love it." She hadn't moved off the bed and Emma sat in an overstuffed chair across from her.

Emma was curious about this woman and thought this might be a good time to ask. "Papa said you were very good at thievery when you were all running around."

Abbey didn't see any malice, just honest curiosity. "Yes," she murmured, "I was quite good."

Was, thought Emma. She asked, "Better than Papa?"

Abbey laughed. "We had similar techniques. Though he never applied himself to the trade like I did."

Emma focused on that last statement and asked the hard question, "Cole and Papa got out. Why did you stay in?"

She gave Emma a long look and finally answered simply. "I was good at it. I liked it. It was exciting."

"I get that," said Emma. "But it wasn't always good."

"No, I occasionally got caught. When I was young, I could cry and get released most of the time. Then I got older," she said and abruptly stood to walk around the room.

Emma watched her for a moment, picking up items off the dresser and placing them back down. "You decided to go to Europe rather abruptly?"

"I did. I had my reasons." She hesitated before she picked up the delicate silver frame. "Is this Mary?"

"Yes, that was Mama."

"She was beautiful," she said sincerely.

"Yes."

Just when they were getting serious, the lunch bell rang downstairs. They both look startled at the sound.

"What was that?" asked Abbey, putting a hand to her chest.

"The lunch bell," said Emma. "We have plenty if you and Papa would like to join us," she offered.

Abbey looked happy at the invitation and responded, "I would like that."

They headed downstairs talking about fashion. Ellis looked up and smiled, realizing they were getting along. He worried about Emma the most. After Mary's death, he hadn't needed anyone but Emma and Dora, but Abbey coming back into his life made him realize he had been lonely. He still loved his work, but she gave him balance.

"Ellis," Abbey said as she stepped down off the last step. "We've been invited to lunch."

"I could eat," he said.

Emma noticed Papa behaved differently around Abbey; he seemed surer of himself and more aware of his surroundings. "Papa, any interesting jobs going on lately?" she asked as they sat down.

"Yes," he said and reverted at least partially to the papa she knew. He went on to describe a project coming up.

Abbey smiled at him, "I'd like to hear more about that also."

Dora was watching with a small smile and fed the baby as she ate.

Emma noticed that smile. *I need to follow up with her. She knows something I don't.* Lunch went by quickly with lively conversation, and each person promised to see each other at the museum event.

Dora and Emma walked them out with the baby.

After they closed the door, Emma leaned on it and said, "Okay, what do you know that I don't?"

"What do you mean?" Dora asked in a coy voice.

"Dora, spill," she ordered.

"It's just that Mama could do that."

"Do what?"

"Pull him out of his engineering world."

"He seems suave," she said incredulously.

"Yes, I remember he was like that with Mama. He would dance with her; he was fully present when she was alive."

"Why is he different with us?"

"He just is," she said with a shrug. "It doesn't mean he doesn't love us; it is a different kind of love." She changed topics. "I noticed you're getting along with her."

"I am," she acknowledged. "I like her."

"That will make Jeremy happy."

"Yes, I think so."

"So, you don't suspect her anymore or think she is after the jewels?"

"Oh, I'm still suspicious," Emma said, not mentioning the man she saw Abbey with that morning.

Dora looked at her but knew the tone, so she left Emma to it.

"I have to head to the museum to help out with the security," said Emma.

"Will you be back for dinner?"

"Philip is providing it for us."

She walked toward the stairs and Dora said, "Aren't you going now?"

"No, I need to be in my delivery clothes. It should be dirty work."

She ran up and changed before heading back down wearing her black jacket, white shirt, pants, and bowler. *You just never know,* she thought. She went out through the kitchen, saying goodbye to Amy and Ethyl as she exited into the backyard to retrieve her bike.

The museum was a few miles away, she pedaled to build up her speed to get there quickly. When she got there, she noticed additional guards standing at the doors and on the street. She knew them by sight and nodded. They waved her up the stairs and yelled at the men at the door to let her in. "Thank you," she said as she entered. The Pinkerton guards were stationed inside as well. One of them took the bike to store it for her.

She gazed into the expanse of the large main room. It had been completely cleared out of the current displays. *Jake will be a bit disappointed that the photos he loves so much have been moved out,* she thought.

"Emma!" called Tony. He had just exited the office and walked over to where she was standing. "Dressed for work?" he asked, smiling easily.

The engagement has been good for him, she thought. "I am," she acknowledged. "What has been done so far?"

He turned towards the main floor and commented, "The floors were polished last night. We have the rugs to layout and the display cases to move. We also have new art to complement the jewels."

Philip had many contacts in Paris to turn to for paintings for various shows. He already had a good reputation as an art authenticator and as a man who could be trusted.

"What artists will be displayed?" she asked.

"James Tissot will be our main focus; his genre is fashionable women shown in everyday scenes."

"That sounds interesting. Can I see them?"

"Sure, they're over here. Follow me."

They neared some paintings lined up by the walls. As they went to each one, he told her the names: *The Traveler, The Two Sisters, Portrait of the Marquis and Marchioness of Miramon and their children, A Luncheon.*

"These are wonderful," she said.

They walked to the additional art that would be displayed three landscapes and three impressionists. She continued around the room, examining each one.

"You won't find Alairs' initials," teased Tony, referencing the forger they had caught in Paris. One of the ways they were able to distinguish the fakes from the originals on the case in Paris.

Emma glanced back with a wide smile. "I would hope not! Isn't he still in prison?"

"Yes, and not likely to get out any time soon."

"Good," she said, happy the man who had tried to kill Philip was out of their lives.

She looked around the room and saw bolts of purple cloth. "What are those for?" she asked curiously.

"Decoration," he said. "Philip told me the color purple has been associated with royalty, power, and wealth for centuries. Queen Elizabeth even forbade anyone except close members of the royal family from wearing it."

"Why is that?" she asked.

Tony responded, "Purple's elite status stems from the rarity and cost of the dye originally used to produce it."

"What will he do with the cloth?"

"He wants it draped on the walls."

"Has he an idea of what he would like?" she asked looking at the fabric.

"I don't think so," he said, frowning. They were starting to run short on time before the benefit.

Emma was thinking and asked, "Would Philip mind if I sketched some ideas on how the draping could be hung?"

"Let me go check with him. He's in his office with Cole and Jeremy reviewing the final plans for tomorrow night." Tony wanted to make sure Philip didn't have other ideas for the fabric. He headed over as Emma continued to examine the room.

Knocking softly on the door, he heard Philip call, "Come in."

Tony entered and said, "Sorry to interrupt. Emma is here and wants to know if you would like her input for the draping."

"Tell her definitely," he said, relieved. There were so many details still to work out. "I will be out in a few moments."

"I will, thank you." He closed the door behind him and went back over to Emma.

"He said yes and he'll be out in a moment."

"Tony, could get me paper and a pencil?" She knew his office was currently off-limits because it was the most secure room in the museum.

He nodded and got the supplies she needed and a book to support the paper. She walked around the room making notes and taking measurements Next, she checked the fabric rolls to see the amount she had available. "Tony, is there additional fabric for the display cases?"

"Well, they already have red felt in them." He saw she was drumming her lips and said, "You have an idea?"

"I do. We could also use the purple in the display cabinets."

Tony smiled, liking the idea. "That sounds amazing."

Philip walked up and said, "I hear you have some suggestions."

"I do." She showed him her sketch; it detailed draping around the room and long lengths between the paintings.

He studied the drawing and said, "Can you demonstrate what you're thinking?"

She unrolled two yards of fabric and set about gathering them. "It will be easier with a bit of thread," she said. "If you could get me a ladder, I can show you the effect." He did as she asked, and she proceeded with the example.

Philip stepped back and said, "I like it. Do you have time to work on this tonight?"

She studied it and said, "If I can get help with the installation of the hangers."

He smiled. "I think we can manage that. What else do you need?"

"I need an iron, ironing board, and my sewing kit."

Tony was making a list and said, "I can go get those for you."

This will be an easier job one day in the future, she thought. She had heard that sewing machines were being demonstrated for at-home use. *Until that time, it's a needle and thread for me.* "Thanks, Tony. I'll measure out the material while I wait for you."

She was still looking at the fabric when she felt herself being embraced from behind. She leaned back and said, "I wondered if I would get to see you."

"Busy trying to make sure this place is secure. What are you up to?" asked Jeremy. She described her project and he said, "Looks like we'll be here a while tonight."

Their group worked into the evening. Jeremy continued to do security scans, evaluating the space. Emma had gotten the fabric cut into manageable sections and ironed them; she had just started tacking together the folds when dinner arrived.

The food was from a local restaurant; they sat down on the floor and enjoyed their meal together. She was sitting next to Jeremy and asked in a low voice. "Any weak spots in the security?"

"I don't think so; we've combed over every inch of this place."

"Good."

The evening wore on. Emma had the drapes ready to go up on the east and west walls. Jeremy helped her move the ladder to each location and provided a hammer when needed to secure the fabric to the walls. She had designed the display so the art was hung between the drapes. The paintings went up next; the purpose was to use the color of the drapes to accent the art.

Once completed, Philip came out to review the effect. "Perfect," he said. He turned to Tony. "Let's get the floors cleaned off and the rugs laid out."

Tony waved to the men working with them and said, "Time to clean up." They moved the ladders and scaffolding from the room. The floors were swept clean and mopped.

While they were waiting for them to dry, Emma saw Cole had arrived.

Jeremy was speaking with Tony about additional security. He had his back to them and didn't notice his arrival. She walked over to Cole and said in a low voice, "Can we step out for a moment?"

Cole frowned. "Yes, of course."

They walked back out the front and stood under the high portico roof. Cole leaned on one of the columns and asked, "Do you have something for me?"

"I do," she confirmed. "I saw Abbey today."

"Yes, I understand you had lunch with her and Ellis at the boarding house."

She looked at him with raised eyebrows.

"I spoke with Ellis this evening before he went out to dinner with Abbey," he said by way of explanation.

"Oh, okay." *Makes sense,* she thought. "No, that wasn't the only time I saw her today." She told him what she had seen.

"The timing of this is suspect," he said, mulling over the information. "Emma, let me look into this. Don't say anything to Jeremy."

She agreed.

"Let's go back in. I'd like to check the security and confirm the plans with Philip and Jeremy," said Cole.

As they went back in, they noticed the floors had dried and the rolls of carpet were being moved to the proper locations. The carpets were rolled out and adjusted. Then cabinets were placed in the center of the room.

"Emma," called Philip. "I have the cases opened."

Emma retrieved purple rectangles and squares she had cut to size. They didn't have to be hemmed; they could be tucked under the existing displays.

Each one was opened, and Emma added the draping. After

everyone left, they would add the jewels to confirm the final setup. Until then, they would be locked up in Tony's office.

A final sweep was completed and the workmen were dismissed. At that time, it was only Tony, Emma, Philip, Jeremy, and Cole. The Pinkerton men were still on guard around the outside of the building.

"Ready?" asked Philip.

They heard a call from the door. Philip went over to find out what was the concern. He came back with Jake, who was carrying his camera. He explained, "After I saw how nice this was turning out, I thought Jake might take some pictures and document the jewels for us."

Good idea, thought Emma.

The museum was locked back down and the jewels were brought out. Philip and Tony had taken time to polish the stones and settings. They gleamed in the light. "We'll need extra light around the cases," said Jake.

"Of course." Philip had arranged for gas lights on stands to be available. Jeremy and Tony moved them close to the cases.

Philip handled the jewels and placed them in each one. "Should we close the lids?" he asked.

"No, leave them open. Otherwise, they may not turn out clear."

"Good suggestion." He completed the arrangements and stepped back to review. He walked around to see the displays from different angles. "Yes, that's it. Jake, you can start now."

Jake was very serious in his work; he gave instructions to have the group help with lifting when he thought it would make a better picture. Once the process was completed, he said, "Philip, would you like a picture with the display board in front of the museum? We could also send them to the paper."

Philip liked the idea and said, "That's a great idea. Tony, would you please join me?"

Tony went red with pleasure. "Yes, sir, thank you."

Their relationship had always been strong, but this was a big step to include him in the publicity for the museum. He felt valued and honored.

The pictures were taken and the jewels were carefully moved back to the safe before anyone could leave. Final security measures were reviewed and confirmed to be in place.

It was quite late when the team headed home, but they felt it would be a nice event.

"Tony," she called, "will anyone be in for a preview tomorrow?"

"No, we're going to keep everyone out until the evening. Philip feels it would be safer that way."

CHAPTER 27

The next night, the family was getting ready for the big event. Emma and Dora were in the attic putting on their dresses. As Emma helped Dora into hers, she said, "There, I have it buttoned up for you." She put on her dress and walked over to Dora, turning around so she could do the same for her.

Once finished, Emma asked, "Do you want some help with your hair?" Both girls were wearing their hair up and it could take a while to style. They completed their task and added makeup to their faces—a mixture made from oatmeal, eggs, honey, and other natural ingredients.

They heard a call from downstairs. "Ladies, Philip and Tony want us there early."

"Yes, well, that's the best we can do," Emma said and Dora nodded. They headed downstairs. Jeremy and Tim were dressed in their tuxedos, looking very handsome.

All motion seemed to stop when they saw each other.

Tim broke the silence and said, "Wow."

Dora smiled broadly. "Why, thank you, sir."

Jeremy couldn't take his eyes off Emma and said, "Beautiful."

Emma smiled softly. "Thank you."

They headed out to the carriage and made their way to the museum.

CHAPTER 28

They were early since Emma and Jeremy wanted to do final security checks. As they pulled up, they noticed the sign outside now included Jake's pictures from the night before. They paused a moment to review them.

Tim commented, "Jake wouldn't agree to come out with us. He said he has a new camera that he's evaluating."

"The pictures did turn out nice," commented Dora. "I'll tell him tomorrow."

They got cleared through the front door and made their way in. The caterers were setting up the hors d'oeuvres and drinks for the guests.

Emma walked over to the display case to view the jewels with Tim and Dora while Jeremy checked in with Tony and Philip. Dora and Tim were looking closely at them, and she commented, "Royal jewels, who would have thought we would be able to see this? Emma, you got to hold these?"

"Yes, and they're quite heavy. I can't imagine wearing them all night."

The guest started to arrive an hour later. Emma noticed quite a large number of them were the same people they had invited to the charity event. There was a large turnout, and everyone wanted to view the jewels. To keep it organized, groups of ten were allowed into the roped-off display area. Other groups were looking at the art on the walls; it had turned out to be just as popular as the jewels.

Philip approached their small group and said, "This is going well. I have some newspapermen here, so this should be in the paper tomorrow."

"How long will you keep the jewels on display?" Emma asked.

"We'll have them for another two weeks." He looked around and said, "I have to mingle," and he moved away.

Emma was looking around and saw Papa and Abbey enter. *They make a very handsome couple,* she thought. Watching them closely, she saw Abbey surveying the room, but not focusing on the art or the people. She was looking at where the security guards were located. Emma would keep an eye on her.

The evening continued. Jeremy walked up to Emma and Philip and said, "All of the guests have arrived."

"Good. Then the building can be locked down. No one in or out until I say so," said Philip, he motioned to the guards with his hands. They barred the door and stepped in front to keep watch.

He went to the front of the gathering and spoke. "Welcome! We are honored to have the French Crown Jewels with us. We would like to thank Tiffany and Co. for choosing us as the first stop. Please review our new French paintings on display as well as the jewels. I hope you enjoy your evening."

Jeremy stood with Emma. She started to say, "Jeremy…"

At that moment, there was a very loud argument at the front door. She glanced to see what the commotion was. Jeremy immediately waved more of his men in that direction.

"You aren't allowed to leave at this time," a voice could be heard saying.

Then, there was the sound of punches landing. The Pinkerton men, in place as undercover guests and museum guards, moved quickly to the door. Emma watched and thought, *This isn't good. No one is watching the jewels.* She pushed her way through the crowds, trying to get to the display cases.

Everyone's attention was toward the door and their backs to her. As she broke through, her worst fears were realized; the glass was shattered and the jewels were gone. Knowing she had to do something to get Cole and Jeremy's attention, she climbed on a chair and said in a very loud voice, "Quiet! I said quiet!"

The room went silent. "Cole." She nodded her head toward the cases.

He and Jeremy ran over. "Gone!" Jeremy shouted. "Philip!"

When he came over Jeremy continued, "Everyone in here will be questioned and searched." That caused a loud murmur among the attendees.

Philip was worried about the important people's responses, but he was more worried about the loss of the jewels. "There's no other way," said Philip. "Please, follow the Pinkertons' direction."

Cole said loudly, "As each of you is searched, you will be allowed to go." They got the people lined up in two lines, one for the women and one for the men.

There was a lot of grumbling from the crowd. "What right do they have to search us?" someone asked.

Cole responded, "We believe the jewels are still in the room. You are all aware of how important this is not only to Tiffany & Co. but to history."

That seemed to calm them down. Philip had screens brought in from the storeroom to help protect the women's privacy. Dora and Emma helped search the ladies.

"I would never do something like that!" an older lady huffed.

Dora caught Emma's eye and gave her a quick smile. Each woman was searched and released. When they got to Abbey, she smiled and said, "Search me." They searched her thoroughly and found nothing.

The men got similar attention from Jeremy and Cole.

Philip and Tony paced at the front doors.

"What do we do?" Philip asked. "How could this happen after all of our preparations?"

"The simpler the plan, the easier to put into action," Cole said. "We need to start letting people go. If the jewels are not on the guests, then they're still here."

"Agreed," said Philip. He announced to the group, "We are very sorry that this event had to end this way. We will find the jewels and continue with the exhibit." He nodded to the Pinkerton detectives to open the doors. The people that had been searched left quietly. Many were not sure what to make of their evening.

Cole spoke quietly to Ellis, saying it would be best if he and Abbey left also. He nodded and said, "I understand. We will head out." Dora and Tim indicated they would leave with them; they had to go home to relieve Amy.

Cole watched them leave and then turned to the group. "We'll need to separate and search the building top to bottom."

The Pinkerton detectives, Cole, Jeremy, Emma, and Tony searched the museum from top to bottom. It was late and they were all exhausted. Suddenly, Emma noticed something. She asked, "Tony, was your office locked during the party?"

"My office? No, there was no reason to. The jewels were out here," he said.

"Hmm," she mused, drumming her fingers on her lips.

"What are you thinking?" asked Jeremy.

"They had to know we would search everyone," Emma said contemplatively.

"Yes," Jeremy said.

She squinted at him. "What's the last place you would think to look?"

Tony's eyes went wide. "The safe!" He called to the others and they all ran into his office. Phillip went directly to the safe to open it.

They held their collective breath as it was opened. Emma had been right, whoever took them knew they would not check the safe for the jewels. Philip removed them carefully for examination. "They are intact," he said, relieved.

"Who did it?" asked Tony.

"Whoever it is will be back to get them," said Cole.

"Yes," agreed Emma.

Jeremy said, "I think I have an idea."

They listened closely and nodded. Later that night, they left the door to Tony's office open. They agreed to go home, each looking exhausted. As they exited, Cole confirmed he would contact the police and have them at the museum first thing in the morning.

DINNER THAT NIGHT

The guards were making their rounds and didn't notice a figure moving around on the roof. That figure dressed all in black entered through the attic vent on top of the museum. They continued down to the main floor and to the office. The office door was left ajar, allowing access to the safe.

When the figure neared the safe, the office chair swung around, revealing Jeremy. It was a toss-up who was more surprised—Jeremy or his mom. He couldn't believe what he was seeing. She was dressed in all black, her hair covered by a black knit cap. Before he could voice his disappointment, she looked behind her and put her finger to her lips. She motioned for him to turn and jumped behind the door.

He reacted automatically and did as she asked. He heard footsteps, then a man's voice as he entered the office.

"So much easier this way," the man said. He made his way to the safe and opened it with no difficulty. When he looked inside there were no jewels. "What! But..."

"Looking for something?" Abbey asked, coming out from behind the door.

Emma was monitoring the room from out in the museum. She had taken out the larger man accompanying the smaller thief as he entered the office. While she tied him up, she listened to the conversation. Cole had the place surrounded, so they were letting this play out.

"What are you doing here?" the small man asked.

"Well, it was easy to let you do all of the hard work," Abbey commented wryly.

"Well, *I* have done the work, so you will give me the jewels. Where have you put them?" he demanded.

"Oh, I don't have them," stated Abbey.

Jeremy turned his chair around at that statement. "No, she doesn't. We do, and you're under arrest." He had his gun trained on the small man.

Emma watched and thought, *There are three scenarios. He can give up, run, or attempt to grab Abbey.*

He picked the third choice and grabbed Abbey. Jeremy didn't want to shoot in the small room; he could accidentally hurt her. Jeremy knew Emma was waiting in the museum and that Cole had the area surrounded. Moving slowly, he placed his gun on the desk and held up his hands. "Just don't hurt her."

The man backed away toward the door, pulling Abbey with him. The thief stood in the center of the doorway with his arm around Abbey's neck, a gun at her throat. The small man suddenly looked surprised. "What...?" He looked at Abbey, then slumped into her, then onto the floor. A knife stuck out of his back.

"Everyone okay?" Cole asked as he stepped over the man and into the room. Abbey looked dazed and kept staring at the knife. *Mom,* she thought, looking at it The knife was exactly the type she used to use. She looked toward the door, expecting her to walk in.

Instead, Emma stepped in and asked, "Mind if I retrieve my knife?"

Cole stopped her and said, "Let's get the police involved first, and you can get it from them."

Abbey frowned at Emma. "What is going on here?"

Jeremy asked her, "Are you okay?"

"Yes, but she's under arrest. Turn around, please," Cole stated coolly. Abbey turned meekly and was escorted from the room. Cole looked back and said, "Emma and Jeremy, we will need you to go to the police station with us."

"But—" Emma said, wanting to stay behind and confirm the place was firmly locked up.

Cole interrupted. "Philip and Tony will take care of it. We need you at the station now."

Jeremy took a deep breath and let it out. Whether Abbey was guilty or not, he would be there for her. He followed them out.

Emma watched Jeremy's face and thought, *This will hurt Papa and Jeremy.*

CHAPTER 30

hen they arrived at the police station, they took all suspects into separate interrogation spaces. Cole was directing everyone in this event.

Before Cole and Jeremy went into the interrogation room with Abbey, Cole looked over at Emma. "We'll start with Abbey, then we'll bring you in next."

She sat on the bench and waited patiently for them to call her. She nodded to the police chief as he entered the second interrogation room. He was personally handling the interrogation of the henchman. They still had to find the inside person who moved the jewels to the safe.

Cole returned and said, "Emma, please join us."

As she walked in, her gaze was blocked by Cole's back. When he moved out of the way, she looked around, not understanding what she was seeing. Abbey was there but so were Papa and the Frenchman. She sent a shocked look to Jeremy and Cole, then she realized they were all smiling at her.

Her observational ability kicked into high gear. Cole, Jeremy, Papa, and Abbey appeared to be very friendly, with none of the animosity she had witnessed previously. "So, all of you were in on this?" she asked, exasperated, but her eyes twinkled.

"Yes, for this to work, we had to keep the number of people involved low," explained Cole.

"How did you get in without me seeing?"

Cole stood up and moved a curtain back, "A second entrance." She eyed him and her family and said, "So, the three of you are not fighting." She zeroed in on Jeremy. "You were in on this!"

He put his hands up. "I didn't find out until we got here."

She looked around, gathering facts. "And since we're in here without a police officer, that would make you French police?"

"You are right. She is good," the French policeman said.

"Was it also a matter of an exchange?" Emma asked Abbey.

Abbey laughed out loud. She had underestimated this girl. "Yes, I came out of retirement for a small job, and it turned out I was set up." She saw Jeremy glance at her and she responded, "Yes, I did one small job for a friend."

"We set it up so she could be blackmailed. It worked that we had a trade to make," the French policeman said.

"And you," Emma looked at Cole, "you were in this all along?"

"No, not initially," he commented. "I reached a point where I thought Jeremy could be hurt if she was here for the jewels, so I followed her. And I saw the same man you did." He nodded at the French detective.

"Yes," the Frenchman acknowledged. "Cole contacted me and we filled him in on the plan."

She looked at Jeremy and said, "Where's the animosity?"

"I'm just glad Mom isn't going to prison," he said sincerely. In response, Abbey took his hand and squeezed it.

"And you." Emma turned to her Papa. "Is this why you were avoiding me?"

He turned red but said, "Yes, little girl. I was afraid I'd give the game away if I spent more time with you."

She looked at Cole. "The man I intercepted at the museum, he is one of the men who attacked us on the train. You should be able to get him for the murder of the other man also."

"Yes, I will inform the chief so he can add the charge," said Cole.

Abbey said, "Can we get out of here now?" Just being there made her nervous.

Cole stood up. "Yes, they're moving the other man. Let me check to see if we can leave without him seeing you." Cole stepped out for a few moments and then returned. "We can go."

Abbey sat next to Emma in the carriage and commented, "So, you're an investigator?"

"You know that also," Emma said, squinting at Jeremy. He squirmed. Emma was used to being the one who knew all the secrets.

It might be a long night, thought Jeremy.

CHAPTER 31

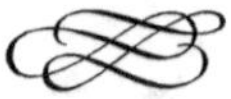

The following week was exciting. They learned that one of the guest's personal assistants had been bribed to take the jewels and move them to the safe. The henchmen in custody gave up his name. He confessed as soon as he was picked up. The personal assistant had paid other assistants to start an argument and create a distraction. They didn't know why, they were just after the pay day.

The week was ending on a happy note for Emma. Friday morning, she and Mr. Pennington were the only guests and witnesses to Mr. and Mrs. Gilmore's second wedding. It was handled quietly in the judge's chambers. "I now pronounce you man and wife," he said and watched as they kissed.

As they thanked him, Emma and Mr. Pennington stepped forward to offer their congratulations. Mr. Gilmore said, "We would like you both to go to tea with us, to celebrate."

Emma said, "I would love to."

Mr. Pennington responded, "As would I."

"Wonderful. I have a carriage waiting for us."

As they descended the stairs, Mr. Pennington offered Mrs.

Gilmore his arm. She took it and they strode off. Emma and Mr. Gilmore followed at a slower pace.

"Emma, I wanted to speak with you a moment," Mr. Gilmore said. His serious tone caused her to pause and look at him.

"Yes?" Emma asked curiously.

"I have something for you. You saved us from prison. You made it so we can finally have a family." He grasped her hands and pressed an envelope into them.

Emma looked down and back up at him. "Thank you, but this isn't necessary."

"We believe it is," he said firmly.

"Thank you," she said and put the envelope inside her jacket. She would enjoy her lunch and check it later.

Lunch was nice, not just the food but watching two people so in love.

Emma got home before her courier work started and ran upstairs to her room. Sitting on the edge of the bed, she opened the envelope and saw there was a hundred-dollar bill there. What to do with it? She made up her mind and moved to the bed, removing the post, and slipped it inside before she went back downstairs. There might be a project where that money could be useful.

CHAPTER 32

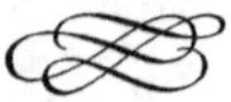

It had been about four weeks since the jewel exhibit and the wedding. The exhibit had been extremely successful, and the couriers had picked up the jewels. It was confirmed that they had made it safely to their next stop.

Jeremy was feeling more secure that his mom was going to stay around for a long time.

That evening after dinner, Emma was working on some lace designs for Abbey's dress in the attic room. She had her initial sketches completed and was ready to meet with her.

There was a knock on her door and when Emma opened it, she was surprised to see Abbey standing there. She smiled. "I was just thinking that I needed to show you my designs for your dress."

Abbey looked very serious. "I think it's time we talked." She closed the door behind her and moved into the room.

"No way out, I suppose," commented Emma, wondering what this was about.

"No," said Abbey. "I want to talk about your knife skills."

"Knife skills?" she echoed, bewildered. "Why would you want to discuss that?"

"Who trained you?" Abbey asked, standing still as a statue without answering Emma's question.

Emma didn't know why she wanted to know, but it wasn't a secret. "We had a specialist who lived with us. She taught me."

"This specialist, what was her name?" asked Abbey, her voice low.

"We called her Miss Marjorie, but I believe it was Marjorie Allen."

Abbey walked over to the chair facing Emma and sat down before she continued. "When did she move into the boarding house?"

"She and a friend moved in 1876."

"A friend?"

"Miss Amy. They were inseparable after their husbands passed."

Abbey's face turned white at that statement. "Her husband? He passed?"

"Yes. Miss Marjorie said it was after their last big job. They both went to prison. She got out and he didn't."

Abbey took a shuddering breath at that statement. Emma watched her, letting the pieces of the puzzle build.

"What was she like, when you knew her?"

That made Emma smile. "Wonderfully brash. She spoke her mind. She taught me about knives and how to use them."

"Yes, I was never good at that. It made her angry that I didn't have that talent," Abbey commented.

"Did you know Miss Marjorie? Papa mentioned when she moved in that he'd known her a long time ago, that he owed her for saving his life."

"She was my mother," Abbey said simply, laying her head back on the chair. "We never got along, too much alike, I suppose."

"Your mother," she said, and something clicked. "But that means Jeremy..."

"Her grandson," she finished for her.

"Did she know about him?"

"I'm not sure. I don't think Jeremy knew, but Cole must have. He and Ellis knew her at the same time."

As Emma thought about it, Miss Marjorie always made herself scarce when they visited. She would have a headache or say she just needed to rest. She hadn't thought anything about it at the time.

"Was she happy?" inquired Abbey.

"Yes, I believe she was."

"When I saw that knife—the craftsmanship and the aim—I knew you were trained by her." She sat up and looked Emma in the eye. "So, tell me. What *do* you do, Emma?"

"I work for Pinkerton and independently on other cases."

"A detective." She laughed. "I should have known Jeremy would pick someone interesting. You asked me about my previous life. Now, I want to know about yours."

They sat up that night, talking and comparing the many stories that had shaped the women they had become. They fell asleep talking.

When they exited the room the next morning, they were as tight as thieves. They walked down together and Emma asked, "Would you like our family to take you to Miss Marjorie's grave?"

"I would," she commented softly.

Dora was surprised to see Abbey walk into the kitchen with Emma. "Visiting early this morning," she asked curiously.

Abbey laughed. "No, visited late. I find I'm very tired and should head back to my hotel."

"I can get Tim to get you a carriage and escort you back," suggested Dora.

"I would appreciate that. I'm not used to these late hours anymore." She hugged Emma. "Thank you for last night." She also walked over and hugged Dora.

Tim came in, and Dora asked, "Can you take Abbey back to the hotel in a carriage?"

"I can." He offered her his elbow. He sent a questioning look at Dora, and she mouthed, "Later."

As she handed Amy the baby, Dora said, "Emma, join me in the sitting room, please."

Emma followed her and sat down, telling her all she'd learned about Abbey and Miss Marjorie.

"All that time, and we didn't know?" Dora asked in amazement.

"She must have made Papa promise," Emma speculated.

CHAPTER 33

After Abbey rested, she got ready for her lunch with Ellis. They arranged to meet in her hotel room. She had not fought with him in all the time she had known him, but that was about to change. All of their talks since she had gotten back, how close they had become, and no word about Mama? If they were to move forward together, there had to be no secrets.

Sitting on a chair near the door, she watched the clock and waited.

Promptly at noon, there was a soft knock on the door. She stood and approached it slowly. As it opened, she saw the smile she had loved always. It was hard to hold her face still and not return that smile.

"Abbey, is everything all right?" he asked, instantly concerned.

"Ellis, please, sit down," she requested.

He looked at her and saw her expression had not changed. He moved to the settee and took a seat. "What's wrong? Has something happened?"

She got right to the point. "Mama."

Ellis' face turned white. "Abbey, I was waiting for the right time to tell you. How did you find out?"

"I saw Emma's knife skills," Abbey said wryly.

"Oh," said Ellis and saw the humor. "I guess that would have been a giveaway."

"I was shocked at how similar her skills are to Mama's."

"Yes, they were very similar people. They really loved each other."

"More than she loved me?" she asked softly.

"No," said Ellis, taking her hand, "just a different kind. That shouldn't take away from your feelings for her."

"Ellis, did you tell Cole or Jeremy?"

"Cole knew as soon as he heard her name."

"Did he plan to tell Jeremy?"

"I don't think so; at least, not at that time. She had been gone for so long, he probably didn't want to stir anything up."

"Yes, Cole would want order." For the first time, she wasn't bitter about it. She said graciously, "Thank you, Ellis, for taking her in."

"I was afraid if I didn't, she may have pulled another job," he teased.

"That she would have. Tell me about her."

"Let's order lunch here, and I'll tell you everything I can remember."

They talked and Abbey cried about missing her mama's last days.

Later, Abbey and Ellis sat down with Jeremy and Cole to explain who Miss Marjorie was. Jeremy was disappointed he hadn't been told that she was his grandmother, but he understood she had preferred to keep it quiet.

"That amazing woman was related to me?" he asked Abbey.

"Yes. I'll tell you more about her adventures and your grandfather later."

"Will we have time?"

She smiled at him and said, "We'll have all the time we need."

CHAPTER 34

bout a month later, Emma opened the door of the boarding house and picked up the two papers that had been thrown on the stoop—two because she usually ended up cutting up one of the papers for potential cases.

Emma moved to the dining room table to review each page of her paper in detail. The clippings she found interesting were kept in her small black notebook. She went through the pages meticulously, reading and discarding the stories.

Occasionally, she kept the things she found that were amusing. Like today, there was an article about a missing dog and, on another page, another about a dog that was found. It appeared to be the same dog. She made a point to contact the individuals and get the dog to its owner.

She continued reading and found a story about the glass factory. There had been an explosion in a furnace used to make the glass, damaging the area and shutting down operations for six months. Luckily, there had been no injuries.

She tapped that one and checked to be sure the opposite side held nothing of importance. When the other side wasn't found to be important, she tore the article out to add to her collection.

Opening her notebook, she filtered through her clippings collection until she found another one about the same glass factory. Comparing the two articles, she thought, *Two rather serious events happened in the last few months that caused the factory to close short term. Hmm—there might be something there.* She made notes to investigate and see if there was a case.

The society page was next. There was an article there that indicated Mr. Baxton was expected to return from his extended European trip within the next few weeks. He had departed after his wife had disappeared a broken man with no answers as to how she had been taken from him.

That had happened two years ago. Emma had wanted to help with the case but, when Pinkerton offered their services, they had been rebuffed both by Mr. Baxton and the police detective in charge of the case.

The notebook she had made for that case was in her desk drawer. Picking up the paper, she took it upstairs to retrieve it. She opened her desk drawer and found it buried under several other notebooks. Sitting in her chair, she reviewed the information she had gathered at that time:

- The Baxtons were rich, with family money and investments in real estate.
- Mr. and Mrs. Baxton had met when they were young; their families arranged the marriage.
- They were both in their early 40s; there were no children and both were active in the community.
- All accounts said they were happy.

On that fateful evening, the servants found Mr. Baxton covered in his wife's blood. He reported two people had broken into their house and taken his wife. The detectives investigated but could not find a body, and the doctors working the case said the amount of blood indicated she probably had not survived. They questioned the servants and found that the husband and wife were having a quiet evening alone and the staff was out of the house. This was something they did occasionally and the detectives didn't think anything of it.

Over the next week, no ransom request was made and no body was found. The case remained open, but there were no additional leads. Mr. Baxton stopped going out in public and stayed inside the house, mourning his wife's death. He only left to attend the dedication of a memorial fountain in her name. Not long after that, he boarded a ship and moved to Europe. The house had been closed up, and no one expected him to return.

She remembered something from an article a month ago, something about that fountain. *What was it?* Making a note, she thought, *I should go by the library to check on back copies.* There should be time after her morning job.

Emma closed her notebook and headed down for breakfast. Jeremy was already in the dining room adding food to his plate. She leaned down to kiss him before sitting. He noticed her notebook next to her. "Do you have a new case?" he asked.

"I'm not sure yet, but I'm looking into a few things."

"Anything you can share yet?"

"I need more data first." She ate quickly and helped with the dishes before heading to her morning job. Jeremy had some interviews to do that morning downtown, so she wouldn't be accompanying him to the trolley.

Her morning position was still with Mr. Pennington; he had made it a permanent one after the last case wrapped up. That morning, the work was routine and the time went by quickly. After she completed her assigned task, she went straight to the library to look for the article she'd thought might be pertinent to the Baxton case.

She arrived and parked her bike outside and secured it to a rail. The library was quiet as she entered and headed to the section where older papers were kept. Flipping through the last four weeks, she read through several until she found the article she had been looking for.

"Aha," she said. There was a story a few pages in about how the memorial fountain had a crack in the foundation and would need extensive repairs. The reporter had interviewed the contractor, who said they would have to dig up the wet ground down to at least six feet to repair and replace the piping. The fountain was important; Mrs. Baxton had been a great lady, giving generously to the community. The repairs would have to be delayed until Mr. Baxton returned from Europe. The article further detailed that he wanted to oversee every detail of the repairs.

Emma sat for a moment and reviewed her notes. She drummed her fingers on her lips and thought, *Is it possible he's coming home because, if they dig there, they might find her body?* It was a long shot and no one was paying her to work on the case, but she would investigate anyway.

She hesitated only briefly before she tore the article out of the newspaper. The papers went back into the stacks. Emma glanced around to make sure she wasn't being watched. The area was empty of people and there didn't seem to be much interest in the back issues, as far as she could tell. Amy would be the next one for her to interview, she usually knew the network of servants in Chicago.

Entering the kitchen she asked, "Amy, can I have a few moments with you?"

"Sure."

"Alone?"

Amy knew that tone. She called over to Ethyl, "Could you dust the sitting room and open the shades to allow some light in?"

Ethyl finished wiping off the counters and said, "Yes, I'll go now."

Amy sat at the table and patted the chair next to hers. After Emma sat, she said, "I get to be involved in an investigation?"

Emma smiled; Amy was normally the one sent from the room. "Yes, I need your help. Please, don't share anything I tell you."

"Of course," she said seriously.

"Do you know the people who worked at the Baxton mansion?"

Amy thought for a moment and said, "It's been a few years but, yes, I knew most of the staff. They were discharged as soon as Mr. Baxton departed for Europe."

"All of them? That's unusual. He didn't take any with him?" Normally one or two servants would accompany the family.

"No."

"No one stayed on at the house to have it ready if he returned?"

"No, I believe another company was brought in to manage it."

"Were they pensioned off?" she asked, having experienced that during a previous case.

"No. Again, it was unusual," Amy said.

"Should I contact the cook?"

"No," said Amy, thinking. "In this case, I think you need to speak with the butler, Mr. Amberson."

Emma noted that and asked, "Would you know where he's working now?"

Amy raised an eyebrow and said, "Let me see your notebook."

Emma laughed and handed it to her. She wrote the address and family name quickly.

Emma read the address and said, "I know that area. It's on par with the Baxton's wealth."

"If you would like to write a note, I can have him meet you."

Emma organized the note and gave it to Amy. She asked him to meet her the next morning at the memorial fountain.

She received a note that evening confirming he would meet her there at 8am.

CHAPTER 35

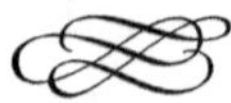

MRS. BAXTON'S CASE — EMMA

*E*mma arrived at the fountain early and walked around it slowly. It was a large, round structure with stone forming the foundation and the walking path around it.

As she reviewed the area closely, she saw there was something wrong with the foundation; it was uneven in several places. She continued to walk around it until she reached the memorial plaque. It read, "This memorial is in place for Diane Baxton, 1885."

A hand reached around her and laid flowers on it.

She turned quickly and had to tilt her head to look into his eyes. "Mr. Amberson?" she inquired

He nodded and respectfully removed his hat. "Miss Evans?"

"Yes. Would you like to sit?" It was a sunny day, but not too uncomfortable. They sat on one of the benches surrounding the fountain.

There was a long moment of silence, and Emma thought he might be praying. She waited until he opened his eyes. "You miss her," she said.

"Yes," he acknowledged. She thought he wouldn't continue, he looked so solemn. Finally, he said, "She was family. I started working there when we were both teenagers. We played in the house; I helped her with her homework. I met everyone she knew, and I was at her wedding."

Emma teared up for a moment, realizing he hadn't just lost a job; he had lost his family. "I'm sorry for your loss, Mr. Amberson."

"Your note indicated that you wanted to discuss Mrs. Baxton's disappearance."

"I think I found a possible lead, and I had hoped you would help me with it."

He'd heard of her through his staff when she was involved in the Millicent Carlyle case. "Do you think you will be able to get him?"

"Him?" she asked, curious to whom he was referencing.

"Yes, Mr. Baxton."

She studied him and asked, "That was your conclusion-that he did it?"

"I lived with them; I saw everything they did."

She nodded and asked, "Could we discuss the night she went missing?"

"Murdered," he stated forcefully.

"Murdered. Yes, I think the amount of blood found proves that," she agreed. "I understand you and other staff members were out for the night?"

"Yes. Occasionally, they asked that they have time alone in the house."

"Did you go out?"

"I did not. I stayed on site. We have quarters outside the main house, so I stayed there."

"Can you see the main house from your living area?"

Instead of answering, he said, "Would you like to go there and see it for yourself?"

She closed her notebook. "Yes, I would." Walking quickly, she retrieved her bike and rolled it over to him.

He glanced at it with a frown and said, "We'll need a carriage. I don't think we'll both fit on that contraption."

She smiled and said, "A carriage will be fine."

"I have one waiting."

She followed him, walking the bike to a very nice carriage waiting on the edge of the park. The driver got down to help her store her bike and helped her into the carriage. Mr. Amberson gave the address, and the driver pulled away smoothly. The drive took about ten minutes; the house came slowly into view.

"There it is," said Mr. Amberson, indicating the grandiose red brick house sitting far back on a manicured lawn.

"It looks like someone is managing the property and the house."

"Yes, Mr. Wright's will mandated that the house be kept and maintained. It's overseen by a management team. Her father always wanted to ensure she had a place to live."

As the carriage made its way up the long drive, she noticed the ornate courtyard. It was lined with the same brick-like that on the house and was set in a herringbone style. It was a circular shape that allowed them to be dropped off at the main steps.

As she descended the carriage, she saw the steps to the mansion were massive, twenty feet across and on two distinct levels. These led to the main doorway, with multiple windows flanked by columns. The house on either side of the columns was red brick, where greenery climbed in a controlled manner.

She stood back for a moment to take it all in. "Three stories?" she asked.

"Yes, the top floor is the large attic space. It's used for storage."

"Just two people lived here?"

"Yes."

She continued to look around outside at the breadth of the estate.

"Would you like to go in?" he asked.

She turned back to him and said, "I would."

The security guards knew him and allowed them to enter. As they made their way into the foyer, what struck her was the attention to detail. The woodwork gleamed and the tile floor shined. "They're maintaining this as well?"

"Yes." He stopped, lost in his memories

She asked gently, "Is this where it occurred?"

"Where he murdered her, you mean?" he asked in a low voice.

She nodded.

"Yes," he said.

"Would you be able to walk it through with me, what you saw in here?"

He took a deep breath and said, "Of course. Where would you like to start?"

"That night, what made you come up to the house? You were the one to find Mr. Baxton lying near the pool of blood."

He looked at her, surprised she knew that. "I was there because I had been told to make sure all of the lights were turned down at 11pm."

"Was that a usual occurrence?"

"No, normally they would have turned them down without help on the nights they planned to be alone."

So, she thought, *he was chosen as a witness.*

"I was part of the plan," he guessed, reading her thoughts.

"It appears so. Go on with your story."

"I entered the back of the house, through the kitchen, and made my way to the foyer. I usually start there, turning down the lights and making sure doors are locked."

"Was the back door locked?"

He had to think. "Yes, I believe it was."

"Were there guards around the house, like there are now?"

"Not like now, no. We had a full staff and they would not have been necessary."

"Okay, continue."

"I walked into the foyer and saw Mr. Baxton. He was lying on the floor and, nearby, there was a large pool of blood. I had never seen so much blood."

"What did you do?"

"I have to admit I panicked for a moment and wanted to run out the way I had come in."

"But you didn't," she guessed.

"No, instead, I went over to Mr. Baxton to check if he was alive. He was breathing, but had been knocked out."

"There was no sign of Mrs. Baxton."

"None at all," he said.

Emma would have to get the police reports to confirm what Mr. Baxton had said that evening. "Could you show me where the servants' quarters are located?"

"Yes," he indicated with his hand, "if you'll follow me."

They made their way through the large interior, then went down a long hallway. She stopped at a portrait of two people. "Is that Mr. and Mrs. Baxton?" she asked.

He nodded, looking only at Mrs. Baxton.

Emma took note of that. She also studied Mr. Baxton's features closely.

They moved on and exited out the kitchen door he'd mentioned. There was a rock path cut into a beautiful garden. "We lived there," he said, pointing to the brick structures set away from the main house. She walked around and saw that their view was cut off from the front drive.

"If there were a second person or persons involved, you may not have seen or heard a carriage."

"Not from back here," he confirmed.

They continued around the garden area. "Mr. Amberson, I'll

have to gather more data. Do you know when Mr. Baxton is arriving?"

"Just what I read in the paper."

"Yes, it indicated we have a few weeks. I understand he asked them to delay any repairs to the fountain until that time? Is it not part of the estate?"

"No, that was Mrs. Baxton's project and was part of the estate that went to her husband."

Three weeks, she thought. She looked at him and commented, "Not much time. I will need to gather information. Would you mind if we meet again, Mr. Amberson?"

"Of course not. I would appreciate anything you can do to help us understand what happened to her."

They went out the front and waved to their carriage driver that they were ready. He dropped her and her bike off at Mr. Pennington's office. She needed to compile her notes for the day and work on her next steps.

CHAPTER 36

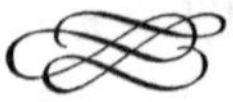

It was late in the evening, and Jeremy and Emma were lying in bed relaxing. "Tell me about the case you started today," he said, propping himself on his elbow and watching her.

She looked over at him. "How did you know it turned into a case?" He drummed his fingers on his lips. She lowered her fingers and grinned at him. "Think you know me so well?"

"Yes," he said. "Now, tell me what you're working on."

She went into detail on what she'd found in the paper, the initial investigation, and the interview with Mr. Amberson.

"So, you think Mr. Baxton, did it?"

"The evidence, though circumstantial, looks that way."

"What are your next steps?"

"I'm going to see if I can get my hands on the will. I'll ask Mr. Pennington for help on that. Then, I'm going to see if I can review the police files."

When she looked pensive at that last statement, he asked, "What's the concern with getting the files from the police?"

"The detective involved in the investigation all that time ago, he's still there."

"Can you work with him?"

"I'm not sure," she said, but she was thinking of going to the chief for this. She had been rebuffed the last time she asked to be involved in the case. The best way was to make the request in such a way that no one was aware she was making it. *Carl,* she suddenly thought. The chief's brother could get her message over to him. She did owe him a Berliner; she'd have to make a point to see him in the morning.

Emma lay back, putting together the information she would need tomorrow. When she settled on a plan for her case, she thought of something Jeremy might be interested in.

"Just a moment," she said. Rolling out of bed, she walked over to her desk. She pulled out her current notebook and clippings.

"What's that?" Jeremy asked curiously.

"When I was looking through the paper, I didn't just see Mrs. Baxton's case. I also saw this." She laid them on the bed. Pointing to one, she said, "I found these two, one about six months ago, about a suspicious fire and another one today about a furnace explosion at the same plant."

He read the first article. The fire had started on the second floor of the building on January 24, 1887. Two men and seventy-five boys barely escaped by jumping into snowbanks or running through flames. The plant was repaired and paid for by insurance. The second one noted that insurance refused to cover the second event. All costs would be covered by the owner. Jeremy asked, "Do you think they might be connected?"

"It's highly coincidental that two such incidents could occur at the same facility in that short space of time. It's a glass company and, if the fire didn't wipe the company out, the furnaces are probably the most important piece of equipment in glass manufacturing."

Jeremy knew something about gas furnaces. They were oven-like structures made for the sole purpose of melting glass in large quantities. The oven could have catastrophic failure due to the design. He mulled it over and asked, "Where's this company located?"

"On the outskirts of town, Wade Street."

"I know that plant, and I believe they supply the local druggist with glass and also ship them to other areas."

"You don't have anything going on right now, do you?"

He thought about his current projects. "No. We're at a stopping point on my cases." He made a decision. "I'll review this with Cole and see if we can approach the owner."

Emma understood. The Pinkertons were a business and would require an agreement to continue.

CHAPTER 37

MRS. BAXTON'S CASE -- EMMA

The berliner box was in the basket attached to the front of her bike. Carl had a weakness for them. She stopped the bike and parked it outside before entering the florist shop. The bell above her head announced her entry and she called, "Carl!"

He stuck his out of the back room and said, "Emma what a nice surprise."

The box in her hands took all of his attention and he went directly to her and took it to place on the counter. "Ahh just what I needed today." And took one out, eating it without hesitation.

Once he had his fill he asked, "What can I do for you?"

"I do have a favor to ask," she admitted.

He nodded, his mouth full of another berliner.

"I need a file from form the police station."

"Why not get it directly from my brother?" Emma and he had a good relationship.

"This one might be tricky, one of his detectives be part of the coverup."

"Hmm. In that case, yes. I will get it for you, I will tell him what I am doing, but I will ask him to give you time to investigate."

"Thank you."

"I will bring it over later today," he promised.

They talked long and then Emma headed off to begin her workday.

That evening Dora called her as she walked into the door, "Carl left something for you. It is on the table."

She walked over and opened the file. The biggest surprise was his conclusions -it was not suspected murder but instead, it was a missing person case. *Wow*, she thought. *I wonder about that detective bank account. I will have Tim check it out.*

CHAPTER 38

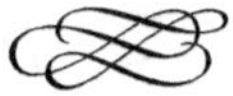

GLASS FACTORY CASE -- JEREMY

The next day, Jeremy met with Cole and showed him the articles. Cole looked at them carefully and asked, "Do you think this is sabotage?"

"I think it might be."

"Okay, make an appointment with the owner. Not on-site, in case any undercover work is necessary."

"I agree." Jeremy sent a note to the owner, using the boarding house as the return address. It would be later that morning when he heard back.

The factory owner suggested an out-of-the-way restaurant for their meeting.

Jeremy agreed and sent back a confirmation.

CHAPTER 39

MRS. BAXTON'S CASE --EMMA

*E*mma was on her way to Mr. Pennington's office that morning. She carried her bike in and was greeted by Ethan.

"Hey, Em, how are you this morning?" They were on better terms now that she was a more permanent part of Mr. Pennington's staff.

"I'm good," she said as she stored her bike and started to her office. She stopped and asked, "Ethan, how would I go about getting a copy of a will?"

"What do you need it for?"

"A new case," she told him. Ethan was the soul of discretion and would not mention it to anyone.

"A will may only be viewed after it has been filed for probate, at which time the document becomes a public court record," he said.

"So, I would have access to it?" she asked.

"Possible. Wills are typically filed in probate courts based on the county in which a deceased person lived at the time of his or her death, or the county in which the deceased person owned real estate. Did they die in this county?"

"I believe so. I know his daughter did," Emma commented.

"You just have to fill out a form and submit it to the court," stated Ethan. "Would you like a copy of the form?"

She smiled and said, "Yes, please." She stepped over to get it from him. "I'll complete this and turn it in after I leave today."

"Just to let you know, it may take a while to get this processed." He lowered his voice. "But I might know someone in the clerk's office who could get you the papers to view."

"If you could set it up, I would appreciate it," she responded in a similar tone.

"You know," he said, "you'll owe me."

She looked at him and said sincerely, "Anything you need."

"I'll keep that in mind."

She went into her office to work. It was several hours later that Ethan stuck his head in and said, "I have that clerk for you."

"Come in."

He stepped inside and said, "You need to see Charlie Livingston at the office next to courtroom twenty-two. He'll expect you at about 1:00 tomorrow afternoon."

Emma documented the time and date. "Thanks, Ethan."

She finished her filing and covered her typewriter. Pushing back from her desk, she took her courier bag, said her goodbyes to Ethan, and headed out for the day.

CHAPTER 40

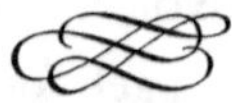

GLASS FACTORY CASE -- JEREMY

Jeremey arrived at the restaurant and gave his name. The host escorted him to a table where an old, rather rotund man was seated. "Mr. Samuels?"

"Yes, are you Mr. Tilden?"

"Yes, Jeremy, please."

"You wanted to discuss the incidents that have occurred at my factory?"

"Yes." He pulled the two articles and laid them down.

"Hmm, yes, those occurred."

"Sir, I'd like to take on the case for you through The Pinkerton Agency."

Mr. Samuels sighed and said, "My boy, I'm going broke trying to stay in business. I don't think I could handle an expense like that."

"Sir, I don't think you can afford not to." Jeremy was thinking and suggested, "What if we agree I only get paid if we find out who the saboteur is?"

As a man of business, Mr. Samuels realized a good deal when he heard one. "That sounds like something I can go along with. What is your plan for getting started?"

"I want to start by seeing the personnel files for that time period and the incident reports."

"I will have that ready for you before you come in."

"Can I have a tour when no one else is there?"

"It is my factory, so yes. Would you like to meet there this evening? The only issue is we run twenty-four hours a day, so there's not a time when there isn't someone there."

"I'd still like to go."

CHAPTER 41

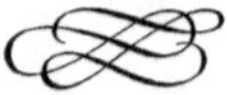

GLASS FACTORY CASE -- JEREMY

That evening, Jeremy dressed in dark clothes and approached the side entrance of the building that housed the factory. They had prearranged the location. He saw a shadow approaching and recognized the owner.

"Let's head in," Mr. Samuels said.

As they entered, Jeremy was surprised; not that they were running at that late hour, but that children appeared to be a large part of the operations. He saw boys as young as nine and ten working near the hot furnaces. They carried materials to the older boys who were blowing the glass.

He would have liked to have investigated the children's working conditions, but he was there for the sabotage case. The owner led the way and showed Jeremy the equipment and explained how his business worked. The children continued to draw his gaze, something had to be done about that.

CHAPTER 42

GLASS FACTORY CASE -- JEREMY

The next morning, Jeremy was speaking with Tim in his study about the factory working conditions. "Do you know anything about the glass factories in the area?"

"Some," said Tim. "It's a hard business and, unfortunately, run with a large number of children."

"Tim, there were boys as young as nine there."

"Yes, and behaving like men. Did you notice that?"

"I didn't."

"Watch next time you're there; they drink, they smoke, and they swear like they are adults."

"Why do parents allow this?" Jeremy asked, bewildered. He looked over at Patrick, working on his letters, and realized he was old enough to work in that factory.

"Money," said Tim simply. "Parents can't make it on their own, so the kids have to go into the workforce."

"They're working them day and night. What about labor laws?"

"There's nothing right now. Most unions protect only adults and oppose child labor reform; they fight desperately to keep the glasshouse boys and others hard at work, day and night. The larger industries are opposing any reform to the child labor law because of the cost it will add to have adults in those roles."

"Why don't the parents say something?"

"Unfortunately, the parents are part of the pushback to keep the kids working."

"Even if they're in danger?"

"Yes," Tim asked. "Any theories if this is sabotage yet?"

"Not yet," he said noncommittedly.

Dora came in holding a thick package and said to Jeremy, "This was just delivered for you."

"Here, let me take that." He walked over to accept it. He opened the side of the envelope and saw it was full of the reports he was waiting for.

"Looks like you have plenty to do today," Tim said.

"Looks like," he said wryly. "I better get started on this now. Would you and Patrick mind if I work here with you?"

"No problem," said Tim.

Patrick mimicked his response. "No problem."

Jeremy smiled and moved to the couch. The package contained engineering investigations of the last two events. Separating them on the table in front of him, he picked up the first one and started to read. The rest of his day would involve him going through reports and making notes. He would need to review the data with Emma and Ellis before he came to any final conclusions.

At last, he finished and put away his files, he needed to check with Dora. She was in the sitting room working on her books with Lottie asleep in her cradle. "Dora, would you mind if we added Mom and Ellis to the dinner tonight?"

"That shouldn't be a problem, just make sure Amy's aware. You know how she plans."

"I will and thanks."

"Anytime," she said softly.

CHAPTER 43

MRS. BAXTON'S CASE -- EMMA

*E*mma had a full morning at Mr. Pennington's office then headed home for lunch, entering through the kitchen door.

"Hi," she said to Amy.

She was cutting up vegetables meant for a stew and said, "Lunch is on the table if you're hungry."

"I am," said Emma. "I'll join them now." She entered and found Jeremy, Dora, Tim, Patrick, and baby Lottie enjoying their lunch. Kissing Jeremy hello. "Well, this is a nice surprise."

He explained, "I got the papers from the case delivered here; figured it would be easier to stay and review them."

"Makes sense," she said as she sat down and started gathering a roll, some cheese, and meat.

"Some fruit and vegetables also," Dora reminded her.

"Yes, Mom," she teased and picked out some fruit and vegetables to eat with her lunch.

They noticed she was eating rather fast. Tim asked, "What's your hurry?"

"New case, looking into some information at the courthouse."

"Anything you can share yet?" asked Dora, knowing Emma's cases could be somewhat secretive.

"Not yet, but soon. Tim, I may need your help looking into something."

"Okay, just let me know."

"What are you doing today, Patrick?" she asked as she watched the boy eat with gusto.

"Grandpapa is picking me up for an afternoon."

"Oh, and what does he have planned?"

"A surprise."

She glanced over at Dora in a questioning manner.

Dora mouthed, "Buildings."

Emma smiled. "I always enjoyed outings with Papa. You should have fun."

"Can I go get ready now?" Patrick asked excitedly.

Dora glanced at his plate and nodded as he jumped up and prepared to run from the room. Tim caught his jacket. "Walk, please. Grandpapa won't leave here without you."

"Yes, Papa," said Patrick and hugged him.

Dora and Emma smiled at how close they had become.

Emma finished quickly and started to do a similar dash when she was also warned by Tim. "Emma, walk, please."

"Yes, Papa," she teased and leaned over to kiss him on the cheek before moving into the foyer. The camera she needed for today was located in the basement. She walked quickly toward it and descended the stairs. The gas lamps were lit, illuminating her path as she made her way down to the locked case where Jake kept his cameras. A key wasn't needed, she picked the lock and retrieved the camera. The camera was kept loaded with film for her to use. Retrieving it, she carried it upstairs and placed it in her bag.

Next, she pulled on her long jacket, and her bowler before she went back through the dining room to access the kitchen door and called out, "I'll be home in a few hours."

"We'll see you then," Dora called back.

255

CHAPTER 44

MRS. BAXTON'S CASE -- EMMA

Emma grabbed her bike and headed down to the courthouse to meet with Charlie Livingston, Ethan's contact. At lunch, the courthouse was very quiet and a good time to meet someone without a large number of people seeing. Checking her notes for the office number, she avoided the elevator and took the stairs. The room was down the long hall-way; she knocked softly on the door and received an affirmative response to enter the office.

Emma entered the room and found it full of filing cabinets. She had seen this type in business offices during her temporary jobs. The man who had called her in was about 5'4", looked to be around 35, and had short, trimmed hair and round glasses. His suit was cheap but well pressed.

"Mr. Livingston?" she asked.

"I am, and you are Emma Evans?"

"I am."

"Good, good. We don't have a lot of time, but you can come through here," he indicated a gap in the long counter, "and view the files on my desk. I'll be over here filing." She noticed he would be across the room and behind additional filing cabinets, giving her privacy.

She smiled and went straight to the desk. There, she found the two wills. The time should allow her to read them closely, but she would be able to take pictures. The sticky gum in her purse would allow her to tack them on the wall to allow for better photos. Taking the pictures quickly, she put the camera back into her bag and removed the tacky material from the back, and replaced them in the folder.

The timepiece pinned to her blouse indicated she had a few more moments. She took the time and started to read through the documents. She saw two things in Mr. Wright's will: 1) all money would go to his daughter and her descendants; her husband would only inherit if there were no children, and 2) he could not be convicted of a felonious act, otherwise, he would be barred from the inheritance.

Hmm, she thought. *What about the daughter's will?* She pulled it up and found the same wording. *He didn't want her to be put at risk because of the money.* She completed her notes and closed the files. Keeping conversations with the clerk to a minimum, she said, "Thanks!"

He nodded, not looking at her as she left.

She thought to herself, *At least I know the reason why he's returning and not just staying in Europe. If his wife's body is found and he's convicted, the money reverts to a trust and it is donated.*

This operation would have taken more than Mr. Baxton. He was knocked out at the scene and, if involved, someone else had moved the body for him. A staff member, perhaps?

She continued her courier duties and swung by Mr. Amberson's house as her last stop.

CHAPTER 45

MRS. BAXTON'S CASE -- EMMA

r. Amberson had a limited window of time, so she arranged to meet him at the residence he was working at. "You won't get into trouble with me coming here?" she asked as he let her into the kitchen door.

"No, not at all. Lunch has been cleared away, and I've informed them I would be delayed for some time this afternoon."

"Wonderful."

"Please, sit," he said and watched as she pulled out her notebook. "What would you like to know?"

"Let's go over who was working at the house during the time the event occurred."

"Yes, I can provide that. There was an upstairs maid assigned to Miss Catherine and a man assigned to Mr. Baxton."

Funny, she thought as she noted the difference in the way he said their names. "Kitchen staff?"

"Two helpers and a cook. For big events, we brought in servers."

"Other inside house staff?"

"Two footmen to assist me and a driver."

"What about outside?"

"There were two full-time gardeners; we brought in help as needed."

She nodded. "Were any of these people new to their positions?"

He looked contemplative for a moment and said, "Cassey. Cassandra Woods. She was only here a few months before the event."

"Interesting," she said. Out of the corner of her eye, she noticed he was happy she had written that down. *Why?* she thought again. "Do we have the names and addresses for where the staff moved?"

"Yes, I can provide all except one."

"Which?" she asked.

"Cassey," he said simply.

When she continued to look at him, he said, looking uncomfortable, "She didn't leave a forwarding address and she disappeared at the same time as Mr. Baxton left the country."

"I'll do some checking and see if I can find out if two tickets were purchased for them to come home." *Also,* she thought, *I'll bet the lawyer has their last address. I can check to see if he has remarried since he left. The fact he would remarry isn't suspicious; many men do after their wives have passed. What is suspicious is who he might have married.* "Mr. Amberson, I know this makes you uncomfortable, but were they seeing each other while his wife was alive?"

"Yes, I'm sure they were."

"Did Mrs. Baxton know?"

"No, no. She would never put up with that," he said a little too quickly.

She kept her face blank as she took notes.

He checked the time and said, "I will have to get back to my duties."

"Yes, thank you. Oh, one more thing. You indicated that you

found Mr. Baxton lying near a large pool of blood and that you were inside to turn down the lights?"

"Yes," he confirmed.

As Emma left, she thought, *I need to interview the staff and find out what was happening in that house.*

She grabbed her bike and headed home.

CHAPTER 46

GLASS FACTORY CASE -- JEREMY

The dinner table was full of family and conversations with each talking over one another. As dinner wrapped up, Dora said, "Everyone take a platter and move them to the kitchen." Abbey and Ellis were there for dinner and pitched in to clean up.

As dishes were completed, Ellis looked at Jeremy and Emma. "You have some papers for me to review?" he asked.

"I do," said Jeremy. "In the study."

"Right behind you." He looked over at Abbey and asked, "Will you be okay here?"

"I'll be okay with Tim and Dora." She had picked up baby Lottie and was enjoying the wriggling child.

He smiled at her fondly and followed Jeremy and Emma into the study.

As they entered, Jeremy immediately went to the desk. He had his notes and portions of the furnace inspections laid out.

Ellis picked up the files and studied them. He saw from Jeremy's notes that the two investigations showed similar defects. The manufacturer said the furnaces were fully inspected before leaving and that the defect was not there at that time.

"Were there other furnaces sent out at the same time as these?"

"Yes," said Jeremy. "The files are here." He pulled one out and showed him the report.

"Have you confirmed with the people in this report?"

He nodded. "I sent out the telegrams this afternoon. I should have that information in a few days."

Emma spoke up. "The theory is that, if they don't have any issues with their furnaces, is that they were sabotaged after they got here?"

"Yes."

"How long were these in place?" Emma asked.

"Just a few weeks each. So, whatever happened, it was during a short time period," said Jeremy.

"Is there an employee list available from that time?" asked Emma.

"I can get the list from the owner," said Jeremy.

"Good. Compare the list and see who may have only been there for short durations," said Ellis.

"I will, thanks for the input."

"Can I take these to examine more closely?" Ellis asked, indicating the files.

"What are you thinking?"

"I wanted to look at how the defect might have occurred; how would someone have done it?"

CHAPTER 47

GLASS FACTORY CASE -- JEREMY

Jeremy received the list the next day with the names and addresses of the employees. Most were located in the Hells. He would need Tim to move easily in the area. That morning, he asked, "Tim, could you accompany me to these addresses?"

"How's tomorrow?"

"I would appreciate it."

They headed down to the Hells early the next morning. There were twenty to investigate. While reviewing the list, they had removed the children who were steady workers. That reduced the list to five temporary employees there around the time of the malfunctions.

They left the first house, feeling dazed after realizing their child had died at the factory.

It was the same for the next three. They went to the fourth house and knocked on the door. A girl of about twelve answered. "Yes?" she asked.

"Can we speak to your mother?" asked Tim.

She looked them over. "She's in the kitchen if you want to

come in." She watched them closely. "Ma, there is someone here to see you."

"Yes?" the woman asked as she walked out of the kitchen. "Henrietta mentioned you needed me for something?"

"Is your husband here?" Jeremy asked.

"No. He delivers ice and won't be back for a few hours. Is there something I can help you with?"

Jeremy nodded and pulled out the paper. "Is there an Aiden living here?"

The woman's eyes filled and spilled over. The girl darted forward. "Ma, sit down."

She took the seat offered and explained, "Aiden died at the glass manufactures."

"We had a second child listed that worked there on these dates, a Brian. Do you have another son?" asked Jeremy.

"No no. We only have a daughter."

Jeremy noticed the girl had looked away when they were asking questions. "I hate to ask, but when did your son pass?"

"It was a little over a year ago," she murmured, looking toward the mantle, where a baseball sat. She went silent.

"I think it would be best that you leave now," the girl said.

They exited and checked their list; there was one more child to check on.

As they exited the last house, Jeremy said, "That was a depressing day."

"Yes, so many children have died at the glass factory," said Tim.

"All of them had parents," said Jeremy.

They silently made their way back to the boarding house. Patrick was running around and saw Tim. "Papa, you are back." Tim swung him up and hugged him tightly. *He will never have to work as a child*, he promised himself. "

"What will you do now?" he asked Jeremy, still hugging Patrick tight.

"Continue watching the workers and see if there are any other issues with the furnaces. I'm also putting in an inspection process to have the entire furnace walked around before each shift starts."

He nodded. "Will they, do it?"

"I'm going to explain the dangers."

CHAPTER 48

GLASS FACTORY CASE -- JEREMY

That night, Jeremy talked to the men and boys on the shift. "We need you to walk around each furnace and inspect it as you come onto your shift."

They were snickering at him and continued to smoke. One of the boys said, "Can we get back to work now?"

"Yes. Just a minute, does anyone remember a Brian working here?" he asked.

One of the older kids stood. "Listen, man, we don't get paid if we don't work. We only know the kids who are around all of the time. The temp kids come in and out when they can't handle the job."

Jeremy was watching children as small as nine smoking and demonstrating mannerisms of much older men. "Ok, you can go, but please check around the furnaces. It could save your life."

"Yeah, sure," commented one of the older boys. They headed back into the factory, immediately going to each of their assigned job areas.

Jeremy watched and saw they didn't inspect the furnaces as asked. He would do it himself; he spent a lot of time going around each one, realizing they were not going to do anything that wasn't productive toward their paychecks.

Jeremy walked home slowly, thinking about the loss of childhood these kids were enduring. *There must be a long-term solution for this.*

CHAPTER 49

GLASS FACTORY CASE --JEREMY

When Jeremy got home, it was late and the house was quiet; everyone appeared to be in bed for the night. He was about to head up when he saw the light on in the study. When he pulled open the door, he saw Ellis sitting at the desk.

"Ellis. What are you doing here so late?"

"Oh, Jeremy," Ellis said absently. "I was waiting for you. I wanted to cover something I found."

"What type of thing?" Jeremy asked and walked over to the desk to look at the materials lying about.

"I think I have the cause."

"Didn't we know the cause was a defect in the furnace structure that allows the flammable material to eventually breach and crack the exterior, leading to an explosion and eventual fire?"

"Yes, that's correct," said Ellis, "but I reexamined the engineering review that described the parts they found. The integrity of the furnace was breached. It looks like it was probably a small defect that someone widened. Notice the hole; see how smooth and completely round the opening appears to be?"

"No one noticed this?"

"No, but I think they should have."

"What kind of tool were you thinking could make this type of hole?"

"An ice pick. They're reinforced and sharp."

"An ice pick. Could it get through the furnace?"

"I believe it could if the defect was already there. It may have been done over a series of weeks or months so the hole was made bigger each time. "

"I did notice the helpers were moving around most of the time and would have access to that area. Ellis, thank you for bringing this to my attention."

"It's not a problem. It's interesting work."

They both said goodnight and Jeremy headed up to bed.

He got cleaned up and climbed into bed with Emma. She snuggled closed. "How was it tonight?"

"Pretty bad," he admitted. "Something needs to be done about the hazardous working conditions."

"It's big business," she murmured, half asleep. "It would also be a political issue."

"Yes." He laid there thinking as she went to sleep.

CHAPTER 50

GLASS FACTORY CASE -- JEREMY

Emma woke slowly and realized Jeremy wasn't in the bed. She searched the darkroom and saw him standing by the window. "What is it?" He had his hands clenched tightly as he looked out the window.

"The person involved in this is too young to be responsible."

"Who did it? How did you work it out?"

"Ellis came by this evening. He had a theory of what may have occurred to cause the design problem and that led to the explosions and fires. It was an ice pick."

Emma knew where he was going; one of the kids had a father who delivered ice. "Oh, no."

"Yes, I think she was avenging her brother by sabotaging the plant and trying to get it to shut down."

"Now that you know, what are you going to do with this information?"

"The owner will want to prosecute her and send her to the workhouse for most of her life. Emma, he's stealing so much of these children's lives. He already has five deaths directly attributed to his business practices. They're babies," he said helplessly.

Emma was thinking ahead. "Let's go see her, hear her side of this."

"Yes. It's time. I'll go and see if I can get her alone and away from her mom."

"Jeremy, I should probably come with you," she suggested, thinking about the child.

"Yes, you're probably right," he said. The last thing he wanted was to scare the girl.

Emma asked, "What time are you thinking?"

"Can we do this in the early afternoon?"

"Yes. I can meet you here."

The next day, they stood on the child's doorstep, waiting for the door to open. It opened slowly, they couldn't see who held the door.

"Henrietta, is that you?" asked Jeremy leaning forward.

"Yes," came the low answer.

"Can we come in?" he inquired.

She begrudgingly moved back out of the doorway for them to enter.

"Are your parents here?" asked Jeremy.

"Ma is out picking up some sewing, and Papa is due back soon from his job. "

Emma held out her hand. "We haven't met. My name is Emma."

Henrietta did not make a move toward the hand she extended. She just went to a chair and sat down, not looking at them.

Jeremy nodded at Emma to try again. "Henrietta, where does your papa work?"

"Ice truck," she said slowly.

"Have you ever worked with him?"

"Sure, he lets me go sometimes when it's hot. The ice feels nice," she said, looking up at them for the first time.

Emma asked softly, "Have you ever used an ice pick before?"

Henrietta froze at the question, and her eyes darted around the room,

Jeremy said, "Don't run. I don't feel like chasing you down today."

Emma asked again, "Have you ever used an ice pick?"

"Yes, Papa showed me," she said slowly.

Jeremy thought it was the right time. "How did you make a hole like that? The furnaces are brick-lined."

"They have defects when they come in. I've noticed before; the workers installing them are lazy and don't always do a good job. I brought the pick out and started to jab at the defect."

"How long did it take?" asked Jeremy, curious about this girl's commitment.

"Months," she said. "It was slow."

"But you stuck with it. Why? Were you angry at the glass factory when your brother died?"

That got her up, and she said passionately, "He was killed by that horrible boy."

"You mean during an accident at work?" inquired Emma.

"They weren't accidents. They caused those deaths, making those little boys move heavy equipment, and work around boilers that are so hot you can't think straight. It was the older boy, a foreman."

"You blame him. Why?" asked Jeremy.

"One of the other boys told me my brother tripped and knocked over some expensive glass. The foreman grabbed him and threw him at the furnace," snapped Henrietta.

"Are you sure about that?" asked Jeremy. She nodded. "Who was this other boy? Can we speak with him?"

"It's no use. He wasn't held responsible," she mumbled.

"What was his name?"

"Josiah," she said. It was on their list but had no address listed. He would have to speak with him at the factory.

"So, what was your plan?" Jeremy pressed.

"Destroy the business; stop the kids from working there," said Henrietta.

"Henrietta, why didn't you tell your parents? They would have helped," said Emma.

The look she gave them made them pause. "Who do you think makes those boys go there? It is the parents. They don't want reform; they want money."

"Surely," said Emma, "that can't be all true."

"It is," she said shortly.

"You can't continue on this path; you could hurt the boys still working there," Jeremy said.

"I have to go to work," she said, getting up, not wanting to answer any more questions.

"Work?" Emma asked.

"Yes, I work in the cloth factory at night," said Henrietta.

"Okay, we will leave. Don't mention we were here," said Jeremy.

"Why would I?"

They exited with her and watched as she locked the door.

Emma checked her watch. "I have to get moving. Can we head back now?"

"Yes, I have some thinking to do," said Jeremy.

CHAPTER 51

MRS. BAXTON'S CASE -- EMMA

Jeremy dropped Emma off at the boarding house. He needed to head into the office to check on other cases in development.

She tapped her notebook and thought Dora and Amy could help her find the servant on the list Mr. Baxter had provided. She headed into the kitchen to have Amy review it.

Amy saw her come in and asked, "Did you have a good day?"

"Not great," she admitted. "I was hoping you had time to review a list of people with me."

"Well," she said. "I might be able to help."

"Good." Emma pulled out her notebook

"But I'm going to need a dessert tonight. Can we work out a trade?"

Emma smiled. "Amy, you're catching on. Yes, I can help with dessert; what would you like?"

"Heidesand—German Sugar Rolled Marzipan Butter Cookies."

Emma nodded and got to work and the cookies were being placed in the over as Dora entered the kitchen with Lottie walking in front of her. "Emma, you are back?"

"I am."

"How did you get wrapped in making dessert today?" asked Dora, seeing Emma wipe down the table.

"Amy figured out our give-and-take system for information," said Emma with a smile.

Dora grinned and said, "Smart girl," winking at Amy.

Amy sat at the table with Dora and Emma. "What can I help you with?"

"Well, I could use you both."

"Hmm," said Dora, "if I'd known I was part of this, I would've gotten myself in on the dessert deal."

Emma laughed and handed Amy the list first.

Amy looked it over and said, "I can give you most of the locations, except for the gardeners." She handed it to Dora for her review.

"I might have an idea on that," said Dora thoughtfully. "Let me check with Tim."

Emma took down notes on the household staff. "Have you heard anything bad about anyone in particular?"

Amy said, "Not bad but I have heard something about Cassey. She wasn't a maid for very long, and she disappeared soon after Mrs. Baxtons disappearance. I haven't heard of her getting another position."

"Did she have any family here?" Emma asked.

"No, not that I'm aware of. I didn't know her very well," Amy explained.

"Okay, I'll see If I can talk to the other personnel." Emma looked at Dora. "Let me know if you hear anything about the gardeners."

Several people on the list we're working in the neighborhood where Cole and Ellis lived. Notes were sent over to them asking for some time to talk. Once she received a confirmation note back, she headed over to the houses where they were working.

First up were the helpers, Todd and Scotty, who had found a job in the same kitchen. They sat with her. "You said in your note that you are looking at Mrs. Baxton's disappearance?" Scotty said.

She noted the way he said that. He didn't say her first name. "How long were you both at the house?"

"We've worked together since we were kids," Todd said, and his friend nodded.

"That's right. We were there about five years," added Scotty.

"For a long while then," she commented. "Did you see anything unusual with Mr. Baxton and Cassey?"

They looked at each other and back at her. Servants normally kept to themselves and rarely gossiped outside their group. But in this case, they didn't feel any loyalty to Cassey. "She thought she was better than us," said Scotty.

"What makes you say that?" Emma asked curiously.

"Upstairs maids tend to put on airs. They think they're better than the kitchen staff," Scotty explained.

"Did you interact with her socially?" she asked.

"No," Scotty said shortly.

"Not that you didn't try," Todd teased him.

"Yeah, sure, I asked, but she had her sights on the boss," Scotty said.

"In what way?" Emma asked.

"She always did a little extra for him and, if she thought she could catch him outside by himself, she would," Todd said.

"Like where?"

"The gardens, mostly," stated Scotty.

"And her quarters," Todd said.

"Yes," Scotty confirmed.

"Did Mrs. Baxton know?"

"I'm not sure about that," Todd said. His friend shrugged in response.

She thought to ask, "Mr. Amberson, did you know him well?"

"Yes," they said at the same time.

"Was he a good boss?"

"He was fair," Todd said.

"How was he with Mrs. Baxton?"

"You mean Miss Catherine," Scotty snickered.

"I heard him call her that," she commented.

"He felt that he had a close relationship because he was there for such a long time," Todd said.

"Did she feel close to him?" Emma asked.

"She treated him like a servant; he just didn't want to see it," said Scotty.

"Now, that's not fair," Todd protested. "She *did* use a different tone with him."

"What kind of tone?" asked Emma, curious about what they heard.

"Softer, maybe," Todd said.

"He was also the only one allowed there when they wanted to be alone," said Scotty.

Emma thought she heard wrong and asked, "Are you saying on the nights they were by themselves, he was also there?"

"Yes," Todd confirmed. "He would serve them dinner and wait on them until they went to bed and then he would turn off the lights."

"Did you mention that to the police?"

"Oh, we weren't interviewed. Mr. Amberson took care of that."

"He was sure surprised when he lost his job," muttered Scotty.

"Yes," Todd agreed.

Emma thought about that, adding it to what she had learned. She asked bluntly, "Do you think Mr. Baxton killed his wife?"

They hesitated before saying anything. Talking about the

people you work for or have worked for could lead to a swift termination.

"I won't mention who told me," she said in a low voice.

Todd muttered, "He just wasn't in the same class as her. He spent too much money and then that whole Cassey thing started."

"He wasn't a bad person but I'm not sure he cared enough about her to kill her," said Scotty.

"He may have cared enough about her money," commented Todd.

She agreed silently with them on the possible motive. She asked a final question. "Was there anything else you would like to share with me?"

"No, I don't think so," said Scotty.

"Me either," said Todd.

"Thank you," she said and got up to leave.

"Did we give you anything important?" asked Scotty.

"I believe you did," said Emma with a slow smile. She thanked them again and exited. *Who next?* she thought, looking down at her notebook.

She located the two footmen and the cook and got similar stories of the household dynamic.

Dora and Tim located the gardeners and they confirmed that Cassey and Mr. Baxton were seen kissing and touching inappropriately in the gardens.

The manservant was the last person she needed to talk to, but it was getting late in the day. The next conversation should be able to provide some direction in the case. After all, who would be more intimate in a man's life, other than the man who helped him dress each day? She had sent a note to the address provided by Amy but had not received a confirmation that it was okay to visit.

CHAPTER 52

MRS. BAXTON'S CASE -- EMMA

*I*t was the beginning of the evening shift and Jeremy sat in the corner, watching the boys working around him. One of the younger boys waved an arm toward Jeremy and said, "Josiah, that boy isn't working."

Josiah went over to stand in front of Jeremy and said, "You aren't here to sit. You're here to work. Go over there and start helping to move the bottles."

Jeremy stood slowly and asked, "Who me?" He straightened to his full height. "Were you wanting me to do something?"

The foreman realized it was the man that had given them instructions on safety inspections. He said, "No, no. Are you supposed to be here? Does Mr. Samuels know you are here?"

"He does," Jeremy confirmed.

"Well, I'm in charge here," the boy blustered.

"I've heard that," said Jeremy.

The foreman said, "I am going to check and see if you are allowed to be here." When he started to move, Jeremy stuck out his foot and tripped him. He fell on his face and the boys in the area started laughing.

"Stop laughing at me, or I'll…" the foreman threatened as he waved his fist at them.

"You'll what, kill them?" Jeremy asked.

"What? No, I didn't kill anyone." He was starting to look nervous.

"No, but you did make the already hard job more unsafe."

"I was doing as I was told, to keep everyone working. So many of the kids are small and can't do the work," he complained.

"So, you get angry," he guessed.

"Yeah."

Jeremy realized he was just a kid that had come up through the same system these little ones had. "How long have you been here?"

"Since I was nine," he said.

"Did you kill Aiden?"

"Aiden?" His eyes filled with tears. "Mister, I pushed him, and he hit the boiler. The vent pipe was loose and hit his head. It wasn't murder. I didn't mean to hurt him. I have done the same thing to many boys. I had it done to me."

Several other boys walked up and one said, "Mister, that was an accident. We were here. He didn't do it on purpose."

Another boy said, "Yeah, he even picked him up and ran him to the hospital."

Josiah said, "When I realized he was hurt, I got him there as fast as I could. The Sisters there said there was just nothing they could do."

Jeremy let him go. *This whole thing is just so sad. Boys having to make a man's decision.*

CHAPTER 53

GLASS FACTORY -- JEREMY

*H*e met with Mr. Samuels at his office. Jeremy looked around, noticing all of the fine items on display. "Very nice place."

"Thank you. Are you here to tell me the outcome of the investigation?" he asked.

"We examined the furnaces and believe it was localized to inadequate maintenance and installation," Jeremy said smoothly. "Defects in the design combined with blockages inside the furnace can build up pressure over time, causing the furnace to develop holes." He spun the tale. There was no way he was going to disclose Henrietta's part in this.

"What can we do to prevent this from happening?"

"If you don't want to lose the entire place, you will need to clean up all of the areas around the furnaces and start more routine maintenance. When new installations are going in, hire an engineering firm to inspect prior to use. I also have further suggestions about routine cleaning and inspection of the furnaces."

He nodded and said, "If it saves the business, I'll do it."

"I will have Ellis Evans come over for an evaluation," he said smoothly.

He nodded.

Jeremy knew there was not an easy way to get the children out, but he could make the environment as safe as possible.

CHAPTER 54

FINAL GLASS FACTORY CASE -- JEREMY

Henrietta looked shocked at Jeremy's news. "He didn't kill him?"

"It was an accident," he confirmed. "He even tried to get him help at the hospital." Jeremy had confirmed with the Sisters that the boy who had brought him in had stayed with him and cried when he died.

"And you helped the kids that have to go there?"

"Yes, and we will keep an eye on them to make sure they follow through with our recommendations."

She nodded and asked, "You aren't turning me in?"

"No. Henrietta, we would like to help you," said Jeremy.

"I would like that," she said.

"What do you want to do?" he asked curiously.

"I want to be smart enough to stop children from having to work. We have a right to an education."

"I agree. I would like you to meet a friend, her name is Clair. Emma and I think we three can help you take the first step. We can help you with your education and pay you at the same time," said Jeremy.

Henrietta looked like he had handed her the world

We can't save all of the children, but maybe Henrietta can, thought Jeremy.

CHAPTER 55

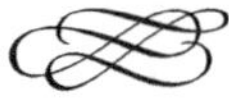

MRS. BAXTON'S CASE — EMMA

The following day, Emma waited outside the house where the last employee to interview worked. The man she was there to meet had sent word he was not available. The information he could provide was too important to the case so she stayed and waited, in clear view of the front windows. Her patience was infinite, aided by a book and snacks.

He watched from the window and waited for her to leave. When she didn't, he tried to ignore her. *Why is she still here?* he wondered.

"Justin, you should go down and take care of that issue," said his employer.

He would have preferred to leave her sitting there all night, but now he had no choice. He headed downstairs, exited through the kitchen, and called over to her, "Come here, I will see you now."

Emma took a long moment to finish her apple and deliberately closed her book. Standing, she started toward him. His body language was defensive; this would not be an easy conversation.

"Follow me," he said and they walked through the kitchen;

she noticed the staff were watching them curiously. They trudged through the dining room to a study, where he closed the doors quietly behind him and turned toward her.

She noticed his clothes and his manners. Servants at this level of society were well educated and could easily pass for the same people they served. Sometimes, that closeness caused trouble. *Like in this situation,* she thought.

He didn't offer, but she went to the long brown couch and sat. He frowned when she didn't wait to be asked. Reluctantly, he joined her there. "What do you want?" Justin asked brusquely.

Lost his manners with me, she thought. "I wanted to ask you about the time you worked at Mr. and Mrs. Baxton's house."

"Why?"

"I'm looking into her murder."

"Someone is actually going to ask some questions?"

"What do you mean?"

"The detective in charge of the case didn't want to talk to us at all."

"Well, I do. I want to hear more about what you saw in the house. What was the relationship between Mr. Amberson and Mrs. Baxton?"

He looked shocked. He had expected another question.

When he didn't answer, she asked, "Who did you think I was going to ask about?"

"Cassey and Mr. Baxton."

"Why is that? Because of the affair?"

"You know about that?"

"Yes, I've interviewed some of the other staff."

"Who?" he asked.

"Two kitchen helpers."

"Yes, Scotty and Todd." He chuckled suddenly. "Yes, they saw everything."

"Back to my original question, Mr. Amberson and Mrs. Baxton," she prompted.

"That was an odd relationship."

"Why use the word relationship?" she asked.

"Because that's what it was. There was always something a little extra. She brought him special things if she traveled; he would be invited to her private sitting room to talk."

"Did he have a similar relationship with Mr. Baxton?"

"No, he felt Mr. Amberson was beneath him."

"What about Cassey?"

He grimaced. "Yes, well, I thought we were going to get married, but she was playing me as much as Mr. Baxton was playing Mrs. Baxton."

"When did you find out?"

"Oh, I found out when everyone else did—when she disappeared at the same time as Mr. Baxton."

"Did you suspect Mr. Baxton of harming Mrs. Baxton?"

"Yeah," he said. "I mean, she disappeared and all that blood and then he leaves the country with Cassey."

"Why didn't you want to see me today?"

"I'm engaged to a member of the staff here and I didn't want any previous gossip about me and Cassey to ruin that."

She nodded. "I shouldn't have to bother you anymore." Standing up to leave. "Oh, one more thing, were you there that night?"

"I was with Cassey; we went out dancing."

She thanked him and he escorted her to the door.

CHAPTER 56

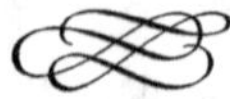

That night, she and Jeremy were at the dining table. She was reviewing her notes and Jeremy was reading. He looked over and asked. "Any updates on the Baxton case? Did you ever get a copy of the file from Carl?"

"I did. It didn't have much in it. Based on my interviews, I believe I have," she said absently, "two suspects?"

"Two? Didn't you think it was the husband?"

"He is suspicious," she conceded. "He was having an affair, and the will gives him the money as long as he didn't kill Mrs. Baxton. No felony, he keeps the money."

"Who else are you considering?"

"The butler."

"Why him?"

"There is something odd about Mrs. Baxton's relationship with him. They seemed overly close."

"Is that all you have? No motive?"

"Well, the butler did lie to me when he said he wasn't in the house when she died."

"That is suspicious. What is your next step?"

"I need to get another look at that fountain. I'll be heading over tomorrow morning."

289

"I need to get another look at that fountain. I'll be heading over tomorrow morning."

CHAPTER 57

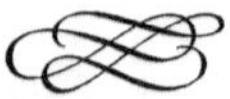

MRS. BAXTON'S CASE—EMMA

It all comes back to this fountain, she thought as she walked around it slowly, looking at the structure and the cement in place around it. The leak was a slow one, and it appeared to be coming out of a long break in the stone. The more she looked at it, she thought, *It is too straight and too clean.* The leak only appeared to be in the one area.

Who built this? Papa would know, she thought. *He could pull the permits.*

She headed over to the house he shared with Cole, his lab was set up in the basement. It allowed him to continue his engineering work without having to go back and forth to the boarding house.

At this time of day, he would be in the basement and wouldn't be able to hear her knocking. She looked around and didn't see anyone, so she pulled out her lockpick kit and went to work on the door. Opening it quickly, she went inside. As she moved toward the basement door, she heard a murmuring coming from downstairs. "Papa," she called, hoping to give him a moment to stop whatever he might be doing that would embarrass her or him.

She paused and heard her papa say, "Emma, is that you?"

"It is, may I come down?"

"Sure, just a moment." She waited, and then he called, "Come down."

Abbey must be here, she thought. As she entered the room, Emma looked toward Abbey and saw not a hair out of place. She smiled inwardly, but outwardly, she said, "Hello, Abbey, Papa."

Abbey sent her a quick smile. "Hello, Emma."

"Hi, little girl. Visiting today?" asked Papa.

"No, Papa, I have a case I need to review with you. Could you access the drawing for the memorial fountain located at Kingston Square?"

He frowned and said, "Yes. What are you looking for?"

"I'm looking for anyone involved in the design and build. If possible, the present management company."

"When do you need it by?"

"Soon would be nice. I'm kind of on a deadline," she said, thinking Mr. Baxton's ship had made it in and he would be there later that week

"It may take some time, but I'll see if I can get it today and bring it by this evening."

"Thanks, Papa," she said and kissed him quickly. He gave her ponytail the familiar tug as she was leaving. She called over her shoulder, "It was good to see you both."

"You, too," Abbey said quietly.

"Lock up on your way out," Papa called.

"I will," she answered back.

CHAPTER 58

MRS. BAXTON'S CASE—EMMA

Emma was busy for the rest of the day. She had a few pickups to make and some additional deliveries. She pulled up to the boarding house stoop and saw Papa assisting Abbey out of the carriage.

"Emma," he said." I have those items."

"Wonderful, Papa. Hello, Abbey," she said, getting off her bike and kissing him on the cheek. "I'll go put my bike up and meet you in the study."

"We'll see you there." Papa walked up the front stoop with Abbey and knocked on the door. Patrick opened it and shouted, "Grandpapa and Abbey!"

Emma came through the dining room at her customary speed and headed to the study. When she got there, she saw Tim at his desk. "Hey, Tim, can we use the study?"

Tim looked up. "Sure, I could spend some time with Dora and the kids."

He saw Ellis and Abbey in the foyer. "Hello, so nice to see you both. Would you like some tea? Will you be staying for dinner?"

"No, we don't need tea or dinner. We plan to go out after we talk," said Ellis.

Tim smiled and went past them to find Dora.

Emma moved the items on the desk, making room for the papers Papa had with him. He rolled out the design drawings for the fountain, then went on to explain, "The original design was signed off by Mrs. Baxton and Mr. Jeffers."

"Do you have the date?"

"The original submittal was April 1885."

"Well before she died. Had they started the work?" Emma asked.

"The work was started before her death; the holes were dug for the plumbing."

"When was the cement poured?"

"I pulled the permits." He flipped through the pile of papers until he found the right one. "It says here that it was poured August 15, 1885."

"That's the day after Mrs. Baxton disappeared and was presumed to be dead. Hmm... we're getting somewhere. Who was the responsible party for putting together the project?"

"It is Jeffers construction. The owner is Mr. Jeffers."

"I don't think that would be him. He is the owner, I need the man in charge of the project," said Emma thoughtfully.

Ellis looked closer at the signatures of the engineer assigned to the project. He said, "The person who signed the engineering drawings was Mike Smothers. If she is buried there, he would know."

She went to the door and called, "Tim, could you come in for a moment?"

Tim joined them and they gave him some background on the project. "Tim, could you check the bank for payments to Mike Smother's account? I would assume it would be a routine payment."

He said, "I have someone at the bank who can look into any irregularities for me."

"Thank you," Emma said.

"I can let you know tomorrow. If that is all you need?"

"It is."

Papa said, "Emma, you mentioned the leak looked man-made."

"It did," she acknowledged.

"Then he is probably involved, he would know where to cut to have a leak like that."

One last thing, she thought. *I need to check on Cassey's whereabouts.*

CHAPTER 59

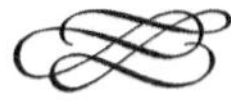

MRS. BAXTON'S CASE — EMMA

It was days later and Emma was waiting at the train station for Mr. and Mrs. Baxton to exit. She had confirmed with Cole that there was no employment record of Cassey in town since Mr. Baxton had gone to Europe.

She watched as each person exited the train and did not see anyone who looked like Mr. Baxton. When it looked like the train was empty of passengers, she approached the porter and asked, "Was that everyone?"

"Yes, were you waiting for someone specifically?"

"I'm looking for a Mr. Baxton."

"Oh, he was on board, but he and his family departed at the last stop."

"His family?"

"Yes, his wife and young child."

"Can you describe the wife?"

"Young, blonde hair, and very pretty."

That must be Cassey. "Thank you for your time."

"You're welcome."

Hmm, I will go to the house and see if I can question him, she murmured to herself.

CHAPTER 60

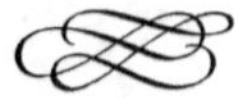

MRS. BAXTON CASE -- EMMA

She organized a note to Jeremy, asking him to meet her at the Baxton estate. She might need some backup if things turned bad. As she rode out to the estate, she went over the questions that she wanted to review.

The guards were not in place at the door. She approached slowly, looking around. At the door, she had her hand raised to knock and heard arguing and a baby crying. She didn't wait; she pushed the door and it swung open. Two men were there struggling and fighting to get a gun. She put a hand into her pocket to access the hidden knife, she heard a shot ring out. Her body jerked back as the bullet entered her arm. She glanced down and saw blood spurt; the room spun for a moment.

As soon as she could steady herself, she ripped her sleeve off and wrapped it around the wound, pulling it tight with her other hand and her teeth. They didn't notice her and continued to struggle. On the far side of the room, Emma saw the woman and baby. She motioned for them to exit the hallway. The woman looked desperate but followed her directions. Another shot rang out, and one of the two men struggling fell to the floor. She recognized the man holding the gun; it was Mr. Baxton.

He seemed in shock as she watched him drop the gun. Emma picked it up and pointed it at him. She said, sensing he would rush her, "Mr. Baxton, I don't like guns, but I do know how to use them."

He decided he would take the chance and went after her; Emma shot his leg, causing him to fall to the floor. She was losing some blood, and she needed to sit. With the gun still pointed at him, she let herself sink to the floor, listening to him scream in pain.

The door slammed open to reveal Jeremy. "Emma, are you okay?"

"Yes, I think so. Feels like a flesh wound," she said, shaking off her grogginess.

He took off her bandage and said, "I think you are right. It should be cleaned, though, and a proper bandage applied. What happened?"

"The two men were arguing, and I got hit by a stray bullet. The man on the floor. Mr. Baxton shot him when they were struggling. It is probably Mr. Smothers, the engineer."

"And who shot Mr. Baxton?"

"Oh, that was me. He wouldn't take direction."

Jeremy laughed.

CHAPTER 61

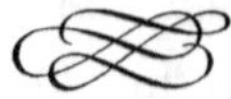

MRS. BAXTON CASE -- EMMA

Emma and Jeremy were transported to the police station by the officers who had responded to Jeremy's note. As they went in, they were greeted by the police chief. It was an important case and one of his detectives might have been bribed to cover it up. His thoughts turned to worry when he saw her arm. "Emma, are you okay?"

"It is just a flesh wound. I'm all right," she said.

He looked her over and she seemed steady on her feet. "Okay, what do you want to do?"

"I have some questions that may lead to who killed Mrs. Baxton."

He nodded, knowing she had the original detective's file. "This way. Jeremy, will you be accompanying her?" Emma saw the detective assigned to the original case, he avoided her gaze. The police chief made note of that and waited for Jeremy's answer.

"I will," he confirmed.

"We have Mr. Baxton and the new Mrs. Baxton. Which would you like to speak with first?"

"The husband," she said firmly. "The man that got injured, that was Mr. Smothers?"

"Yes," the police chief confirmed.

"How is he?" she asked

"He will be fine. The Sisters said he fainted when he got shot," he commented.

"You will want to contact Tim. He has some information about Mr. Smothers' involvement in this and a blackmail scheme involving Mr. Baxton," commented Emma.

He smiled and said, "Didn't I tell you years ago to stay out of dangerous situations?"

She laughed. "I didn't take your advice then, either."

He laughed loudly. The officers in the area looked on in amazement; Emma was the only one who could get him to do that. "Go on in."

She and Jeremy entered the room where Mr. Baxton was cuffed to the table. They had bandaged his leg; his was also a flesh wound.

He had the grace to look embarrassed when he saw her bandaged arm. "I'm sorry about that; I wasn't aiming at you."

"At least not the first time," she commented wryly.

He stayed silent so she continued.

"I know the first one was an accident. I walked in when you were struggling with Mr. Smothers."

"Yes, they haven't told me, is he okay?" he asked in a pleading voice.

"We understand the damage was minimal and he fainted," she commented.

"Thank goodness for that," he said, grateful he hadn't killed him.

Emma looked at her notes and back to him before saying, "We haven't met, but I am Emma Evans and this is Jeremy Tilden. I would like to ask you some questions, and I hope you can be truthful with us."

"I will try," he said, meeting her eyes.

"Did you murder your wife?"

He looked helpless for a moment and said, "I don't know."

"Could you explain that?" she asked.

"No, not really," he said, a bit helpless.

She took a deep breath and said, "Let's go back to the night of your wife's disappearance. Let's go through this step by step. You were having dinner with her. Were you alone?"

As he remembered, he started talking. "It was a special night. Catherine had just told me we were going to have a baby. She was so happy. I had Mr. Amberson open some champagne for us."

Emma knew that part. "What happened next?" she prompted.

"We started to talk about our plans for us and the baby. We wanted to raise her in Europe. It was our dream coming true," he said.

"Mr. Baxton, weren't you having an affair with Cassey during this time?" she asked abruptly.

He had the grace to look embarrassed. "I was," he said truthfully. "It was a dalliance, something to distract me."

"Why did you need a distraction?"

"We weren't able to conceive the baby for years. We started to think it wouldn't happen, and Catherine started to turn away from me."

"So, you found solace with someone else," Emma asked.

"Yes."

"Go on with that night," she told him.

"We drank, danced, and had a wonderful time."

"What happened next?" she asked.

"I don't remember."

She frowned and asked, "What is the very last thing you do remember?"

He thought back. "Mr. Amberson was talking in a low voice to Catherine. He looked upset; I don't know what it was about."

"What would happen to the servants if you went overseas with Catherine?"

"Probably the same thing that happened when she died. We would have let them go and have a management company takes care of the house."

"Hmm. Would Mr. Amberson be upset at being separated from you both?"

"Well, not from me, but he was very close to Catherine."

"What is the next thing you remember?"

"Mr. Amberson woke me up and told me I had killed her," he said, putting his head in his hands.

"Mr. Baxton, you said you were drinking. Is it normal for you to have blackouts or loss of memory for periods of time?"

"Unfortunately, it was at that time," he admitted.

"You don't remember killing her?"

"No, just being woken up by Mr. Amberson."

"Whose idea was it to hide the body?"

"Mr. Amberson," he said, not having thought this through before.

"Who arranged for the carriage to transport her?"

"Mr. Amberson."

"Whose idea was the fountain?" asked Emma.

"That was mine. I involved Mr. Smothers. It was all I could think of. I liked the idea of her there."

"Why did Mr. Smothers agree to help?" asked Emma.

"Money," he said simply. "Money that has turned into a very long agreement."

"Is that what you were fighting about?"

"Yes, he has been asking for more and more money." He hesitated and said, "I think that trouble with the plumbing was him."

"That would make sense," said Emma. "We had a structural engineer review it and determined it was sabotaged."

"Yes, I thought he might do something like that."

"What happened when you got to the fountain?" Emma asked.

"All three of us dug the existing hole at the fountain deeper by six feet and put her in." He was openly crying at this point. He had lost his wife and baby that night.

"If you will excuse us," said Emma, nodding at Jeremy.

"What are you thinking?" Jeremy asked as they left the room.

"Once we confirm the same story with Mr. Smothers, I think I know who to go to next."

CHAPTER 62

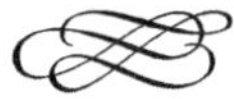

MRS. BAXTON CASE -- EMMA

"Mr. Amberson," she said quietly, sitting down on the bench next to him. He was staring at Catherine's fountain, he had been crying. Emma saw the Pinkerton men behind them and waved them back. She started with a blunt question, unsure of how he would answer. "How did you get Mr. Baxton to believe he murdered his wife?"

He didn't look up from where they'd buried his Catherine. "Oh, that was easy. He was a drunk. I had seen him have black-outs and no memory of what had occurred. It was so easy."

"Did you plan it?"

"No."

"What happened?" she asked.

"They were celebrating. I had served them dinner and opened many bottles of champagne for them. They ignored my presence and started talking about moving to Europe. At first, I thought I heard wrong, but they kept going on about closing up the house."

"Did you speak to Miss Catherine?"

"I did. I waited until we were alone, and I asked if I was

303

going to accompany her overseas and be there when the baby was born."

"What did she say?"

"She said only her family would be going. Her *family*. Who did she think I was? After all that I did for her."

"What did you do for her?" Emma asked softly.

"She wanted, a baby so badly, so I helped her," he explained.

Emma asked, keeping the amazement out of her voice, "The baby was yours?"

"Yes, that husband of hers couldn't give her one. Miss Catherine said I was special and I was her family, that it was natural."

"So, she got the baby she wanted and was leaving you behind?"

"I just couldn't believe she would leave me."

"What did you do?"

"I was carving up some meat for the next day's sandwiches when we started arguing. I remember glancing at the knife and picking it up to follow her to the foyer. The rage just overtook me and I reached up and slit her throat."

That explains the amount of blood, thought Emma.

"Where was Mr. Baxton?"

"He was dancing in the sitting room," he said. "I went up behind him and knocked him out and dragged him into the foyer. I woke him up and told him what he did. It was so easy."

"Do you regret what you did?"

He didn't answer her question instead he said, "I miss her so much."

She saw his hand raised but did not see the wickedly sharp knife he was hiding. He brought it up and slit his throat. The blood poured out and she tried to stop the bleeding as he fell back onto the ground. She got on her knees and put her hands on his neck, trying to stem the flow. The men ran up, trying to help. Jeremy also put his hands on the man's neck, but it was no use. He bled out in a matter of minutes.

Jeremy took his bloody hands away, while Emma continued to try to talk to him. "You will be okay; can you hear me?"

Jeremy could tell it was over. "Emma." When she didn't look up, he said louder, "Emma!" That finally got through and she pulled back, her bloody hands falling to her knees.

"Jeremy, I didn't know."

"No, you didn't."

"Why did he do it?"

"Perhaps he saw no other way out?"

"He missed her so much, considered her his family." She looked at him and said, with tears falling from her eyes, "Jeremy, she was having his baby."

That shocked Jeremy into silence as they watched the men lay a coat over Mr. Amberson's head.

"What will happen next?" Emma asked.

"The coroner will come for his body. There will probably be questions from the police."

"Okay," she said and took a deep breath.

"But not now," he said firmly, seeing she was in shock. "First, we go home and take a long hot bath and a nap. The police can wait until this evening."

She stood and was too calm. He held her close and summoned the carriage home. "Do you think they could add his name to the fountain?" asked Emma drowsily.

"We will ask Clair to look into it for us," he murmured.

He took her out of the carriage and they walked into the boarding house. They must have been a sight, blood on their hands, face, and clothes.

Dora turned white when she saw them. Jeremy shook his head at her and mouthed, "We're okay. Bath."

"Yes, of course. We will get that started now. Ethyl," she

called. "Could you draw Emma a bath? Take the back stairs." She didn't need her fainting at the sight of these two.

CHAPTER 63

MRS. BAXTON CASE -- EMMA

*E*mma sat quietly; with the police chief at the police station. He was giving her an update of the events she had missed." Mr. Smothers is at the hospital; officers are with him. He will have to answer for his actions the night Mrs. Baxton went missing." Tim had sent over the bank files confirming the blackmail accusations Mr. Baxton had made against Mr. Smothers. He looked over at her and asked, "Emma. I believe you have something for me?" She nodded and pulled the updated detective's file out of her jacket pocket.

"You will find the actual events the night Mrs. Baxton died in this file," she commented The chief looked across the room at his detective. He squirmed at the attention being aimed at him. The chief asked, "Was there anything else?"

"Yes, Tim asked that I give this to you." She pulled an envelope out and gave it to him.

He opened the envelope and saw it was bank transactions That belonged to his detective. "He was involved?"

"Yes, in the coverup; not the actual murder. What will you do?"

"Oh, I will take care of it." What he did was take the detective into custody with the other conspirators.

Mr. and new Mrs. Baxton were released and allowed to move into the estate. He would still face some charges but probably not receive any jail time. Now that there were no felony charges, his inheritance wouldn't be questioned.

Later that evening she was taking notes on how the case had ended, wishing she could have prevented Mr. Amberson's death, but he was with his Catherine now.

Jeremy sat next to her and took her hands in his. They were still cold. "Do you want to go lie back down?"

"No, I have had all the rest I can take." She shook her head. "Jeremy, I didn't see the signs. I didn't know he was going to do that. I should have known."

"Emma, you are not a mind reader."

"I know, I know. I just wanted to help him."

CHAPTER 64

FINAL MRS. BAXTON CASE -- EMMA

Clair had made arrangements for Mr. Amberson's name to be added to the memorial. Mr. Baxton agreed to the request, but would not be in attendance for the reveal. He asked that it be turned over to the Carlyle Foundation permanently. He would continue financial support for any future repairs.

Emma stood with Jeremy as the service drew to a close. It was only their families in attendance. "I am glad he is with her."

"Me, too," said Jeremy.

CHAPTER 65

She was sewing the final elements on the dress. "Can I look now?" the bride asked excitedly.

"Of course, turn around."

She turned and saw herself in the mirror. "Oh, Emma, it's so beautiful."

"Thank you. But it is you that looks beautiful."

Dora spoke up and said, as she blotted her eyes, "You hair should go up, and maybe some flowers?"

"Can you show me?" asked Abbey.

They pulled it back to show her. The wedding would be in a few days, and the family would all be together to celebrate the event.

Notebook Mysteries

Books
1 - 2 - 3

KIMBERLY
MULLINS

ABOUT THE AUTHOR

Kimberly Mullins is the author of series of books titled "Notebook Mysteries". Her stories are based on historical events occurring in 1871-1890's Chicago. She holds a BS in Biology and a MBA in Business. She lives in Texas with her husband and son. When she is not writing she is working as a Process Safety Engineer at a large chemical company. You can connect with her on her website www.kimberlymullinsauthor.com.

Photo Credit: Blessings of Faith Photography

twitter.com/kremullins_kim

www.ingramcontent.com/pod-product-compliance
Lightning Source LLC
Chambersburg PA
CBHW071356300726
48976CB00006B/1901